The Square

Jean Illingworth

The Square

Jean Illingworth

Copyright © 2022 Jean Illingworth

Kirkbee Books

All rights reserved.

ISBN: 9798839211841

The Square

Jean Illingworth

DEDICATION

Dedicated to DJ and Jamie O. Illingworth
and in loving memory of Lexey O. Illingworth

The Square

Chapter One

"It is my great pleasure to declare Lady Kirkby Square, open," Jack announced with a big smile.

The small crowd of local residents, allotment holders and dignitaries clapped loudly, the volume rising as Lily and little Dottie stepped forward and cut the flower-woven ribbon.

A champagne cork popped, Jack kissed Kara and everyone's phone cameras captured the moment.

Jack was slim with arresting clear, grey eyes and Kara was curvy with long, wavy, auburn hair; together they made a striking couple and a lovely photo, lit as they were by the early spring sunshine.

"Lady Dorothy would have loved this," said Kara, squeezing her husband's hand.

"I wish she could have been here," replied Jack sadly, "but that would have made her 104, which even for someone as stubborn as my great-grandmother, would have been expecting a lot!"

"At least she lived to see her great, great, granddaughter," said Kara, her face filling with love as she watched four-year-old Dottie, or to use her full name, Dorothy Rose, as she sneaked one of Kara's famous brownies from the waiting buffet table.

"There is so much of her in this plan," said Jack, looking around at the beautiful quadrangle of neat houses built out of Yorkshire stone. "Just a week before she died, I went over the plans with her for about the hundredth time, and she was so enthusiastic. She loved the idea of multi-generational living, of those most in need having somewhere beautiful to live, rather than beauty and comfort being the privilege of the wealthy."

"She was one very special lady," agreed Kara.

Jack nodded, wishing he'd had longer with his great-grandmother whose existence he had been unaware of until a series of events brought them together in her ninety-ninth year. He was the grandson of a daughter she thought had died at birth and finding him had given Lady Dorothy so much joy and contentment in her final years. Jack had been homeless and broken, lost and alone after everyone he ever loved had abandoned him. Meeting Kara and his great-grandmother had given him love and hope, whilst working at the allotments and with children at the local school had given him purpose and a sense of belonging.

Lady Dorothy Kirkby had died peacefully in her sleep at the age of 102, Jack beside her, holding her hand. A bed had been set up for her in the window of her sunny sitting room at Kirkby Manor from where she could see the carriage house where she had last seen her beloved fiancé, Henry. She could also see the beginnings of hers and Jack's dream, Lady Kirkby Square, the beautiful building rising slowly at the bottom end of the allotments in what had formally been the grounds of Kirkby Manor.

The whole town had turned out for her funeral, lining the streets and packing the ancient church at the heart of the moor side town. "The end of an era" was what most people said, and so it was, as the time when most towns and villages had their own gentry whose influence shaped everyone's lives was well and truly over. Although Jack had inherited the manor, he would not be lording it over the town, he would continue being a part-time teaching assistant at the local school and also running his small gardening company, 'Brown's Green Gardening'. All the money he had inherited from his great-grandmother he had used to build the Square in her memory.

The fund that Lady Dorothy had set up over 70 years ago to support the allotments would now be used to subsidise the rents where needed, so that local people in need of support could find a welcoming home in Kirkby, just as Jack had done. Ground source heating, photovoltaic roof panels and high levels of insulation meant that the cost of heating and hot water was almost nothing, making living there much easier for those on low income.

There were eight terraced houses of varying sizes on each side of the Square, some just one bedroom, and others two or three bedrooms to meet different family's needs. A couple of the properties were split horizontally creating a double-width, wheelchair-friendly, ground floor apartment with a more traditional apartment, accessed by a separate entrance, above it.

At the centre of the Square was an accessible communal garden, divided into quarters separated by wide, level paths. One quarter was just grass, somewhere for children to play in clear sight of their parents. Two of the quarters diagonally opposite each other were filled with raised beds, ready and waiting for the residents to grow their own vegetables, in the tradition of the allotments on whose land they now stood.

The final section was for flowers, with meandering paths through it to access the many borders. A few trees for spring blossom and to give shade and autumn colour had been planted, but other than that, the beds were empty and waiting for the new residents to make it their own garden. Several of the former allotment holders who had given up their plots to make way for the development had volunteered to assist and guide any of the residents who were new to gardening.

Jack was very grateful for their generosity, as he and the Allotment Association's chair, his dear friend Josie, had had the difficult job of deciding which of the allotment holders would lose a plot to make way for the housing development. Only half of the allotment plots would remain, but to Josie's surprise, several allotment holders volunteered to give up their plots straight away. One of those, much to everyone's astonishment, was John, the association's treasurer for as long as anyone could remember. John was going to help his friend, Sarah, a wheelchair user, at the accessible allotments which had been constructed in memory of his late wife, Mary.

A few of the other former plot holders opted to care for the children's garden or the sensory garden which were located within the allotments, instead of having their own plot, and others were going to share allotment plots with friends or family. For the last few that were needed, plots that were clearly neglected were an easy decision, and then, in fairness to everyone else, the remaining plot numbers were put into a hat and drawn at random.

Those affected were disgruntled but appeased somewhat when Josie had her own name drawn. Seeing the stricken look on her friend's face, Kara immediately offered to swap, but then Hugo stepped in, put his arm around Josie and said that there was no need as she could share his. This caused a bit of a stir, as at that point the growing romance between Josie and Hugo wasn't common knowledge.

In the middle of the Square was a paved area with a beautiful eucalyptus tree at its centre surrounded by a curved bench.

Around the bench was carved a quote from a poem: 'The kiss of the sun for pardon, The song of the birds for mirth, One is nearer God's Heart in a garden, Than anywhere else on earth.' There were also benches around the sides of the paving, so that residents could sit and socialise, as Jack and Dorothy had been very keen for the Square to be a community where residents would get to know each other. One bench was dedicated to the memory of Lady Dorothy, another to her daughter, Rose, and a third to her granddaughter, Jack's mother, Hope. The fourth bench had no memorial dedication on it, and Jack hoped it would stay that way, as he had lost enough people in his life already.

"What we need now are some residents," said Jack, sitting on his great-grandmother's bench with his arm around Kara.

"I think the first one moves in this week," replied Kara, taking a welcome sip of her champagne. She fished her phone out of her pocket and scrolled through messages.

"Yes, Joy and her little girl, Mia, move in tomorrow. I understand that they have few possessions, so we've put her in one of the furnished houses and made up the beds ready for her. Josie has also put some basic supplies in the fridge, and, as we are both at work, she is going to welcome Joy and see if she needs anything else."

Jack nodded, pleased that they could give the tiny family a safe place to start over. Local people could apply to the Square's trustees for a home, but fifty per cent of the houses had been set aside for Social Services to allocate. They would draw from those most in need, the homeless, the abused and the lonely. After much thought, Jack and Dorothy had agreed that allocation could include ex-offenders who had served their time, as everyone deserves a second chance, but not anyone who'd committed a violent crime or were paedophiles.

A condition of accepting a place at Lady Kirkby Square was that everyone must help in the communal garden, not just to be more self-sufficient, but because Jack and all the allotment holders knew the therapeutic value of gardening, something that would help the residents heal from whatever traumas that they had experienced in their former lives.

Chapter Two

Joy sat on a bench in the centre of the Square and looked around nervously. Mia was leaning against her, fast asleep, and at her feet was a bin-bag containing all their worldly goods. Joy thought without any regret about all the stuff she had left behind, the glamorous dresses, the Gaggia coffee maker, the cinema sized TV... The only thing she had made sure they had brought with them when she had fled from her abusive husband was Mia's favourite cuddly, Pink Rabbit.

The sun was warm on her face, and she closed her eyes for a moment, luxuriating in its warmth and the feeling of peace and safety that was beginning to settle on her in this lovely place. Her fingers traced a word on a plaque on the bench: Hope. Joy smiled at the aptness of the word; for the first time in a very long time, she dared to feel hopefully.

A gentle voice woke her, and she jumped, reaching blindly for Mia, panic making her heart thump. She couldn't believe she had fallen asleep out here in the open where anything could happen. It had been so long since she had just dropped off to sleep like that: for years she had lain awake every night in terror of her husband, and even when 'safe' in the women's refuge, the comings and goings and muffled crying had kept her awake. Then today, bundling a four-year-old and a bin bag on and off three buses to get here had also taken its toll; Joy realised she was mentally and physically exhausted.

"It's okay," said the lady, sitting down next to her on Hope's bench and holding out her hand. "I'm Josie, one of the trustees of Lady Kirkby Square, and I'd like to welcome you to your new home."

Joy took the outstretched hand and looked into Josie's face, noticing the twinkle in the deep brown eyes behind her glasses, and her warm smile. She was probably over retirement age as she had short pure white hair, but with a healthy outdoor tan and very few wrinkles, she looked younger. Something about her reminded Joy of her favourite teacher at primary school and she instantly felt safe.

Josie in turn studied Joy, and her heart went out to her as she was so pale and thin, dressed in borrowed clothes that were too big for her, the cuffs hanging to her fingertips and the baggy trousers turned up several times. Her long, almost white-blonde hair was tied back with a piece of string, and she had massive shadows under her eyes that were the same colour as the bruises just starting to fade on her neck, the only bit of skin visible. Josie wondered how far the bruises extended, and she felt anger rising up inside her at the thought that anyone could hurt this woman-child who looked like a broken doll.

Mia stirred and started to cry, so Joy lifted her onto her lap and cuddled her. She was soon settled and staring at Josie with open curiosity in her large blue eyes. She looked to be about Dottie's age with beautiful blonde curls just a bit lighter than little Dottie's strawberry blonde curls, in fact the two little girls were remarkably similar. However, unlike Dottie who was always beautifully turned out, little Mia was dressed in badly fitting hand-me-downs like her mother.

"And who's this lovely young lady?" asked Josie, producing a wrapped lollipop from her pocket, handing it to the child once Joy had given a nod of approval.

Mia carefully unwrapped it, handing the wrapping to her mother before popping the sweet into her mouth, never once taking her eyes off Josie.

"This is Mia, and I'm Joy. I'm afraid Mia's not talking at the moment, but hopefully she will start again soon," said Joy in a quiet voice.

"I'm sure she will once she settles in. There are lots of other children around, so it won't be long before she'll be running around making lots of noise with the rest of them," said Josie with a reassuring smile.

Joy doubted that, as poor Mia had seen and heard too much in her short life to be carefree; as well as having 'selective mutism', Mia was frightened of men and didn't like to let her mother out of her sight.

Josie saw the shadow cross Joy's face but didn't want to probe.

"Let me show you your new home," Josie said with a smile, picking up the bin bag and leading the way.

Having shown Joy the location of the stop cock, gas and electricity meters, and pointed out the folder full of other information, Josie didn't stay long, knowing that Joy would want to get settled in, but she left her phone number in case Joy had any questions or needed anything.

Once they were alone, Joy wandered around the house, Mia on her hip. It was about half the size of her marital home, but more than adequate. Downstairs, as well as a tiny utility and toilet, there was a large, light-filled kitchen diner cum sitting room and a small 'snug' that she thought she'd use as a playroom for Mia. Upstairs there were two bedrooms, the larger one with an en-suite shower, a house bathroom and a storeroom.

Their few pathetic possessions looked lost, but as soon as Mia was settled into the local school, Joy would find a part time job and hopefully then they could start to make it look like their own home. At the moment however, what she was more concerned about was security, and Joy was pleased to see that the windows had locks and that the door was solid looking with a good lock and a security chain. There was also a panic button by the door, and Josie had explained that any resident that needed it could also have an emergency button on a bracelet or necklace. This was more for elderly residents in case of a fall, but Josie had said that if Joy wanted one, that could be arranged.

After a quick sandwich and double checking the locks, Joy and Mia curled up together in Joy's bed, and although it was only the middle of the afternoon, both fell into a deep sleep, safe at last.

Chapter Three

"I hope she'll be okay," said Josie, cradling a cup of tea and gazing out across her flower filled garden.

"Who?" asked Hugo, coming up behind her and wrapping his arms around her.

Josie leaned back and rested her head on his chest. She gave a sigh of contentment, luxuriating in the pleasure of Hugo's strong arms around her. Four years ago, she had been sad and lonely, missing her late husband, Keith, who had passed away just a couple of years after she had retired from being the headmistress of Kirkby's school. They never had the chance to fulfil all the retirement plans that they had made, and Josie, who never expected to find love again, was facing a long, solitary retirement.

And then, after almost a year when they constantly missed each other like ships in the night, she'd met fellow allotment holder, Hugo, at Kara and Jack's Wedding. They both felt an instant connection, and six months later, to everyone's surprise, they too were married. As Hugo had said, at their age, they didn't have time to waste.

"Joy, the young woman that's just moved into the Square," replied Josie, shaking her head sadly. "It's none of my business, but she is covered in bruises; I think she must have run away from an abusive partner. She has a lovely little girl, Mia, who has stopped speaking, which can only be a response to trauma."

"They'll be safe here, love," said Hugo.

Josie turned and smiled at him, thinking how handsome he looked today, with his thick grey hair more unkempt than usual and a smile in his clear blue eyes. Like her he was slim and tanned, as when he wasn't volunteering at Crisis Line, he spent a lot of time outside at their allotment or helping his son, David, at his own allotment.

David had lost both his legs in an improvised bomb blast during a tour of duty in Afghanistan, and his army mates had helped the people of Kirkby create accessible allotments for David and other wheelchair users. It was this community spirit that made the moor side town of Kirkby so special, as although you would always get Yorkshire bluntness, it came with great kindness and a clear sense of 'doing what was right'.

When a corrupt councillor had tried to sell the allotment land for a luxury housing development, Josie, Kara, Jack and a small group of allotment holders had worked together and found the evidence to stop it. Some good had come out of that battle; instead of houses that only the very wealthy could afford, Lady Kirkby Square had been built, giving a home, and hope, to those that needed it most.

Chapter Four

Zoe took the opportunity of her daughter, Saffron's, afternoon nap to update her allotment blog, dropping in the pictures she had taken of the opening of the Square. She particularly liked a picture of Jack and Kara sharing a kiss, the sun catching Kara's auburn curls and their children, Ronan, Lily and little Dottie sunlit in the background.

If you looked closely, Ronan must have just confiscated the scissors Dottie had used to cut the ribbon, as he held them safely behind his back, away from her outstretched hand. Ronan and Lily were Kara's children by her previous marriage, Ronan a young teenager and twelve-year-old Lilly already acting and dressing like a teenager too. They could have been resentful when their mum remarried and a new baby came along, but they just adored their half-sister and were always looking out for her.

Zoe, a website designer and blogger, and her husband Ben, a cyber security expert, had moved to Kirkby from London about five years ago, and couldn't imagine living anywhere else now. Zoe was slim with masses of red hair and very pale skin due to her Scottish roots, and Ben was broad shouldered and dark skinned due to his families' Caribbean heritage. At first their striking appearance and London accent was a bit of a novelty in Kirkby, but now they were just part of the community, a very valuable part, as their skills had helped save the allotments.

Having an allotment had been an important part of their dreams of rural living, but since the arrival of baby Saffron, Zoe had hardly been there, but she was hoping to get there today once Ben returned from overseeing the fine tuning of the security system at the Square. The all-encompassing demands of having a baby were taking a bit of adjusting to and Zoe felt the need to just get her hands dirty, to have nothing more important to think about than weeds and seeds.

With Josie, Kara and Jack's help, the young city couple had gone from being novice gardeners to competent allotmenteers, growing all their own veg. Now that Saffie was starting to have some solid food, Zoe was keen to have a good supply of organic vegetables underway to ensure a healthy diet for her baby. Zoe planned to batch cook and freeze tiny portions of puréed fresh veg so there would always be something nutritious ready to zap in the microwave when a hungry baby was crying to be fed.

She knew that Ben had arrived before she saw him, as Saffie, now awake and zipping around in her baby-walker, started to shout "Dada, Dada," and lift her arms to show she wanted to be picked up. Zoe couldn't help being a bit peeved that Saffie still hadn't mastered 'Mama', but the bond between dad and daughter was lovely to see. She watched with a big smile on her face as Ben threw a giggling Saffie into the air, caught her and spun her around before holding her between them as he kissed them both 'hello'.

"A few more people have moved into the Square," he said as he put Saffron back into her walker and picked up the cup of coffee Zoe had just made for him.

"Oh! Anyone interesting?" Zoe asked.

"Well, there is a very old lady, not long out of hospital, moving in today, but there's already a young Asian couple just starting out together who are very sweet. Then there's Bert, an elderly gentleman who's recently lost his wife. He had that lost look that John had when Mary died, but he seemed friendly and keen to get started on veg growing, so I'm sure he will soon fit right in," replied Ben.

"That's good," said Zoe, "and talking of veg growing, I'm off to the lottie - beetroot, carrots and parsnip to plant out."

"Okay, see you soon, love. Oh, can you feed the tomato seedlings in the greenhouse, please?"

"Sure," replied Zoe, giving him and Saffie a kiss before heading out into the sunshine.

Chapter Five

Elsie sat on the old farmhouse bench and waited for her life to change. The seat was rough under her hands, the wood badly cracked in parts and, when she looked closely, starting to rot. She wondered how she hadn't noticed that before and how much longer it would last, but then, that wouldn't be her problem any more. She remembered her dad painting it. White she seemed to remember, but the paint was long gone, just the memory of it in cracks and hollows.

Her old sheepdog, Blue, sat at her feet, and she fondled his ears and wondered if he would miss the farm, the fields, the sheep. She wondered if she would too and lifted her gaze to stare at the familiar view, green as far as the eye could see, a multitude of different shades. The strong green of the hedges, the soft green of the meadows sprinkled with dots of yellow, pink and white flowers, the dull green of lichen creeping across old stone walls, the brownish green of the higher fields dotted with white sheep and the almost black-green shadows of the woods.

Elsie had looked at this view every day of her life and had once thought she would never tire of its beauty, but now she realised that she was bored of it, and probably had been for a very long time. When she had fallen four months ago and had lain on the cold ground unable to move, all she could see was this view as the painful hours passed and she waited to die. Blue had curled up next to her, faithful to the last, and she knew now that it was his warmth that had kept her alive.

The view that day had been shades of white, remnants of snow, frosted grass, glistening ice and a little mist drifting in the hollows. Then there had been a flash of red as the post lady, Sandra, arrived to deliver an unsolicited seed catalogue.

Sandra took off her red fleece with its embroidered Post Office logo and wrapped Elise in it, reassuring her gently that everything would be alright. Failing to get a mobile signal, Sandra went into the empty farmhouse to phone for an ambulance and to fetch more blankets whilst they waited for it.

A broken hip and hypothermia kept Elsie in hospital for months, and apart from Sandra, her only other visitor was the neighbouring farmer who had been renting her lands for the last few years. He offered to buy the land from her to extend his own farm, and also wanted to buy the farmhouse as a wedding present for his son. Much to her surprise, Elsie's immediate feeling was relief, followed swiftly by guilt as Darnton Farm had been in her family for generations.

Her small tartan suitcase was beside her on the bench, and Elsie rested her hand on it and thought about what was inside. Not much to show for 85 years, because in the end, she realised there was very little she wanted. Inside the case were a few items of clothing including the new nighty that Sandra had brought for her in hospital, her winter boots, a small clock, some documents and a photo of her late parents. On her right hand she wore her mother's wedding ring, and on her left wrist, her father's old watch.

Inside the farmhouse everything had just been left, and picturing it in her mind's eye, Elsie thought it looked more or less the same as it had done in her mother's day. She'd never had the time, energy or the money to redecorate, and now she certainly didn't have the energy to clear it out. A clearance company were arriving to make a start that afternoon, and once they'd done, the builders would arrive.

They would be ripping out her dirty old kitchen cupboards, knocking down the wall between the kitchen and the never used dining room, putting in much needed new bathrooms, and installing a wall of glass in the lounge to 'maximise the view'. The young couple had told her of their plans for her home and 'hoped she didn't mind' and said they would 'retain the original features'. Elsie found that she didn't mind at all, in fact she didn't give a damn. She had dedicated her whole life to the farm and all she had to show for it was loneliness and near death on the cold farmyard cobbles.

When social services had assessed her before her discharge from hospital it was decided she was too frail to live alone on the farm. They showed her a brochure of a new development, Lady Kirkby Square, and her heart leapt at the prospect of having neighbours, someone to talk to. She didn't think she'd be able to do much gardening now, but she would enjoy sitting in the sun watching others and would enjoy seeing the end results of their work. However, what she would be looking forward to most was watching children play, and she was so pleased that their play area was right outside the apartment she was moving into.

She had always wanted children of her own, but living on an isolated farm, working from dawn to dusk, three hundred and sixty-five days of the year, had given her little chance to meet a man, and those she did meet she knew were more interested in getting their hands on the farm than on her body. When her mother had died, Elsie had just stepped into her shoes, cooking, washing and cleaning on top of helping her beloved father on the farm. Many years later, right in the middle of the lambing session, her father had been found dead in his tractor which had got stuck in a snow-filled ditch. She'd no choice but to carry on, alone, helping to deliver lambs as the howling wind drowned out her crying.

Elsie heard her taxi approaching and stood up with difficulty, leaning heavily on her sticks. The driver took her bag and helped her into the car, Blue jumping up with some difficulty onto the seat beside her. As they drove away from the dark old farmhouse where she had spent her entire life, Elsie never once looked back, but watched the fields flash past and thought excitedly about her bright, clean, new home.

Wanting everything to be fresh and modern, Elsie had ordered new furniture, bed linen, towels, pots and pans, curtains - a whole house full of stuff - and was looking forward to seeing it all in place. Not having any broadband at the farm, Sandra had brought her an Ikea catalogue to look at for ideas. Loving the simplicity of the furniture lines and the bright colours, Elsie had spent days looking through it, marking the items she wanted. It had been a very long phone call to place all the order, and an eye watering amount of money at the end, but, with the sale of the farmhouse, for the first time in her life she was rich and had no one to tell her how to spend her money.

She knew that the accessible apartment was all on the level and had a wet room which had a walk-in shower with a seat in it, which meant that for the first time since she got back from the hospital, she'd be able to get a shower. When she came home from hospital, she hadn't been able to manage the farmhouse's steep stairs, and although they'd brought a bed downstairs for her, she'd had to get washed at the scullery sink the best she could.

The taxi driver stopped in the car park behind the Square, and kindly carried her case to her front door. She paid him with a large tip and waited till he was gone before putting the code into the key-safe, as instructed, to get her new door key. Arthritis and excitement made her hands clumsy, and it took several attempts to get the box open and then fit the key into the lock. The door opened at last, and slowly, with Blue at her heels, Elsie stepped into her new life.

Chapter Six

Jack had spent the morning at the local school where he worked part time as a teaching assistant. On the death of his beloved great-grandmother, he had become Lord Kirkby, but never used the title, and was just 'Jack' to the children he supported. Having taken his diploma in 'Supporting Teaching and Learning' and additional courses on working with children on the autism spectrum, Jack had decided against taking a teaching degree whilst he focused on his family, his gardening business and building the Square.

The Square was now finished, and Brown's Green Gardening Company was doing very well, employing three men and with a full order book. It was a bit different to a few years ago when he had tried to get established and had been thwarted at every turn by a rival gardener, Poppy Gilbert, aka 'The Gardening Venus', who had constantly maligned him on social media. Poppy had also conspired with a corrupt councillor, Smythe, to sell off the allotment land in order to get a big backhander from an equally bent property developer, Julian Fernsby.

When Jack's magnificent great-grandmother had taken on Smythe and exposed the plot to the council, the three conspirators had been arrested. Fernsby was fined heavily and Poppy and Smythe went to prison. Although Poppy had only got a short prison sentence she had not been seen in Kirkby since, much to Jack and everyone's relief, as she was a nasty piece of work who enjoyed making other people's lives miserable.

Two of Jack's workforce, Alex and Adam, or the 'A Team' as they called themselves, had learning disabilities, as Jack believed strongly in focusing on ability not disability. His foreman, Todd, had many years gardening experience and Jack knew he could trust them to just get on with the work. Jack spent as much time as he could working alongside them, but with so many other demands on his time, it wasn't as much time as he'd have liked. Having his hands in the soil, watching a tiny seed grow into a healthy plant, feeding his family with home grown goodness made Jack happy, and he very much hoped that today he'd get the chance to join Kara and Dottie at their allotment.

First though, he just wanted to check on the new residents to the Square, to make sure they had everything they needed and were settling in okay. He got no reply at Joy's house, but met with another new resident, Bert, who was outside inspecting the empty raised beds. Bert confided sadly how much his late wife would have loved his new house, but then brightened and chatted enthusiastically about what they could plant in the communal garden.

Young first homers, Nadia and Amir, proudly invited Jack in to show him their new home. Everything they had was second or third hand, sourced from charity shops or from Freecycle, but the use of brightly coloured throws and a few cultural family objects made it personal and welcoming. Jack declined a cup of tea but resolved to invite the charming couple to tea with his family at Kirkby Manor as soon as possible, as he knew Kara would love them.

Jack's final call was on Elsie; he heard her shuffling slowly towards the door and waited patiently, knowing she was very frail. He was shocked at her pale, distressed face, and even more so at the piles of boxes, large and small, behind her in the open plan lounge.

"Is everything okay, Miss Darnton?" asked Jack, although clearly it wasn't.

Elsie shook her head and looked close to tears.

"I ordered furniture, and there are just boxes," she said, indicating them behind her.

Jack looked over her shoulder and read the large logo on the boxes and realised what had happened.

"Ah. There is furniture in these boxes, Miss Darnton, but it needs assembling," he said.

"Oh!" Elsie replied. "I didn't know. I've never bought furniture before. Do you know a local handyman who can help me? At least to get the bed made so I have somewhere to sleep tonight?"

"I'm local, and I'm here, so very handy," said Jack with a grin.

Elsie tried to laugh, but it came out as a sob. Jack realised she was looking very shaky, and with nowhere for her to sit, he took her arm and guided her to Dorothy's bench in the middle of the garden. He then knocked on Nadia and Amir's door and asked if they would be so kind as to make the cup of tea that they had offered him, but for Elsie, not him.

Jack then phoned Ben.

"You busy, mate, I need your help?" he asked. Jack explained what the issue was, and then listened for a moment whilst Ben said something. "That's fine, Ben, just bring her with you, and bring your tool kit, please" he replied

Jack phoned Kara.

"Hi love, are you at the allotment?

"I am," replied Kara. "We're just having a break and catching up with Zoe who's just arrived."

"Is there any cake left in the tin?" asked Jack.

"Yes, but you'll have to get here quick before Zoe and Dottie have it all," replied Kara with a laugh.

"Great! Can you bring the cake, Zoe and Dottie down to the Square? We need you."

Jack cut the call without explaining why, but Kara knew that he would have a good reason for asking her, so they quickly cleared up and locked the shed then set off down the hill, swinging Dottie between them as they walked.

As Ben had to find his toolbox and then pack Saffron and all her paraphernalia into the car before driving to Kirkby, the ladies got there first. Kara looked quizzically at Jack who was sitting on a bench drinking tea with an old lady.

"Where's the emergency?" she asked, plonking herself down next to them and introducing herself to Elsie.

"It's me, I'm afraid," said Elsie. "I've done a very silly thing, and your lovely husband has offered to help."

"We're very happy to help," replied Kara, "once we know what the problem is."

"Come with me," replied Jack, taking her hand and leading her into Elsie's house.

"Oh," said Kara immediately. "I see!"

Nadia and Amir were already there, trying to locate which box had the bed frame in it, and Jack introduced Kara to them. He smiled when she immediately invited them to tea as soon as they were settled in. Zoe and Dottie arrived, having stopped to speak to Bert, and Jack gathered his little girl up in a big hug.

"Ooh," said Zoe, looking round the room. "Ikea furniture. I love putting this stuff together!"

"Good," said Jack, "because we have a great deal of it to do, otherwise poor Miss Darnton isn't going to be able to go to bed tonight."

"Right," said Zoe. "We need to move everything into the room it's going to be going in, to give us some space to work, and then split into teams and get the big stuff built first."

"Zoe taking charge already?" said Ben, who had just arrived. He had Saffie's baby carrier in one hand and a toolbox in the other and put them both on the floor gratefully. Dottie ran straight over to Saffie and started playing with her, gently tickling her little toes and making her laugh.

"Dada," said Saffie.

"Yes darling, Dada," said Ben, smiling at her.

"Dada," said Saffie, again, pointing excitedly past him.

"I think she means the dog," said Zoe with a laugh, and they all turned around to see Blue cowering in a corner.

"Oh, poor dog. I think all this is too much for him – he's used to sheep and silence. I'll take him outside," said Kara, who was an RSPCA officer and used to handling animals.

"Can I play with him?" said Dottie, jumping up and down in excitement, Saffie now forgotten.

"Yes, love, but I just need to check he's safe to play with first, so stay here please," said Kara.

Kara picked up Blue's lead that was hanging on a coat hook in the hall and then walked slowly towards him, talking gently to him as she approached. She stopped a couple of feet away and held out her hand for him to sniff, and when he did, she moved it slowly to stroke his head and fondle his ears, before clipping his lead onto his collar. Blue trotted meekly behind her with Dottie following less meekly behind. Blue sped up when he saw his mistress and jumped up beside her on the bench.

Dottie clambered up next to him and politely asked Elsie if she could stroke him. Elsie was as pleased to see the little girl as Dottie was to see Blue, and Kara left them sitting happily together and returned to help with the furniture building.

Nadia was busy putting crockery and saucepans away in the kitchen, and Amir and Zoe had unwrapped a two-seater settee and were turning it onto its side to attach the feet. Jack and Ben were in the bedroom checking they had all the pieces before starting to make the bed frame. Kara went in search of the mattress and then slid it along the floor in its plastic wrapping, leaving it outside the bedroom, ready for once the frame was assembled.

The lovely rich blue settee was upright again and had been placed against a wall and Amir was busy attaching the feet to a matching armchair. Zoe had located a pale ash table, and Kara helped her fit the legs on to it before they went in search of chairs. These needed very little assembly, so soon the pretty dining set was complete and placed under the window.

The trickiest task was the chest of drawers, especially as the instructions were missing, or possibly just lost amongst the growing pile of packaging. Zoe pulled her tablet from her bag and in a few swipes had the instructions up and was enjoying supervising Ben and Jack step by step.

Nadia and Kara made the bed with crisp white linen and put fresh white and blue towels in the en-suite wet room. Amir had hung some pale lilac curtains in the bedroom but needed help to hang the larger blue flowered curtains in the lounge. Empty boxes were piling up outside, but there were still more waiting to reveal their contents. The next three opened were a coffee table, a bedside cabinet and a TV table, none of which were too fiddly to put together.

That accomplished, Amir and Kara tackled a bookshelf, whilst Nadia unpacked the last few bits and pieces, placing a beautiful blue glass vase on the table and the last bits of kitchenware in the cupboards. Thankfully there was a built-in wardrobe, so having finished the tricky chest of drawers with only one piece left over, the men ferried the empty boxes to Ben's car and squashed them inside. Whilst Ben took them to the nearby council recycling centre, Jack helped finish the final bits and Zoe changed a grizzling Saffie's nappy.

When Ben returned, bringing a couple of bottles of prosecco and a bottle of elderflower fizz, everything was finished, and the group were outside on the benches eating Kara's lemon drizzle cake. Elsie was looking flushed and happy, with her arm around Dottie on one side and a gurgling Saffie in Zoe's arms on the other side. Blue was waiting eagerly for any cake crumbs to fall, and Kara and Bert were discussing vegetable growing.

"Mama," said Saffie suddenly in a loud voice, "Mama."

Ben turned from pouring drinks, expecting to see a delighted smile on Zoe's face, but he had to laugh as Saffie was pointing at Elsie, and Zoe was looking decidedly peeved.

A movement in the window of Joy's house caught Jack's eye. He'd had a feeling that someone was in when he'd called earlier but hadn't got a reply. Not wanting to leave Joy and Mia out of what was turning into a party, he decided to employ his secret weapon and sent Dottie to knock on the door. It was opened almost immediately, and Dottie found herself face to face with a little girl who looked very like her. They stared at each other a minute, and then Dottie held her hand out towards her.

"Do you want to come out and play?" asked Dottie.

Mia nodded, and before her mother, who was standing behind her in the shadow of the door could stop her, Dottie had taken Mia's hand and pulled her outside. Sensing that his little girl may have gone too far, Jack went to check if it was okay with Joy and see if he could get her to join them. She was clearly very nervous, but seeing as Mia was already outside, Joy took a deep breath and stepped outside too. Jack introduced her to her neighbours, Ben gave her a paper cup of prosecco, and Kara gave her the last slice of cake.

Whilst a silent Mia, a noisy Dottie and an excited Blue ran around on the grass, the adults finished their cake and fizz and got to know each other a little. As the sun started to go down and the children started to droop, Elsie was helped back to her new home. She couldn't believe how beautiful it now looked and thanked her saviours profusely, her eyes shining with tears.

Elsie sat on her new blue settee and looked out at the garden framed in her fresh new curtains as it slowly emptied of her kind neighbours. She realised she was still smiling, in fact hadn't stopped smiling all afternoon, and couldn't remember when she had last smiled so much, or even smiled at all. She was happy and she was home.

Nadia and Amir walked hand in hand back to their house. They hadn't known if they would be accepted in this mostly white neighbourhood, but they hadn't cared as long as they were together. Today they felt as if they belonged, and it felt good.

Joy ushered Mia in, locked the door and put the chain on, but somehow didn't feel quite as scared or alone as she had the night before. She had a home, she had kind neighbours and she was safe.

Chapter Seven

Poppy impatiently picked up a newspaper whilst she waited in the Leeds city centre sexual health clinic. She didn't like to be kept waiting, and a 'walk-in' clinic should be just that, come in, get the treatment, and get out, not left to wait her turn with these lowlifes. She'd probably had chlamydia for months, but despite her lifestyle, she hadn't bothered to get checked out until she'd started to get a bit of pain and bleeding.

She didn't think of herself as a prostitute, but ten minutes on her back whilst some fat, bald man sweated and grunted over her was a quick way to make some money when she needed it. Most of the time she got by on her benefits and a bit of drug dealing. Apart from some weed and magic mushrooms (which she considered to be healthy options as they grew naturally), she didn't partake herself, but if others weren't so sensible, that wasn't her problem.

She'd quite enjoyed her short stint in prison for 'conspiracy to defraud', and she'd made some useful contacts, but was still seething as without those interfering do-gooders in Kirkby she would have been rich now, and not living in a scruffy bedsit in Leeds. Poppy scowled at the thought, her thin eyebrows almost meeting in the middle, but then rising again in surprise at a picture in the paper in her hands. Jack, bloody Lord Kirkby, and that fat cow Kara kissing in front of an elegant square of houses – just where her and her accomplice, Smythe, had planned to build million-pound executive houses.

Poppy read the article praising Jack for his social conscience and she mimed being sick, but then the details of eligibility to move into the houses caught her attention, and a plan started to form in her devious mind.

Chapter Eight

The Square was starting to fill up: every new resident had a story, and every new resident was very welcome. The trustees, Jack, Kara, Josie, Hugo, Zoe and Ben, met weekly to look at the applications for the local resident's places, but had no overview of the applications being handled by Social Services. This was deliberate to afford confidentiality for people in difficult situations in order that they could make a fresh start at the Square, leaving their past behind them.

Tonight, the trustees were meeting in the ground floor apartment of the manor that had been Lady Kirkby's own home until her death. Jack and Kara lived in the penthouse apartment on the top floor, but Jack hadn't wanted to rent out his great-grandmother's rooms. During her final years her spare bedrooms had been used as offices whilst planning the Square, and they had continued as such as Jack and his friends project managed the build after Dorothy's death.

Jack still kept one room as an office, and the rest was used for guest accommodation, with the extended family that Josie had tracked down in time for Dorothy's hundredth birthday visiting often. Dorothy's old sitting room was a lovely large room with wood panelling, high ceilings and large French windows framed in heavy pale yellow silk which gave a lovely view across the allotments. It made a perfect place to hold meetings, and it was there that the friends were gathered to go through the latest applications.

Places were subsidised if the applicants were on low incomes, but those who could afford it, like Elsie Darnton, paid the full rent. Lots of applicants put forward a case for reduced rent, and so it was important to undertake financial checks, as too often it was a fraudulent attempt to get cheap rent. Of tonight's pile of applications, six had already been rejected for 'trying it on', but the seventh one, a young man named Will Appleby, wasn't asking for any rent reduction, he just wanted to leave home and have some independence at last.

"Oh, he's an artist," said Zoe, reading through his application.

"Seems a nice young man," said Kara.

"Let's put him next door to Joy," they said almost together.

"I hope you two aren't matchmaking?" said Josie.

"Of course not," said Kara with a wink. "Just thought it would be nice for her to have someone of a similar age next door."

"Hmm," replied Josie, knowing what they were like. "Are we all agreed to offer Will a place?"

They all nodded.

"Next door to Joy?" asked Zoe.

They all nodded again.

"Okay," said Jack, "That's settled then. On a different matter, I think we should encourage the residents to set up a Resident's Association."

"As long as I don't have to be Chair," said Josie with a laugh.

Josie, who had been the Chair of the Allotments Association for over 20 years had only just managed to pass that role over to Zoe and was enjoying having one less responsibility.

"No," replied Jack, smiling at her. "It's for the residents to set it up and organise, and for us to meet with them and hear any grievances or ideas for improvement."

"Hopefully they won't have any grievances," said Josie, "but it's important they have a voice and feel listened to. I'm all for it."

"Me too," said Hugo, smiling at his wife, knowing how passionate she was about fairness and equality.

"Shall we ask Bert to set it up?" suggested Ben.

"Yes, as most decisions are hopefully nothing more than what to plant, I think he'd be good at it as he's chomping at the bit to get started," said Jack.

Official business over, Kara went to check on the children and returned with a couple of bottles of wine. She poured everyone a glass and brought one over to Jack who was looking down the valley, watching the setting sun gild the walls of the Square far below them. The sun lit up the greenhouses across the allotments, turning them into a string of glowing lanterns connecting the Square to the Manor. Jack put his arm around Kara and pulled her close, and she leaned against his side and sighed happily.

"We are so blessed," she said.

"We are," Jack replied, kissing the top of her head.

They went to join the others who were passing around a postcard from John and Sarah who were currently in Thailand.

"I still can't believe that she's persuaded John to travel the world with her!" exclaimed Josie.

"Had he even been out of Yorkshire before?" ask Zoe, teasingly.

"Not much," admitted Josie with a laugh. "He and Mary used to go up to Scotland for their holidays every year, but he always said he was glad to get back to 'God's own country' afterwards!"

"It's astonishing how much Sarah has broadened his horizons - mentally as well as geographically that is," said Jack.

"Considering that she is a wheelchair user, she's an inspiration to us all, not to let anything stop you from doing what you want to do," said Kara.

They all agreed, and Josie privately wished she had half of Sarah's 'get up and go'. On reflection, though, being home with Hugo, tending her garden and allotment, being part of this wonderful thing that was the Square, was more than enough for her: she was content.

Chapter Nine

Will didn't know if his mum was relieved or upset that he was leaving home at last, but she hugged him for longer than she would normally, and, although she said it was just some dust in her eye, it looked suspiciously like she was crying. It was a big step for him too, he and his mum had always been close, and he was comfortable at home, but that was the problem – he was too comfortable. He was 27 and too old to still be living at home; if he didn't leave now, maybe he never would.

His new one-bedroom house at the Square was lovely, full of light with a view over the communal gardens, even if there wasn't much growing out there just now. He'd never done any gardening, but was keen to learn, and he could imagine how charming the garden could look if they all made an effort with it. He hoped it would be an inspiration for his painting as he'd suffered from the artist's equivalent of writer block for a few months now. He had plenty of book illustration work to be getting on with, but nothing to supply to the gallery that regularly sold his own work.

It was two years since he'd split up from his fiancé, but in a small town like Kirkby there were very few unattached ladies, and those that were he'd known all his life - going out with them would be like going out with your own sister. It was strange to think that had things worked out, he would have been married for over a year now, with a house of their own and perhaps a baby on the way. They had been together for three years, until she'd ditched him for someone she'd met online that she thought had more money and more prospects.

Will had been far less upset than everyone thought he'd be, which made him wonder if he'd ever really loved her. He didn't miss her, but he did miss having someone in his life to talk to after a bad day, or to cuddle up with on the settee to watch an old film. Online dating wasn't for him - there was too much fakery and self-editing - but as a self-employed artist working from home, opportunities to meet women were few and far between.

His mum was turning his old bedroom into a sewing room, so Will had been able to bring his bed and chest of drawers with him, along with his swivel chair and the desk for his computer and drawing tablet. In his old room, the computer desk has been squeezed into a corner and he'd had to climb over his bed to get to it, which was a bit of a pain seeing as he spent all day there. Here, the bedroom was big enough for a king-sized bed, so as his was only a single, he had plenty of room to put his desk under the window where he could look out onto the garden.

Will's easel and paints were set up in front of the window in the open plan kitchen / dining / living room, but the rest of the room was empty, apart from a small table and two chairs he'd bought from the second-hand shop in Kirkby. He'd ordered a settee online, but it was going to take six weeks to be made, so in the meantime he'd have to sit on a dining chair or his bed. Even once his settee arrived, Will reckoned that he'd have room to do his daily Aikido practice, something he'd struggled to do in the lounge at home without knocking a lamp over or stepping on the cat.

Will suddenly realised that he didn't have any curtains, something he'd not given a thought to. He'd have to ask his mum to make him some - her first project in her new sewing room - but in the meantime, he'd just have to stay away from windows when undressed so as not to shock the neighbours. Will didn't mind the austerity of the house as just having a place of his own was a luxury; he could take his time to make it a home.

Chapter Ten

It wasn't long before Bert called the first meeting of the Lady Kirkby Square Resident's Association. Zoe had printed some flyers for him, and he'd put them through his neighbour's doors and was now waiting nervously on Rose's bench in the centre of the garden to see if anyone turned up. Jack, Kara and the children arrived first, Dottie to play with Mia, and Jack and Kara to give Bert moral support and answer any questions, should they arise. Ronan and Lily had come too, as Jack had promised them a pizza afterwards, but in the meantime, a disinterested Ronan plonked himself on a bench, pulled out his phone and put in his earbuds.

Next to arrive was Elsie, wearing a large hat and walking unsteadily down the central path on two sticks with Blue at her heels. Bert rushed to assist her, letting her lean on his arm as he matched his pace to hers. He settled her on Dorothy's bench, and Jack felt a lump in his throat seeing her sitting there regally, very much like the bench's late namesake. Lily perhaps thought the same, as she went to sit next to Elsie, and soon they were chatting away as if they were old friends.

Kara had to hide a smile when she saw that Bert was wearing a jacket and a bow tie, taking his position as nominee Chair very seriously. It was a warm Saturday afternoon, and poor Bert was obviously sweltering, red faced and regularly tugging his bow tie away from his neck. Much to Bert's relief, gradually the seating area filled up with his neighbours and he cleared his throat and called the meeting to order.

The first item on the agenda was the appointment of the Chair, and a show of hands very quickly voted Bert into that position. He wasn't sure if he was pleased or relieved, but was happy to move onto the next, and only, item on his agenda, which was which vegetables to plant in the raised beds. Suggestions came in thick and fast, a long list was drawn up, and then there was a bit of a debate, with Jack and Kara advising on what would grow best, before a final shortlist was agreed.

"Who's going to pay for tools, seeds, pots and stuff?" asked someone from the back.

Bert looked flummoxed for a moment, and Jack was just going to step in and offer to assist, when it was suggested that they all contribute what they could afford, and this was agreed. They had just moved on to discuss flower planting when Josie and Hugo arrived laden with trays of vegetable seedlings.

"I hope you don't mind us offloading these," Josie said, putting her trays down, "but we planted far too many, so if you can use them, you'll be doing us a favour."

"We certainly can!" replied Bert, his eyes lighting up. "Let's get stuck in, folks."

Bert quickly took off his jacket, pulled off the bow tie and rolled up his sleeves. Hugo produced a bag of old trowels that gardeners who had given up their allotments had left behind, and Bert handed them out. Very soon everyone was busy planting with Josie and Hugo staying to give guidance if needed. Nadia was very sceptical at Hugo's insistence that you shouldn't put more than two marrow seedlings into one whole raised bed, but months later, when their big leaves filled it all and overflowed onto the path, she understood why.

"Do you think we have any 'extra' seedlings, darling?" Kara asked Jack. He grinned at her, knowing full well that Josie had planted them specially, and that he had done the same. Checking that Dottie was playing happily with Mia and Blue and that Lily and a reluctant Ronan were helping planting, hand in hand the couple walked up the hill to their allotment to load themselves up with spare plants. It was about fifteen minutes later when they arrived back and were quickly surrounded by eager gardeners who had finished with Josie's donations and were ready for more.

As they handed them out, Kara became aware of Blue barking loudly, but couldn't see him through the crush of people. Elsie was struggling to her feet to see what was the matter with her dog, but not being able to see him, put her fingers in her mouth and gave a piercing whistle. Trained as a sheep dog Blue knew the signal and weaved around the legs of the gardeners and was at her side in seconds. People jumped back as he brushed past their legs, and Kara had a line of sight to the children's play area, which was completely empty apart from Mia's Pink Rabbit, abandoned in the centre of the grass.

Spotting Joy chatting shyly to Will, Kara dashed over and asked her, as calmly as she could, where the girls were. Joy went white and spun round to look at the deserted play area before running towards her house, Kara at her heels. They quickly searched from top to bottom, but there was no sign of the children. Will had alerted Jack and he joined them at the door, but one look at Kara's shocked face told him they weren't there.

"Listen up everyone," shouted Jack, jumping onto a bench. "Dottie and Mia are missing. Can you check your houses, please?"

Everyone rushed to do so but were quickly back again shaking the heads. Jack and Kara were already frantically searching and calling, Josie was comforting Joy, so Hugo took charge. There were four arches in the centre of each wall of the square: the south arch led to the car park and then onto the town, the west arch took you to the main road, the east one to a back road and the woods, and the north one to the allotments. Hugo quickly split the neighbours into four groups and sent them off through a different arch to search in each direction. Ronan and Lily he kept in his team, not wanting them to go missing too.

They all set off rapidly, searching and calling, but when half an hour had passed with no sighting, Jack decided to call the police. Two police cars arrived quickly, followed shortly by two more and then soon afterwards a van containing a police sniffer dog. The dog was given Pink Rabbit to sniff, and after walking around in a circle, nose to the ground, he set off towards the allotments. News of the missing girls had spread rapidly, and dozens of Kirkby residents started to arrive to help in the search and were formed into teams, briefed by the police, and given areas to slowly re-check.

Josie had phoned Zoe and Ben and they soon arrived, Ben joining the search whilst Zoe did what she did best, got out her tablet, and resting it on the baby sling containing a sleeping Saffie, started to work the local social media. She soon got a report from a Kirkby resident who had been crossing the road in town about the time the girls had disappeared and had nearly been knocked down by a speeding car. In the back of the car had been a little girl in a pink sun hat who was screaming loud enough to be heard in the street. Although the lady didn't note the number plate, she did remember the model and colour of the car.

Zoe passed that information straight on to the police, who said they would inform Joy and Kara who were sitting together in the back of a police car, their hands clasped tightly, fighting to remain calm but jumping every time the police radio burst into life. Jack had refused to wait in the car and continued to search, so he didn't hear the message over the radio that the dogs had found a little girl hiding in the old carriage house at the top of the allotments.

Joy and Kara looked at each other, both hoping it was their own daughter, but both hoping for the other woman's sake it was not. They were out of the car and running up the hill before anyone could stop them and burst through the gathering crowd outside the carriage house and into its dim interior. Late afternoon sun through high half-moon windows was sending faint shafts of light through the gloom, lighting up dancing dust motes and glowing like a halo on the fair hair of the child crying in the arms of a policewoman: Mia.

Chapter Eleven

Mia sat on her mother's knee at their kitchen table, Pink Rabbit clutched tightly to her chest and a policewoman at their side. Josie had taken Ronan and Lily home, and Jack, Hugo, Ben and Zoe were still out searching for Dottie as the day faded to twilight and hopes faded with it. Kara stood rigid in the kitchen doorway, clutching a cold cup of tea, willing Mia to say something, anything, that would help find her beloved daughter. Despite the policewoman's gentle probing and Joy's pleading, Mia remained silent.

Faintly above the pounding of her heart and panic in her head, Kara heard Blue barking a few doors down. She wished the dog could speak and tell them what had happened, but there was as much chance of that as there appeared to be of Mia speaking. The policewoman had put a piece of paper and some crayons on the table and was gently asking Mia to draw what had happened, but the traumatised little girl just turned her head away and clutched her rabbit tighter.

Kara heard Blue bark again, and an idea occurred to her. She put the mug down and left the house, returning a few moments later with Blue on a lead. Blue went straight up to Mia and licked her hand and the little girl's face relaxed.

"Do you want to play with Blue?" Kara asked, ignoring the cross look from the policewoman.

Mia nodded and climbed down from her mother's lap and Kara gave her Blue's lead, took her other hand and walked her to the other side of the room where there was room to play. Kara knelt down next to the little girl and stroked Blue's head.

"Do you think you can tell Blue what happened?" she asked quietly.

Mia looked at her solemnly for a moment, and then gave a tiny nod. Kara stood up, placed her phone on the arm of the settee next to them and walked back to Joy and the policewomen, putting her finger on her lips as she approached to signal that they needed to stay quiet. The three women sat in silence as Mia stroked Blue's silky fur and spoke quietly to him, her voice rusty from lack of use and the words inaudible to those desperately needing to hear them.

Blue sat very still and appeared to be listening, and when Mia finished, he looked at Kara and gave a single bark. Kara retrieved her phone, and whilst child and dog played, the adults listened to their conversation, the phone on maximum volume. The first word that leapt out was 'Daddy', and if it was possible, Joy paled even further. They listened through a couple of times before the policewoman went outside to radio her colleagues and Kara went into the hall to phone Jack.

"Mia's father has her," she told Jack without any preamble. "He must have thought she was Mia as she'd put on Mia's pink sun hat. Mia had just gone into her house at the opposite side of the square to get them both a lolly and saw him just as she came back out. She is terrified of him, and just ran in the opposite direction, through the arch into the allotments, then as far as she could get to find a hiding place. Joy has confirmed that the make and colour of the car seen in town was his, and she knew the number plate, so the police are looking for it now."

Kara ran out of steam, and Jack could hear her crying.

"I'm on my way, darling. Hang on," he said.

Through the long dark hours of the night, Jack and Kara waited at home for news, huddled on the settee, hands held tightly, hearts beating so fast Kara feared she would have a heart attack. Josie and Hugo had taken Lily to their house, but Zoe and Ben waited with them, Saffie asleep in a travel cot in Lily's room.

Ronan was hunched on the settee, his ever-present phone in his hands, this time not playing games but sending messages out across his social media for a sighting of his little sister. Zoe sat next to him, contacting her far wider network, even though they both knew the police would be doing their best, but sitting doing nothing was not an option.

CCTV footage from the square had shown a man come through the arch from the car park and grab Dottie and, with his hand over her mouth, walk calmly back the way he had come. The man had a hood pulled well down and the angle of the camera made it impossible to see his face. Jack was blaming himself for placing the children's play area near to the arch that led to the car park, where someone could sneak in and then away again quickly, and Kara was too distressed to reassure him it wasn't his fault.

The police family liaison officer kept bringing them cups of tea, and the cups sat in a row on the coffee table going cold. Every time her radio cracked into life, and she stepped into the hall to take the call, Jack and Kara jerked upright, their hearts hammering even harder as they strained their ears to hear the news that never came.

"What I can't understand is how he didn't recognise his own daughter," said Ben quietly to Zoe, when they had moved out onto the balcony for some fresh air.

"Well, they do look very similar, and she was wearing his daughter's sun hat, one I understand he bought for her, so if he just grabbed her quickly without a proper look, I suppose it's understandable," replied Zoe.

"Yes, but as soon as she spoke, or he looked at her properly, surely he would have realised?" asked Ben.

"You'd have thought so," replied Zoe. "And then what would he have done?"

"Do you think he would have just turned her out of the car?" asked Ben in a shocked voice. "A four-year-old?"

"It's possible. Mia told Blue that the last time Daddy hurt Mummy, he told her if she told anyone, he'd kill her Mummy. He terrified his own daughter into being mute, so I doubt he has any scruples about the safety of someone else's child," said Zoe.

"What a monster!" exclaimed Ben. "So, Mia could tell Blue because he wasn't a person, so that didn't count?"

"Yes, it looks like that. Kara didn't know that of course, she's just used to working with therapy dogs, so she must've thought it might help," replied Zoe.

"If the bastard threw her out of the car, where would he have done that?" asked Ben.

"Well, we know she was in the car when he drove through town. Wait a moment whilst I check what the witness saw," said Zoe, fetching her tablet. She fired off a quick direct message to the witness, and an answer came straight back as everyone in Kirkby was up late, watching social media and praying for the safe return of the little girl.

"Okay. The witness said the driver was half turned toward the child in the back which is why he nearly ran her down. I asked her specifically what kind of expression he had, and she said he looked shocked. I'd say he'd just realised he'd kidnapped someone else's child," said Zoe.

"So, if he realised when driving through town, he couldn't dump her there where there were witnesses. Where is the next place he could have stopped unobserved?" asked Ben.

Zoe brought up a satellite map on her tablet and enlarged it around Kirkby.

"Assuming he turned right at the roundabout to head back towards Leeds, the next place he could have stopped is here," she said, pointing to a long lay-by on the side of the A road. She zoomed in further and studied it. "It's where lorries tend to stop over at night, but if I remember it correctly, there are seldom any vehicles there during the day and its fairly well screened by bushes. A perfect place."

"Come on then," said Ben, taking her hand. "It's worth a look."

Ronan looked up bleary eyed and nodded when they asked him quietly to give Saffie her bottle if she woke. Kara and Jack barely noticed them leaving, and although the policewoman raised an enquiring eyebrow, they said nothing, not wanting to get anyone's hopes up if it was a false alarm. Ben tore down the main street, turned right at the roundabout and then slowed down so as not to miss the lay-by. As Zoe had said, it was screened by bushes and he did nearly miss it, pulling into it just in time. He left the headlights on full beam, and they ran the length of the lay-by, calling Dottie's name. The layby was empty and silent and however much they strained to hear, no reply came.

"Let's just check under the hedge," said Zoe, fetching a torch from the boot.

They re-covered the ground slowly, peering under the hedges as they went. There were scurryings and scratchings as they disturbed night creatures, and once a bird flew out into their faces, making them jump.

"What's that?" said Ben suddenly, as something light caught the torch beam. He reached into the hedge and pulled out something made of fabric. A hat. A child's hat. A child's pink sun hat.

Ben yanked the hedge apart as much as he could and pushed through, just stopping himself from falling onto the deep ditch on the other side. Zoe passed him the torch and he shone it into the ditch, a drainage channel that in wet weather would be full of water but tonight was thankfully dry. The torch beam picked up a small shape in the bottom and Ben jumped straight down, shouting to Zoe to call an ambulance.

The little girl lay absolutely still, and Ben's heart felt like it was breaking: how on earth could he tell Jack? Ben picked her up carefully, a dead weight in his arms, and passed her through the hedge to Zoe.

"Oh no, no," cried Zoe, taking the still, cold form in her arms. She sank to the ground, her knees giving way and she held the dear little girl close, rocking her and crying. Ben climbed out of the ditch and picked up Zoe's fallen phone, giving directions to the ambulance before speaking to the police. Very soon the distant wail of sirens sliced through the silence, the growing noise almost drowning out a small voice.

"Auntie Zoe?"

Chapter Twelve

As Will and Joys' houses were both on the north side of the square, facing south, the early morning sun shone through the central archway on the opposite side, sending a beam of light creeping across the garden and straight into Will's lounge. Will focused on this growing path of light as part of his early morning meditation before undertaking his daily Aikido practice.

After a late night out searching for Dottie, and a sleepless night worrying about the little girl, it was a huge relief to check his phone and see the posts on the Kirkby Facebook site saying she'd be found, alive, but suffering from concussion and hyperthermia. Will needed his morning meditation more than ever today and, wearing only his boxers, he had just settled cross legged to meditate, when the beam of sunlight was broken by a shadow slipping through the archway.

Knowing no one else would normally be up and about so early in the morning, Will stood up and watched from one side of his window as the man made his way across to Joy's house. Will could no longer see him, but he sensed he was there, just feet away outside Joy's window. There was noise that Will instantly recognised as the sound of packing tape being pulled off its reel, from a part-time packing job he'd had when he'd been at college. Puzzled, Will strained his ears, but then the next sound made it clear what was going on. Someone was breaking Joy's window, using the tape to muffle the sound of breaking glass.

Grabbing his bokken, the wooden sword used in Aikido practice, Will dashed outside, and found the man half in and half out of the window.

"Oi! Get out of there," cried Will, grabbing the man and pulling him out. The man spun round angrily, but laughed when he saw Will, slim, almost naked, fair hair in a top knot and brandishing a wooden sword.

"You think you can take me, kid?" he asked, puffing out his broad chest and taking a boxer's pose.

The man lunged at Will, but in one fluid move, Will stepped and twisted and the man found himself falling without knowing exactly what had happened. The man pushed himself up and lashed out at Will, but found himself again on his back, the bokken touching his throat. Every move he made he ended up on the ground and the angrier he got the faster it happened.

Joy had sat up all night watching her daughter sleep, her ears pricked for any small sound out of place. As soon as she heard the window break, she had dialled 999 and locked herself and Mia in the bedroom, knowing without seeing him exactly who it was. She knew a locked door wouldn't keep him out for long as her husband was strong and hated to be thwarted; she just prayed the police would arrive before it was too late and this time he'd get away with Mia. She knew he didn't really want Mia, he never had, but it was his way of punishing her for having the audacity to leave him and file for a divorce.

Sneaking a look through the window Joy couldn't believe what she was seeing - her big beefy husband being beaten by her neighbour, delicate Will the artist. At the sight of her red-faced, sweating husband being knocked down time and time again, Joy could feel a laugh bubbling up inside her – he looked so ridiculous! For so long she had been terrified by this man, constantly trying and failing to please him, taking the beatings time and time again without crying, as crying only made him hit her harder. It was only when he started to threaten Mia that she had run away, but now, seeing him lying pathetically on the ground begging for mercy, she couldn't understand why she hadn't done it sooner.

Joy found herself mesmerised by the sight of Will's beautiful slim body, his muscles gently defined by the rising sun as he moved with such deadly grace. Something she hadn't felt for a very long time started to spread through her body like warm honey, but she was brought back to reality as the quiet of Kirkby was once again disturbed by police sirens.

Joy unlocked the door, came outside and spat on her cowering husband, all his power over her now gone. The police came streaming through the sun filled archway and stopped, bemused, at the scene in front of them – a half-naked man with a stick, a radiant lady with flowing blond hair, and a fat, crying man on the ground.

As the police handcuffed Joy's husband and took him away, Joy turned to Will to thank him, but he simply bowed and returned to his own house to start the day as if nothing had happened.

Chapter Thirteen

Poppy stood at the window and looked down over the gardens at the centre of the square. There was an old man pottering about amongst the vegetable beds and the old hag downstairs sitting on a bench chatting to him with her stupid dog sitting at her feet. A woman wearing a hijab was on her knees in the flower beds, planting some bright orange flowers, and Poppy scowled. 'Filthy Muslims - I thought I'd left them behind in Leeds,' she muttered to herself.

She watched what was being planted with vague interest, having run a gardening business of her own for years, until that stuck-up cow, Zoe, and her fit black husband, Ben, had outsmarted her online and ruined her. Still, she'd learnt a thing or two at the prison IT classes, so maybe she would outwit them when the opportunity arose. Anyway, gardening was too much like hard work and her exclusive catering business, 'Dinner+', was going well. They didn't come for the food, which was just as well as her cooking wasn't much better than her gardening, but a sprinkling of magic mushrooms in every dish meant her clients soon didn't care and were eager to get to dessert - her.

Thinking of Ben made her horny, and Poppy picked up her binoculars and focused them on the bedroom window of the house opposite, hoping to catch her fit young neighbour half naked, or preferably, fully naked, again. She'd been woken a few days ago by a commotion in the square and had looked angrily out of her window to see two men fighting. Her annoyance soon passed as she watched the youngster thrash the older man, finding his half-naked body, fluid movements and total control very erotic. Now that was an improvement on the old, flabby bodies she usually had to put up with!

Much to her delight, he didn't appear to have any curtains, and she'd been able to catch several glimpses of him, and particularly enjoyed watching him doing his daily martial arts practices. Poppy hadn't been happy when Social Services had offered her a first-floor apartment in the square, but she was pleased now as it made her more anonymous, and she could watch the goings on without being seen and without people seeing what she was up to. Another advantage was that she could see straight into her fit neighbour's bedroom, and on a couple of occasions, had been able to watch him undress before he got into bed, naked.

Feeling frustrated that so far, she hadn't had the chance to get into his bed too, Poppy scowled and looked again at the email to all residents from the 'Tramp', Jack bloody Lord Kirkby. It informed the square's residents that he was having gates fitted to the arches into the square and that all residents would be issued with their own keys. It was bad enough she couldn't park right outside her own house, without having to mess around with keys to get from the car park into the quadrangle. Just because his dippy daughter had got herself kidnapped, it wasn't fair that they would all be inconvenienced in the name of 'security'.

The email said they shouldn't give the keys to non-residents, but there would be an intercom and they would have to go and let visitors in. Balls to that! Her guests usually slipped in discreetly and it was going to be a right pain running up and down stairs to let them in. Poppy deleted the email and opened the Kirkby Facebook page: time to get her own back and have a bit of fun.

Chapter Fourteen

After a couple of days in hospital, Jack and Kara never leaving her side, Dottie was home, and apparently, none the worse for her experience. Her parents weren't so sure, and watched her like a hawk, as did Ronan and Lily who wouldn't let her play outside without them present. Thankfully Jack's mornings at the local school coincided with Dottie's half days there, so he was on hand if she needed him, and either him or Kara arranged it so they were with her the rest of the day. Physically she was probably recovered, but she wasn't her usual boisterous self, and Jack and Kara wondered about getting her some counselling.

When she'd been dumped out of the car in the lay-by, Dottie had had the sense to keep away from the busy 'A' road and had crawled under the hedge where she thought it was safe and she could hide from the bad man. She hadn't known there was a drop on the other side, and she'd fallen into it, hitting her head on a rock. Unconscious, she hadn't known the passing of time or felt the chilling of her little body as the cool evening turned to a cold night. If Zoe and Ben hadn't found her, it was unlikely she would have survived until morning, something her family couldn't bear to think about.

The local community had been wonderful, almost the whole town had arrived spontaneously to help search for her, and as Jack watched Dottie play with her dolls, he opened his laptop to post heartfelt thanks on the Kirkby website. He immediately saw a blurry picture of Dottie and frowned as it wasn't done to post children's pictures without their parent's permission, but what was written shocked him even more. Someone, calling themselves 'The Square Insider' had written a scathing attack on him:

'Too busy swanning around being Lord of the Manor to look after his own daughter, the poor girl is abandoned, alone, in the empty square. Then when she wanders off with the first person to be kind to her, the whole town is obliged to turn out and look for her. When will this feudal obligation end and the lazy Lord look after his own?'

As Jack stared at it in shock, the phone rang, and he was relieved to hear Zoe's voice; if anyone could sort it out, she could.

"Don't look at the Kirkby Facebook Jack," said Zoe, without preamble.

"Too late, I've just seen it. Who would do this Zoe?" asked Jack.

"Four years ago, I could have told you straight away, Jack, but she's long gone, so I've no idea. I've just contacted the website adjudicator, and it'll be taken down very soon," she replied.

Although Zoe couldn't see him, Jack just nodded, too busy staring at the picture to speak.

"Jack – you there?" asked Zoe.

"Sorry Zoe, yes. I'm just trying to work out when this was taken as we would never have left Dottie alone," replied Jack.

"Could it have been on Saturday at the Resident's Association meeting?" asked Zoe.

"Yes, that's most likely, as she was playing with Mia and Blue whilst we planted," agreed Jack. "Oh my god, Zoe, I've just remembered, we *did* leave her for five minutes whilst we went to get more plants. They are right, we are terrible parents!"

"Jack, that's not true. Josie and Hugo were there and loads of others, all in an enclosed, safe space," replied Zoe soothingly.

"Not that safe Zoe, seeing as someone just walked in and took her from right under their noses!" replied Jack.

"Hmm," said Zoe. "I'm looking at the picture and have enlarged it. It's been taken from above and probably from the same side of the square. There are some blurry areas in the adjacent vegetable gardens, which tells me that people have been Photoshopped out - badly I might add, but good enough to make Dottie look abandoned. Someone's gone to a lot of trouble to have a go at you, Jack!"

"But who, Zoe? The whole point of the square is to help people, and all the residents I've met have been lovely!"

"Are there any you haven't met Jack?" asked Zoe.

"Yes, two or three that were placed by Social Service and didn't need help to move in, but I've got their names, and there is no one I know."

There was pause as they both pondered on who could have made the post and why. As Jack watched his precious daughter playing happily, a sudden realisation made him gasp.

"What is it, Jack?" asked Zoe.

"Whoever took this photo saw her being kidnapped and did nothing!" said Jack, shocked. "If they'd rang the police, we wouldn't have wasted time searching for her locally, and she may have been found hours earlier."

"Good God - you're right Jack. The bastard. This is someone with no heart or conscience. We need to find them, as who knows what else they could do?" replied Zoe, equally shocked.

Chapter Fifteen

Nadia stood back to admire the flowers she had just planted. She thought it looked lovely and hoped the other residents would like the bright colours she favoured; orange marigold, magenta nicotiana, purple phlox and bright yellow coreopsis. It would be a little while until they were fully out in all their colour-clashing fragrant splendour, but the thought of that glory to come made her smile. She realised that creating a garden was about visualising it, putting everything in place to facilitate it, and then waiting and watching, fingers crossed, as that vision emerged, and others could finally see the picture that had been in your head.

Nadia picked up her kneeler and trowel, stretched out the kink in her back and looked around the square. Bert was busy amongst the vegetable beds, Elsie and Blue his companions as usual. The lovely stone of the buildings was pale gold in the sun and Nadia wondered if it reflected back heat, making a sort of microclimate in the square, helping the plants to thrive. She would Google that, and also check out local, or online, gardening courses that maybe she could do - perhaps something with a qualification that would give her a career away from just stacking shelves. Nadia smiled at the thought: back in Bradford her family had had a small, paved yard without so much as a plant pot in it, and here she was getting into gardening!

Glancing at her watch, she just had time to do a bit of research over a coffee before her shift at the Co-op started. Bert and Elsie waved at her as she passed, and Nadia smiled and waved back, realising that she was 'home', accepted and part of this wonderful community. When she and Amir had fallen in love, they had been ostracised by her own community as he wasn't a practising Muslim. She wasn't either really, but had had no choice at home, and still wore the hijab out of habit. Maybe, one day, she'd be brave enough to take it off, feel the sun on her hair and not care.

Sipping her well-earned coffee, Nadia opened her laptop to the Kirby Facebook page she'd been browsing earlier. She refreshed the screen and a picture of Dottie popped up. The awful post shocked her, and from the comments, clearly outraged the rest of the town. Nadia refreshed the screen again to see any new comments and was even more stunned when a picture of herself appeared. It must have been taken only minutes earlier when she was kneeling in the flowerbed, but the flowers had been sort of merged and a vague line drawn around them, so it looked like she was kneeling on a rug, a prayer rug. Someone called 'The Square Insider' had captioned it:

'Lord Kirkby has brought Muslim terrorists to live amongst us right in the heart of our beloved Kirkby.'

Nadia was so distressed that she couldn't breathe and for a moment she thought she would pass out. It was bad enough that her illusion of being accepted, of being home, had been shattered, but worse still the picture would tell her extended family where she and Amir were. Whilst her parents had eventually accepted their relationship, her uncles and cousin had not. Instead of the traditional Nikah ceremony involving all their extended family and three days of celebration, their marriage in York registry office had been quick and simple and witnessed only by Amir's parents and sister. It hadn't mattered as they were just so happy to be together, but now that could all be taken away.

Knowing she couldn't ring Amir at work, Nadia had no choice but to bottle up her fears and go to work. A couple of colleagues noticed her red ringed eyes and asked if she was alright, but she just nodded, unable to speak her fears. Towards the end of her shift, she didn't realise she'd stopped motionless in the aisle, a can of beans clutched in her hand, until a pale liver-spotted hand patted hers and a very elderly lady asked if she could do anything for her. The kindness brought fresh tears, and Nadia dashed to the toilets, where her manager, alerted by the customer, found her and kindly suggested that she took the rest of the day off.

Nadia was desperate to speak to Amir, but he was fast asleep, and she didn't have the heart to wake him, knowing he'd need to be up at five for his early shift the next day. She hated when they were on opposite shifts, but the shift patterns changed every week and most weeks they did have some time awake together, but not when one was on earlies and the other on lates like this week. Nadia pulled off her clothes and crept into bed beside her sleeping husband: he stirred, turned, and wrapped her in his arms but didn't wake.

For hour after long hour, Nadia lay awake, safe in her husband's arms, but for how long? Her tired mind conjured up increasingly terrible scenarios and when she did eventually fall asleep, she dreamt that her uncle came crashing in through the bedroom window to tear her from Amir's arms. Waking with a start, alone, for a terrible moment she thought Amir had been taken from her, but then realised he'd just gone to work. Feeling very guilty, Nadia rang in sick to work – her sympathetic managers making her feel even more guilty. She was worried that the lie could cause her to lose her job, but her priority was to speak to Amir as soon as he came home.

Tired and hungry though he was, Amir took one look at his wife's distraught face and held her tight against his chest, rubbing her back and rocking her as she cried. Through her sobs Nadia explained what had happened, but couldn't show him the post as it, and the one of Dottie, had been taken down. Amir thought for a moment and then made a phone call, before telling her to wash her face and put on something smart. He was going to do the same, and then they were going to Kirkby Manor.

The couple were nervous as they rang the bell but relaxed a little when Jack welcomed them warmly and ushered them into his apartment. They were both drawn immediately to the window with its view over the allotments, the Square, and then over the town and onto the hills beyond. Jack urged them to sit and brought tea and brownies, and almost immediately Dottie came running in from her bedroom to steal a cake. She looked at Nadia with solemn eyes and Nadia found herself drawn to the child. Whilst the men spoke in quiet voices at the other side of the room so as not to concern Dottie, the little girl climbed up on the settee next to Nadia and held out a story book.

Jack decided they needed Zoe's help and went to phone her. Amir stood still and watched his wife as the distress on her face lifted, replaced by a smile as the little girl cuddled up to her whilst she read to her. Not for the first time, Amir thought what a wonderful mother Nadia would be, and fervently hoped they would have the chance.

Zoe arrived before long, bringing with her printouts of screen shots from the two vicious Facebook posts. Dottie had fallen asleep on the settee, so Nadia covered her with a soft mohair throw and then joined the group at the table to study the picture. Jack had produced a plan of the square, and Zoe had marked with a cross the rough position that Dottie and Nadia had been in when the pictures were taken.

"Looking at the angle of the photo of Nadia, I'm pretty sure it was taken from above," said Zoe. "The picture of Dottie is also taken from high up but at a more acute angle and from much closer, which is why we can clearly see it's her whereas Nadia's picture is more out of focus."

Zoe drew lines of sight from the crosses onto the plan.

"I think the photos were taken from either an upstairs window of a house on the south side of the square or from a drone," she said. "If it's from a house, it's one of the four central ones on that side: do we know who lives there?" she asked Jack.

"Let me see," said Jack, opening a folder. "That's Bert's," he said, adding a 'B' to the plan.

"We're next to Bert's," said Nadia, picking up the pencil and putting A&Y on their house "and I don't think anyone has moved in next door yet.

"We don't need to worry about that one anyway, I don't think," said Zoe, "it's too far over."

"Who is the other side of Bert?" asked Amir.

"No one yet," said Jack after consulting his list. "A family with three children is moving in next week."

"The other side of that one is Elsie," said Zoe, adding an E to the plan, "and any after that are too far.

"Could anyone have a key for the empty properties?" asked Nadia.

"Unlikely," replied Jack. "I keep all the keys for unoccupied properties and one of the trustees meets either the new resident or one of the social services team to hand over a key when someone is moving in. The keys are restricted, all numbered, and only I have a master key for emergencies."

"A drone then?" asked Amir.

"It would have had to come in fairly low, and someone close by would have had to operate it, so I think that's unlikely without someone seeing it or them. Zoe, what do you think?" asked Jack.

Zoe had been quiet as she studied the photographs, a frown of concentration on her face.

"Nadia," she said suddenly, ignoring Jack's question. "There is actually nothing on this photo that identifies you, or the location apart from the post saying it's Kirkby."

She pushed the photo across the table to Nadia and she and Amir stared at it. Zoe was right! The blurry picture of Nadia was side-on to the photographer and for once in her life Nadia was grateful for the hijab as it obscured her face. The tapestry of flowers, edited to look like a rug, could have been anywhere.

Nadia and Amir hugged each other, feeling like a weight had been lifted off their shoulders.

"Not only that," continues Zoe, "but in the unlikely event someone recognised your side view or your clothes, surely the fact you are depicted in prayer would be seen as a positive thing by your community?"

"This is our community," said Nadia, her eyes shining. "And no one is going to frighten us away!"

Chapter Sixteen

When the doorbell rang, Will was relieved as he was getting nowhere with his commission. A reimagining of the flower fairies was so not his thing, but the author had asked for him by name having seen his work on other children's books. He's researched Cicely Mary Barker's original illustrations, and they were lovely, but how he was going to produce anything just as good, but up to date and different, was currently beyond him. He bounded down the stairs two at a time and flung open the door and was greeted by an enormous chocolate cake. Underneath it was Mia, looking really cute in a pink dress, the image of a flower fairy.

Joy appeared next to her daughter and smiled shyly at Will. She looked so different, her face relaxed and glowing, and later Will realised that the arrest of her husband must have freed her to relax and be her own beautiful self.

"For you," said Mia, thrusting the cake at him. "As a thank you for saving us," added Joy.

Before Will could protest that he'd done nothing, he saw that the cake was in danger of slipping off the plate and grabbed it quickly, realising as he did so that it was the cake itself that had a slightly tipsy look to it, rather than a sloping plate. He dashed into the kitchen to put it down before it landed on his door mat and returned to the door to see Joy and Mia about to go back into their own house.

"Please come and have a slice or two with me," Will called out.

Mia didn't need asking twice and had turned around and was in Will's house before Joy could answer. Joy gave an exasperated look, but quickly followed her daughter.

"Oh, your house is different to ours," Joy explained, looking around Will's sparsely furnished lounge cum kitchen.

"Well, yours is a two bed, I assume, and this is just a one bed, so everything is smaller, but after living in my bedroom at home for years, it seems like a palace!" said Will, grinning.

"My last house had six bedrooms," said Joy with an expressionless face.

"Gosh, it must've been hard to downsize," said Will.

"On the contrary, it's wonderful," replied Joy, a smile lighting up her face. "A home is not made up of rooms and possessions, but love, and wherever Mia is there will be love and it will be home."

Will found himself transfixed by her beautiful face which was lit by love as she looked at Mia. Her smile turned to a frown as Mia tried to pull the cake towards her, and both adults leapt at once and got there just in time to prevent a disaster.

"My favourite," said Will, and although it was nearly lunch time, he fetched plates and a knife and served them all a large slice. They sat around Will's tiny table, Mia on Joy's knee as there were only two chairs, and quickly demolished slices of cake. Will, who was usually tongue tied in the presence of pretty women, found himself chatting away easily, enjoying Joy's dry sense of humour.

Will looked at Mia's cake smeared face and laughed.

"She doesn't look like a flower fairy any more," he said.

"A flower fairy?" Joy queried, and Will explained about his commission and how he was struggling.

"With the garden coming on outside, I've plenty of inspiration for flowers, but cute little girls were in short supply until this one rang my doorbell," Will concluded.

"Well, I'm happy to lend her to you as your muse should you need it,'' said Joy, gathering up the plates.

"Can I be a fairy please mum," asked Mia who'd been half listening to the conversation.

Will looked from mother to daughter.

"Would it be possible to take a few photos of her in the garden for reference please?" asked Will. "I'll show you each shot after I've taken it to make sure you are happy with it, of course, and delete them after I've done the drawings."

"No need for all that – I trust you. But I think we'd better wipe her face first," replied Joy.

Whilst Joy cleaned Mia up, Will got his camera, an old Nikon that had once belonged to his late father. Mia was as precocious as any top model, posing and prancing amongst the flowers as Will snapped away. Joy sat on a bench and watched for a while, before going in to make her and Will a cup of tea to wash down the cake.

It was whilst she was inside that Amir returned from work and stopped in astonishment to see a man crouched in the flower beds photographing a little girl. The child's mother came out with a tray of tea, so Amir went into his house without saying anything, but a doubt kept nagging at him: was this the person who had photographed Dottie and Nadia?

Chapter Seventeen

Amir wasn't the only one watching Will. Poppy stood at her window and watched as he moved gracefully amongst the flowers. If it hadn't been for that insipid neighbour of his and her sprog prancing about, she'd have been straight down there and invited him up to her apartment to take some far more interesting photos. To make up for her disappointment she started to photograph the photographer, some close up for her personal use, and others with the brat in shot perhaps for another bit of fun.

Looking at her watch, Poppy decided she'd create her post later, as she needed to start preparing for this evening's guests. She wasn't cooking anything complicated but hoped to forage some ingredients from the woods alongside the allotments. She'd got to know the woods well from when she'd last lived in Kirkby, so she knew exactly where to look. Not only were foraged ingredients free, but they made her recipes sound more exotic, important as she had an 'old flame' coming tonight.

The last time she'd seen him they hadn't parted on the best of terms, but he had a lot of contacts and could be useful to her. She knew what turned him on and knew how to make him beg for more: before long he'd be eating out of her hands, obeying her every command. Poppy checked if the coast was clear and as soon as the sexy photographer, the insipid cow and her irritating sprog had gone back inside, she slipped out unnoticed, smiling to herself like the cat who'd got the cream.

Chapter Eighteen

The photos of Mia had come out well and Will had the inspiration for his flower fairies. He had been painting since dawn, the brush flying across the paper, a single photo on the windowsill next to him. The image, however, was of Joy, a picture sneaked when she wasn't looking. Upstairs, next to his computer and drawing tablet were the photos of Mia and there was a half-finished flower fairy on the screen, but when he woke up that morning, it was Joy he had been inspired to paint.

Unusually for him he was using watercolours, Joy's beauty too fragile for heavy oils. He had sketched her in really easily and was happy with the way he had painted the waterfall of her hair aglow with sunlight. Her clothes were a mere suggestion of colour, unimportant, but Will was painting the flowers around her in great detail, spilling them across the image so that she looked part of nature. Her face he was leaving till last, almost frightened to begin, not because he thought he couldn't do it, but because he thought he couldn't do it justice.

They had talked for ages in the garden, relaxed and laughing, flitting from one subject to another. They had come from very different backgrounds but had so much in common that Will felt like he had always known her. He had never believed in 'soul mates' but he couldn't shake the feeling that she was just that, the other half of him that he hadn't realised was missing.

Remembering the contentment he had felt last night, Will took a deep breath and dipped his brush into the paint ready to paint Joy's face that was so vivid in his own mind. Just as he was touching the brush to the paper the doorbell rang and his brush slipped, creating a blotch. Cursing, he dabbed it away quickly before it dried and crossly, his mood destroyed, threw open the door. The face he had been concentrating on was in front of his eyes, and Will blinked to check it wasn't an illusion.

"I'm so sorry to disturb you Will," said Joy, "Mia's running a bit of a temperature and I need to get her some Calpol. Would you mind just sitting in my house in case she needs anything whilst I try and find a chemist?"

"The chemist won't be open yet, Joy," said Will, glancing at his watch, "But if you want to stay with her, I can try the Co-op for you, and if they haven't any, I can wait outside the chemist till it opens."

Joy nodded gratefully and hurried back to Mia. Five minutes later, Will was cruising the aisles of the nearby Co-op and quickly found Calpol and then added Lucozade, remembering how his mum used to buy it for him when he was poorly. On impulse, he added a bunch of red roses for Joy, not stopping to think how she might interpret the choice.

Joy had left the door ajar for him, so, not wanting to pull her away from Mia to answer the door, after a moment's hesitation he just slipped inside and put the items on the kitchen worktop. He called upstairs to tell her that he'd been able to get the medicine and told her to let me know if she needed running to the doctors or anything.

Back in his own house, Will made himself a coffee and cradled the mug, stared at his faceless picture. 'What am I doing?' he thought to himself. Joy was first and foremost a mother and should not be the subject of his fantasy, he told himself as he tipped away the paint water and covered the unfinished picture on the easel.

Chapter Nineteen

It was a perfect day to be at the allotments, and Josie and Hugo were not the only ones busy planting and weeding. Josie paused a moment to stretch her aching back and looked around her, spotting and waving to several old friends. Jack was with a small group of school children in the children's garden just below the manor, and their excited young voices carried in the clear air and made her smile.

Hugo's son, David, was busy at the accessible allotment, and they'd drop by shortly to say hello and check on Sarah and John's patch, although there'd be no need as she knew that David would have been looking after it. Zoe was also busy at her allotment, Saffie strapped to her back as she worked. Josie smiled, remembering how she used to put her own baby daughter into an old apple box whilst she gardened, much easier than carrying her around.

"Fancy a cuppa?" Josie shouted across to Zoe, who gave her a thumbs up.

"Yes please," said Hugo, coming up behind Josie and pulling her into a hug.

"I didn't mean you," replied Josie, turning in his arms and kissing his cheek, "but now you're here, make yourself useful and put the kettle on."

"Slave driver," replied Hugo, kissing her on the forehead before going to do as he was bid.

Josie went into the shed to fetch the folding chairs, and spying an empty fruit crate, brought that outside too; she'd show that young Zoe the old way of doing things before fancy baby slings became trendy - much easier on the back!

After muddling through a nappy change on the floor of the shed, Zoe placed Saffie gratefully into the box. Josie had placed it under a tree and padded it with a blanket she kept in the shed to put over hers and Hugo's knees when sitting outside on frosty days. After washing her hands at the allotments cold tap, Zoe gratefully accepted a mug of hot tea and plonked herself down next to her friends.

"As Chair of the Allotments Association, I ought to ensure we have nappy changing facilities here," she said with a smile, knowing there wasn't the room or the money for such things.

"Ha! If you knew how long it took me to get a basic toilet put in when I was Chair, you wouldn't even consider it," exclaimed Josie.

They grinned at each other and went back to drinking their tea, watching Saffie wave her chubby little arms in the air as she watched the dancing leaves above her.

"Are you and Ben any closer to tracing the Square's troll?" asked Hugo.

"Frustratingly, no." replied Zoe. "Whoever it is knows some tricks to keep their identity secret, however, now the police are involved due to the troll witnessing the kidnapping, we hope to make progress."

"No leads at all?" asked Hugo.

"Well, Amir rang me about a man taking photographs of Mia in the square, so we'll have to check that out."

"Do we know who it was?" asked Josie.

"Will," replied Zoe, pulling a face.

"No!" exclaimed Josie. "It couldn't be him, he's such a kind, gentle young man."

"I know it's highly unlikely, but you just never know about people," said Zoe.

"I agree with Josie that it couldn't be Will - what on earth would be his motivation?" asked Hugo.

"Nothing. He was so pleased to get a house in the Square - I can't think of any reason why he'd have a grudge against Jack," said Josie, shaking her head.

Zoe's phone beeped with a notification, and she glanced at it, and then looked more intently.

"Well, we can rule Will out," she said. "He's being trolled as well."

Zoe angled the phone so Josie and Hugo could see it. There was a picture of Will kneeling in the flowerbed taking a photo of Mia and another of him entering Joy's front door looking nervous. The commentary from 'The Square Insider' read:

'The square's resident paedo sneaks in...'

"That's appalling!" exclaimed Josie.

"We need to get this taken straight down before Will sees it – he would be mortified," said Hugo.

"On it," said Zoe, her fingers flying over the phone keypad.

"Gone," she said a few seconds later. "I'm now one of the Kirkby Facebook page adjudicators, so I can take things straight down, but as soon as we close one account, the troll opens another under a different name but still signs off the post as the Square Insider. Short of closing the whole site down, there's nothing much we can do."

Zoe had taken a screenshot before she'd taken down the post and now stared at it intently.

"Both these photos were taken from the same place as the last two, from a drone or from the first floor of a house on the south side of the square," she said.

"There's something we're missing. I know there is, but I just can't put my finger on it, said Josie, perplexed.

"I know what you mean," said Zoe, "but we worked out who the 'Gardening Venus' was all those years ago, so I'm confident we'll soon crack this one."

"These are very like the vicious posts that Poppy Gilbert, aka the Gardening Venus's, used to do, don't you think?" said Josie.

"Yes," replied Zoe, "and talking of which, I'm sure I saw her partner in crime, Smythe, in town the other day.

"Really?" exclaimed Hugo. "I'm surprised he dared show his face around here after trying to swindle Kirkby out of its allotments and Jack out of his inheritance."

"Well, his ex-wife still lives here, so maybe he was seeing her?" suggested Josie.

"I'd be surprised if she let him through the door, after the humiliation of his affair with Gilbert being in every newspaper during the trial," said Zoe. "The stuff that was on the internet was pretty graphic."

"You didn't have anything to do with the video of Smythe and Gilbert's sex games getting leaked, did you?" asked Josie, narrowing her eyes, and looking intently at Zoe.

"Me?" said Zoe, all innocence.

"Yes, you!" replied Josie, still staring at her.

"Well, I might just have had a bit to do with it going viral..." replied Zoe nonchalantly.

Chapter Twenty

As Joy waited in the doctor's surgery with a feverish Mia on her knee, she was aware of the young woman sitting opposite her staring at her intently. Joy was used to being stared at, hearing the whispers as she passed by - all the times she had had a black eye, bruises around her throat or her arm or leg in a cast.

Following her husband's arrest, she had given a lengthy statement to the police, listing the abuse she had suffered over the years, and it had subsequently been backed up by medical evidence. With Dottie's kidnap and the recent break-in on top of her abuse, she knew her husband would be locked up for a very long time. With her divorce petition already in, very soon she would be completely free of him.

Ignoring the rude woman, Joy stroked Mia's hair and let her mind linger on Will and the way he had made her feel special and protected. Maybe, just maybe, she would be allowed to be happy. Her daydream was interrupted by her name being called, and she gently lifted a red cheeked Mia and carried her towards the doctor's room. The woman continued to stare, and just after Joy passed her, she turned to the women next to her and whispered loudly.

"I thought so, that's the child that the paedo was photographing."

"What do you mean?" asked the other woman.

"Ah, you probably missed it, it only flashed up for a moment and then it was taken down. I've been following the goings on at Lady Kirkby Square and I've a Facebook alert set for anything that the Square Insider posts. He or she just revealed that there is a paedophile living there."

"That's disgusting!" said the second woman. "Do you think the mum's brought her for the doctor to check if she's been, you know…"

That was all Joy heard as the doctor closed the door, but it was enough. Her dream of a future with Will was shattered. He was a paedophile, just trying to get to Mia, not her. Joy's cheeks were as red as her daughters as she fought to hold back tears whilst the doctor examined Mia. She couldn't wait to get out of there and back home and lock the door. It would be just her and Mia from now on, she was not letting any man into their lives ever again.

Mia was diagnosed with a chest infection, probably brought on by her falling asleep on the cold stone ground of the carriage house when she had hidden from her father. The doctor assured Joy that once Mia had had a couple of doses of antibiotics her temperature would come down and she'd soon start to feel better.

By early evening there was little improvement, so Joy wrapped Mia in a blanket and settled her on the settee and read to her until she fell asleep, her head on her lap. Not wanting to disturb her, Joy just sat quiet, stroking Mia's hair and staring into space. Having not slept well for several nights, she didn't realise she had nodded off until the doorbell woke her with a start. Thankfully Mia didn't wake, and Joy carefully lifted her head and settled it onto a cushion before going to the door.

Through the spy hole she could see Will on the doorstep, a bag of sweets and an envelope in his hand. Joy made sure that the chain was on, and then opened the door a crack.

"Go away you pervert – you're not welcome here," she hissed at Will before slamming the door in his face.

Will was so shocked he couldn't move and stood frozen on the doorstep. He'd made himself work hard all day spurred on with a promise to himself of seeing Joy once he had finished the first flower fairy illustration. Now with a printout of the finished drawing to give to her, he had finally allowed himself to call round. He wanted to know how Mia was and hoped that he might be able to spend a bit of time with Joy, but she had just made it very clear that he wasn't welcome.

Will racked his brains for what he could have done. Joy had called him a pervert - why on earth would she say that? He'd never been alone with Mia, apart from a couple of minutes in the garden when Joy had gone to make them tea, and that had been out in the open with other residents around. Had he said something she had misinterpreted, perhaps? He couldn't think of anything, and his hand hovered over the bell to try and get an explanation from Joy, but with a sigh, he dropped his hand and turned back to his own house.

Will dropped the picture into the bin and sat down, his head in his hands and his hopes shattered. The silence of his empty house pressed against his ears, a long, lonely evening stretching bleakly in front of him.

Chapter Twenty-One

A couple of years earlier Jack's little gardening company had tendered to maintain the grass verges and public open spaces in and around Kirkby. His proposal had been controversial, creating mini wildflowers meadows on roundabouts and only cutting a narrow pedestrian strip on the grass verges until wildflowers had dropped their seeds. He also proposed working with households and landowners to create a continuous green corridor so that wildlife could move around and have plenty of food. Much to his surprise and delight, he had got the contract and the wholehearted support of the council, the Kirby Environmental Group and most of the residents.

Occasionally someone would complain that the verges looked scruffy in that short period when flowers had finished but not yet dropped their seeds, but overall, the project had been a big success. It was much cheaper for the council and made Jack very little profit, but his motivation hadn't been making money. Since he had taken over the contract, Jack had been running an annual bee survey with the children at the school, and although after only two years it was too soon to tell, there was already a significant increase in the number of bees counted each year.

Cutting the narrow strip of grass verge along a rural road with little traffic was a simple job which Todd entrusted to Adam and Alex on a regular basis. He would drop them and the mowers off and go onto another job, before coming back to check on them and share a sandwich around midday. Today Todd was running late and knew Adam and Alex would be hungry, so after pulling the van into a farm gate, he jumped down and went to look for them rather than wait for them to find him.

Todd was puzzled that they were nowhere in sight, and that a long section of verge hadn't been cut yet. By now they should have been well beyond the farm gate where he'd parked, so he set off up the lane to look for them. As he rounded the bend, Todd couldn't believe what he was seeing; Adam was mowing right up to the hedge and Alex was shouting at him to stop.

"What on earth is going on, boys?" he asked.

"I've been trying to stop him Todd, but he won't listen," exclaimed Alex, looking close to tears.

"Adam, stop!" commanded Todd, standing in front of the mower.

For a moment it looked like Adam would keep going, knocking him over if necessary. At the last moment he stopped and stood still, looking belligerent.

"Adam," said Todd, as gently as he could, "why are you cutting right up to the hedge?"

"She told me too," said Adam, sulkily.

"Who, Adam?" asked Todd.

"The woman," Adam muttered.

"What woman?" asked Todd.

Adam said nothing, just twisted his hands round and round in the hem of his jumper and shuffled his feet.

"Alex?" asked Todd, turning to him in exasperation.

Alex shrugged his shoulders.

"I don't know. I didn't see her," he said.

"Why didn't you see her?" asked Todd, starting to lose his temper.

"I was mowing the other side and was around the corner."

Todd took a deep breath to stop himself shaking one or both of the young men.

"What did you see Alex?" he asked as calmly as he could.

"As I came back around the corner, I saw Adam getting out of a car and then the car driving off. He had a red face and looked strange. He started up the mower and mowed all the flowers down, right up to the hedge, and wouldn't stop when I told him to," replied Alex in a rush.

"Thank you, Alex, said Todd. "Why don't you go to the van and have your sandwiches. We'll be along in a moment."

Alex nodded and walked off gratefully. He was very perplexed at Adam's behaviour and wanted to return to the normal routine as quickly as possible.

Todd put his arm around Adam's shoulder and steered him towards a fallen tree branch.

"Now lad," said Todd, sitting down, "tell me what happened."

"The car stopped, and the lady told me to get in," replied Adam.

"Did you know her?" asked Todd.

Adam shook his head.

"What did she look like?" asked Todd

"She had dark hair and big boobies," replied Adam.

"How do you know she had big boobies?" asked Todd.

"She took off her top and they were spilling out of her bra. A red bra," said Alex, looking more agitated than ever.

Todd's eyebrows shot up, but keeping his voice calm he asked Adam what happened next.

"She put her hand down my trousers and touched my winkie."

"Did she hurt you Adam," asked Todd gently.

"No, I liked it. I didn't want her to stop, but she suddenly took her hand away. I felt like I would burst but she just laughed and put my hand on her boobies."

"What happened next, Adam?" asked Todd.

"She told me that if I cut the grass all the way to the hedge she would come back, and we'd have sex. I've never had sex, so I started cutting the grass, but she hasn't come back yet. Is she coming back soon, Todd?" asked Adam, looking at Todd beseechingly.

"I don't think so, lad. I'm sorry, I know it felt nice, but it was wrong of the woman to do that. Go and have your sandwiches whilst I give Jack a ring," said Todd, feeling sick at what Adam had told him.

Jack had just got home from school with Dottie and was making her some lunch when his mobile rang. He was shocked and disgusted at what Todd had to tell him, and agreed they needed to report the abuse to the police.

"What I don't understand," said Todd, "is why she wanted him to cut the grass verge cut right back to the hedge – it's such a strange request in the circumstances."

"I don't know Todd," replied Jack. "Maybe it was just a control thing – 'I can make you do whatever I want' sort of thing?

"Dunno Jack, seems warped to me. If you'll have a word with the police, I'll take the boys back to the base as I think they're too disturbed to be left to work alone" said Todd before saying goodbye.

An hour later Jack was crossly pacing around his apartment, replaying in his head the conversation he'd just had with the police. As Adam was an adult, they hadn't been particularly concerned about him being taken advantage of, just asked that he would come to the police station later to make a statement. Jack had left a message for Adam's social worker to arrange for him to accompany Adam as an 'appropriate adult', so when his phone rang, he expected it to be him and not Zoe.

"There's been another one, Jack," said Zoe without any preamble.

"What?" asked Jack, his mind elsewhere.

"Another post from the 'Square Insider'. I'm just about to take it down but thought you should see it first," said Zoe.

Jack said he'd ring her back in a minute, opened up his laptop and logged onto the Kirkby Facebook site. There was a picture of a rural road with a freshly cut grass verge, and a second close up picture of a pile of cut grass and wildflowers. Prominent in the image of dying flowers was a rare orchid, which Jack knew was protected under the Wildlife and

Countryside Act. Its presence along the hedge line was one of the reasons that Jack had got support for his strategy of minimal cutting of the roadside verges. With a sinking heart Jack read the post:

'Putting profit before the environment, Lord Kirkby's men destroy our beautiful wildflowers including a rare orchid.'

Although the post had only been up moments there were already a few angry comments, so Jack rang Zara straight back to ask her to take it down. Jack stood at the window and stared out over the allotments at the Square below. 'How could something so beautiful and full of promise conceal such evil?' he asked himself, glad for the first time that his great-grandmother wasn't here to hear of her dream of kindness and community being destroyed.

Spotting Josie tending her allotment, Jack rang her mobile and asked if she could break off for a short while and come and sit with Dottie as there was something he needed to do. Josie readily agreed, as long as there was a cup of tea and a biscuit as 'payment'. Jack laughed and put the kettle on, and as soon as Josie arrived, he set off: he'd tell Josie about the abuse later, as she was very fond of his 'boys' and would be upset.

Jack parked in the same farm gate as Todd had done earlier and walked up the road surveying the length of cut verge. Getting to the end of it, he turned and walked back again, double checking as he went that his hunch had been correct. Returning to his car he rang Todd.

"Hi Todd, is Adam okay?" Jack asked.

"I think so, Jack. He's a bit bewildered, but his social worker is here now and will go with him to make a statement," replied Todd. "Alex is going to go with them as he's got a good memory for vehicles, although sadly he didn't get the registration. They're in good hands so I'll get back to work now."

"Thanks Todd, but before you do, can you check the file for all the orchid locations near where the boys were working, please?"

Jack waited a moment whilst Todd when to look.

"The nearest 'orobanche reticulata' is over five miles away, and no 'orchis mascula' have been recorded along that stretch, Jack," said Todd after a few minutes. "Why do you ask?"

"'The Square Insider' posted a picture of the cut verge with an Early Purple Orchid, 'orchis mascula', prominent in the shot. I've just walked the length of the cut verge, and can't see any amongst the cut wildflowers," replied Jack.

"Bloody hell!" exclaimed Todd. "Well, there won't be any there, and even under the extreme provocation that Adam was under, I know he wouldn't have cut them. We have their locations marked with white sticks, and Adam is always very, very careful to check if they have spread beyond those areas before he cuts - he knows how important it is."

"Yeah, that's what I thought," said Jack. "Let's make a list of all known locations within a ten-mile radius and you and I will split the list and check them all."

There were eight possible sites, and it was at Todd's second site that he found it - a small area of wildflowers and grass cut by hand and placed in a pile, the Early Purple Orchid prominently placed on top. The white stakes that marked the orchid's position had been pulled out and thrown aside so they wouldn't be in shot. Jack had just arrived at his third site when Todd rang to tell him what he'd found.

"Whereabouts is it, Todd?" asked Jack.

"Alongside the road that runs up through the woods at the side of the allotments," said Todd.

"There'll be no CCTV then, said Jack. "Can you take some photos and ping them across to me please Todd. I'll report it to the police, as cutting down the orchids is a criminal offence, and it will also link to Adam's abuse and the missing witness to Dottie's kidnapping."

"Will do," said Todd. "Whoever this Square Insider is, they are a nasty piece of work, that's for sure."

Chapter Twenty-Two

As spring progressed and more people moved into the square, at weekends and warm evenings residents gravitated to the gardens and the seats in the centre of the square, chatting and sharing snacks, the children playing happily together. Jack and Dorothy's vision of a happy community was being realised, and with no more posts from the Square Insider, Jack began to relax a little.

Mia had recovered fully from her illness, and Dottie seemed to be back to her usual self. With more children now living in the square, Jack and Kara decided to have a bit of a children's summer party with a bouncy castle on the children's play area and some old-fashioned games like an egg and spoon and sack races.

Ronan, who was football mad, had set up a football net at one end of the grass and was ready to defend it against all comers in a game of 'beat the goalie'. Lily had helped her mum make hundreds of cupcakes and Mia and Dottie had helped ice them, some not entirely successfully, but no one cared as long as they tasted good.

Ben and Zoe came along with baby Saffie, who for some reason Zoe had dressed as a bumble bee complete with wings. She was now crawling, so Ben had brought a pop-up playpen along for her, setting it up right in the centre of the square so they could see her from wherever they were. Dottie and Mia were dressed as princesses, and Elsie wore a tutu and tiara.

"I feel a bit underdressed," said Josie, looking down at her simple blue summer dress and white cardigan.

"You look lovely, darling," replied Hugo. "Just need one small improvement," he said, tucking a few flowers into the band of her straw hat and settling it on her head. "Perfect," he said, kissing her cheek. Josie smiled at him, thinking how lucky she was to have been given this second chance of happiness. Joining Ben and Zoe on a bench, they accepted a glass of punch and sat back to enjoy watching the children having fun.

"What's the matter with Will?" asked Zoe, nodding towards where he was sat alone on a chair outside his front door looking miserable. "I had high hopes of him and Joy becoming an item but looks like that's not on the cards."

"What a pity," replied Josie. "They made such a lovely couple."

"Do you think they had a falling out?" asked Zoe.

"I don't know," said Ben, "but I do know he looks like a man that needs a beer."

Ben picked a bottle out of the tub of ice next to him and sauntered over to Will, whilst the rest of the friends watched with interest. Will stood up and shook Ben's hand, and after a moment's hesitation, took the proffered beer off him before ducking into his house and returning with another chair for Ben. The two men were soon chatting away between slugs of beer, and Will started to look a little less unhappy.

"Seems like that counselling course has paid off," said Zoe.

"What! Ben's training to be a counsellor?" asked Josie, surprised.

"Yes, surprised me too," said Zoe. "More to my Ben than just a lovely body, it seems."

"Zoe!" Josie exclaimed. "Ben is brilliant, as you are, at all things computer related."

"Thank you – you're right, but he just wanted to do something more meaningful. It's probably becoming a dad that's done it, so now it's just me that's shallow and constantly living in the never-never land of social media," Zoe replied with a grin.

"Thank goodness you do, Zoe," said Hugo. "Without you and Ben we wouldn't have the allotments or the Square, and without you, the Square Insider would still be making people's lives a misery."

"Do you think he or she has moved away, or just given up?" asked Josie.

"I don't know," replied Zoe. "I have an uneasy feeling there is worse to come."

Chapter Twenty-Three

Poppy watched the children's fun from her window, a frown on her face. She hoped the frivolities weren't going on until late into the evening as she had guests coming that night, and she tried to keep her activities out of the public eye. She'd been very busy of late with 'Dinner+', Smythe having proved useful at discreetly spreading the word just as she had hoped. Thankfully the party walls had good sound insulation, and the old bat downstairs was going deaf, so as long as her guests came under cover of darkness, no one was any the wiser.

Picking up her camera, she zoomed in on Ben and Will drinking beer outside Will's house. 'Cor, they are both fine specimens,' she thought to herself, and fantasied about being between them both in bed, Ben so dark and Will so fair and her the meat in the man sandwich. She fired off a few shots for her own private viewing, and grinned when she checked the pictures and saw she had captured Ben putting his arm around Will for a few seconds. Now that was something she could have fun with!

Later that day, Zoe was editing pictures she had taken of the children's fun day ready to upload to the Kirkby Facebook page. It had been a brilliant day, relaxed and fun, even if she'd lost Ben for most of the afternoon. They had been right, and Will and Joy had had a falling out, but Will was unable, or unwilling, to tell Ben why. He was clearly bewildered and deeply sad, as, he admitted to Ben, he was a little bit in love with Joy. Much to Zoe's frustration, rather than probing the reason for the breakup, Ben had spent time teaching him ways of dealing with the grief he was obviously feeling.

"How can I sort it out if I don't know what went wrong?" Zoe asked Ben, exasperated.

"Zoe, Zoe," said Ben, shaking his head. "You can't just interfere in other people's lives all the time."

"Why ever not!" exclaimed Zoe, knowing she had a terrible habit of doing just that, usually very successfully.

Ben just shook his head again and went to run Saffie's bath, leaving Zoe to upload her pictures. Just as she finished her post, she was alerted to a new post that she was tagged into. Her heart sank when she saw it – the Square Insider was back, and it was her lovely Ben in the frame this time. The picture, in slightly blurry close-up, showed Ben and Will sitting closely together, a bottle of beer in their hands and Ben's arm around Will. It was captioned:

"Ebony and Ivory's queer fling shocks the square."

Zoe stared at in horror, before sense took over, and after taking a quick screenshot, she deleted the post and blocked the account it had been posted from. She was staring at the screen shot when Ben returned, a sleepy baby-powdered Saffie in his arms.

"Don't you have a better one of Will and I to post," he asked, peering over her shoulder.

"Too late, it's already been posted, but not by me," Zoe replied, in a flat voice. "The troll is back."

Taking Saffie off him, Zoe went upstairs to put her into her cot, leaving Ben to look at the rest of the post. As she sang a lullaby quietly, she could hear Ben on the phone: she assumed it was to Jack, as that's what she'd have done next. Switching the baby monitor on, Zoe returned downstairs, poured a couple of glasses of wine and handed one to Ben.

"The bastard is like a dementor, sucking all the happiness out of life," said Ben angrily. "This is the last thing Will needs right now!"

"Well hopefully he didn't see it as I was already online when it popped up and I took it straight down," said Zoe. "I wasn't quite as quick with the last post that slurred Will, and I was wondering if Joy saw it, or was told about it, and if that's why she wants nothing to do with Will?"

"I don't know," replied Ben, "but I do know we have to do something about this. I was just speaking to Jack, and he has agreed that I can put in some more surveillance equipment."

"Well, this was taken from the same position as last time, from the opposite side to Will and Joy's houses, so we need more cameras facing that way I think," replied Zoe.

"That's exactly what I was thinking," said Ben, "but I need to install them covertly, so I think Will might just have a visit from a TV engineer this week."

"Oh, I do love it when you go all secret spy!" said Zoe, closing the screen on the laptop and taking Ben's hand before leading him away to cuddle up on the settee.

Chapter Twenty-Four

Holding hands, Josie and Hugo wandered happily around Helmsley Walled Garden, taking their time to look at individual flowers and different vistas. Hugo's favourite view in late spring was looking towards the ruins of Helmsley Castle through a tunnel dripping with yellow wisteria above a border full of purple allium globes. Josie's favourite view was down the long, wide herbaceous borders towards the magnificent glasshouse, especially in autumn when it was a mass of yellow and purple herbaceous flowers in a vibrant repeating pattern. Visiting the walled garden was a favourite day out for them, and having resident's passes, they could visit as often as they liked for free, although they tended not to visit in the height of summer when it was crowded with tourists.

As had become their tradition, they enjoyed afternoon tea at the café, sitting outside the old vine house under a parasol enjoying the garden view. Hugo had his eye on some plants for sale, and Josie was trying to persuade him that there was no room in their garden for more, when she became distracted by a man at the next table; he looked very familiar, but she couldn't work out where she knew him from.

The man, who was sipping a coffee and reading a book, was very smartly dressed and stood out against the more casually dressed customers. Aware of Josie's eyes on him, he looked up for a moment, then snapped his book shut, gave her a disdainful look and then got up and left. As he passed, Josie could see the book was one on local flora and fauna that she had admired earlier in the gift shop.

"You thinking of trading me in for a younger model?" asked Hugo, as Josie's eyes followed the man as he left.

"Never," replied Josie, squeezing his hand. "I just thought I knew him, but he doesn't look like someone I'd want to know. Tell you what, if you get some plants, I'm having the book I looked at earlier – deal?"

Chapter Twenty-Five

Elsie and Bert had become good friends; nothing romantic - she was far too old for that - but 'companions', Elsie thought to herself, a lovely old-fashioned word that was just right for their relationship.

Whenever the weather was dry, Bert would be out tending the vegetable beds, and she'd come out and sit nearby to watch and chat. Occasionally, she'd give a bit of advice, knowledge gleaned from years of tending the farm's vegetable garden with her mother, and Bert would nod and smile, not a bit offended by her interfering.

If the weather turned cold, Bert would fetch her a warm shawl from her house without being asked, or her sun hat if the sun was hot. When she went inside to make them both a bit of tea, he'd come and carry the tray outside if it was warm, or just wander in and sit at her table in the window if it had become too chilly to sit outside any longer. With the town within walking distance for Bert, most mornings he'd visit the local bakers or butchers, bring back fresh bread, cakes or best ham for their shared meal.

A new family with three young boys had moved in across the square, and like Bert, the boys, Finn, Felix and Freddie were cricket mad. Bert had played for Kirkby Cricket Club for years, and was still their secretary, so he was keen to encourage new young players who would perhaps join the team one day. On dry Saturday mornings, Bert would set up stumps on the children's play area and coach the boys in bowling and batting. Ronan, who was in the same class as Freddie, would come along to join in whilst his sister Lily was at ballet class, and Dottie would play with Mia with Blue at a safe distance from the cricket balls and noisy boys.

Kara, Joy, Elsie and the boy's mum, Fiona, would sit and watch before throwing together an impromptu lunch for them all once Lily had arrived back from ballet. Lily was a little in love with Felix, and to Kara's amusement, arrived with her hair released from its ballet bun and wearing what looked suspiciously like a touch of Kara's favourite lipstick. Lily needn't have worried, as Felix was as besotted with her, and once she arrived walking gracefully across the Square, he would miss every ball. Usually at this point, Blue darted in and grabbed the ball, so that was the end of play anyway.

Elsie was loving her new life being part of the community of the Square, and if it wasn't for her noisy upstairs neighbour, who's partying kept her awake, her life would be perfect.

Chapter Twenty-Six

Poppy watched the cricket practice from her window, furious that she had been woken up. Saturday mornings she liked to sleep in, get her beauty sleep ready for a late night as she usually had guests on Saturday evenings. She scowled as one of the brats bowled another out and a cheer went up – no chance of getting back to sleep whilst there was this rabble out there.

Picking up her camera, she zoomed in on the older of the boys; in a few years, they might be worth watching. She'd instructed a few young boys in the art of sex several times in the past, and had enjoyed their puppy-dog devotion, but these were a bit young even for her.

She moved her lens across to Will's window. Damn! She'd just missed him doing his morning Aikido practice – now that was something worth getting up early for! Silly boy still hadn't got himself any downstairs curtains, so being directly opposite, she always got a good view as he ran through his routine, bare to the waist. Like a video playing in her head, she would rerun Will's coordinated movements when she was with her customers and struggling to get in the mood.

This morning he was standing in the window looking towards the group of bitches gossiping and laughing together. He was still bare chested, his hands resting on his silly wooden sword, and Poppy wished those strong hands were on her body instead. His face looked so sad, that for a moment she felt almost guilty about splitting him and Joy up by suggesting he was a paedophile, but then she grinned when that gave her another idea for a post.

Although he wasn't looking at the children, in a close up shot of him looking out wistfully no one would know who he was looking at. Put that next to a shot of the little girls playing with that bloody dog and viewers would put two and two together and make five. Poppy checked the shots on her camera and laughed out loud; in one shot of Will with his hands on the hilt of the sword it looked like he was pleasuring himself - perfect!

Chapter Twenty-Seven

Friday night had been a rare 'date night' for Ben and Zoe, the first one since Saffron had been born. Josie and Hugo had the baby for the night, so the young couple had gone into York for a civilised meal without constant interruptions. Ben had insisted that they turn off all notifications on their phones, apart from any call from Josie, so that they could really relax and be just them for a short while. After two bottles of wine, they were so relaxed that they had to book into a hotel for the night and enjoyed making love slowly without having to keep an ear open to listen to the baby monitor.

They slept so late the next morning that they missed breakfast, and suddenly ravenous, had to find a café where they wolfed down a full English. A call to Josie had assured them Saffie was fine and there was no rush, so keen to enjoy their freedom to the full, they wandered around the eclectic shops in the beautiful mediaeval city, hand in hand. Most of what they bought was for Saffie, but Zoe also got a vintage flower-painted teapot on a bric-a-brac stall in the Shambles Market, which was perfect as a thank-you for Josie and Hugo.

It was only when Ben was driving them home later that afternoon that Zoe switched her notifications back on and the phone started to beep.

"Oh no, there's been another post from the Square Insider!" Zoe exclaimed.

She quickly opened up the Kirkby Facebook and swore at the number of comments and shares the post had got.

"How bad is it?" asked Ben, unable to glance at the phone as he navigated the narrow, windy roads.

"About as bad as it could be!" said Zoe, as she saved a screenshot and then worked to remove the post and block the person who had posted it - again.

Ben saw a farm gate ahead and swerved into it, reaching for Zoe's phone almost before he had the handbrake on. They stared at the screen shot together, and Ben swore loudly.

"Poor Will – she's really got it in for him, hasn't she?"

Under the two side-by-side pictures the text from 'The Square Insider' read:

'Unable to get his hands on the little ones, the square's resident paedo puts his hands on his big one.'

"That's disgusting!" exclaimed Zoe. "But it does look a bit like…"

"It's his bokken!" interrupted Ben. "His Aikido sword – it looks like he's just finished his daily practice and was just looking innocently out of the window when the Insider snapped him. Only someone with a filthy mind would think otherwise!"

"Well, judging by the comments, half of Kirkby have filthy minds then," replied Zoe a little huffily, "not just me!"

"Yours was pretty filthy last night," said Ben with a grin.

"Well, I had my hands on flesh and blood, not wood - but come to think of it…" she said, putting her hand on his thigh.

Ben laughed and turned to kiss her, but the sound of a tractor's horn stopped him, and with a wave of apology he pulled the car out of the gateway, and they continued their journey. Zoe resumed studying the picture as they drove.

"It looks to have been taken from exactly the same point as the last ones, so I think it's pretty safe to say now that it's someone in an upstairs room on the other side of the square," she said.

"Grab my phone and log onto Will's camera feed will you darling?" ask Ben.

Zoe did so, and then ran through all that morning footage slowly.

"It looks like a great morning of cricket so far," she said. "Wow - the 'triple F boys' are pretty good players – I think you might have some competition on the Kirkby team before long, Ben."

"Anyone at the upstairs windows on the south side of the square?" asked Ben.

"No one yet," replied Zoe. "Right, I think I've got to around the time that the pictures were taken, as the girls and Blue are in about the right place. I'll slow it down and watch it frame by frame.

"Okay, I've just seen a movement at the upstairs window in Elsie's house, but Elsie is outside with Kara. Definitely a figure now - difficult to say if it's a man or a woman. Oh! There was a flash - not a photo flash, but light catching the lens of a camera, perhaps. I think we can be pretty sure this is the Square Insider at work!" exclaimed Zoe.

"I know Elsie's old, but why would she let someone into her house when she's not there?" asked Ben.

"Duh!" exclaimed Zoe, hitting her forehead with the heel of her hand. "We have been so stupid. Josie said there was something we were missing, and she was right. It's so obvious now."

"What?" asked Ben, mystified.

"Elsie's is an accessible apartment - ground floor only. There's a separate apartment upstairs - someone else is living there, someone with a grudge against Jack and everything he has tried to do at the square," explained Zoe.

"Of course!" exclaimed Ben, shaking his head. "We've all been so stupid."

"I'm going to text everyone and see if we can meet at Jack's - Josie can bring Saffie there," said Zoe, already typing a group text to the square's trustees.

Chapter Twenty-Eight

"Mama, mama, mama," said Saffie, toddling towards Zoe's with outstretched arms.

Zoe swept her up and spun her around and then cuddled her close.

"Oh, I've missed you, darling girl," she said, covering her in kisses.

"I'm sure she's grown an inch overnight," said Zoe as she handed her to Ben to say hello to as well.

"Well, she's learnt to say your name at last," said Ben.

"You clever girl, Saffie," he said, tickling her tummy whilst she squealed with delight.

"Did you have a nice time?" asked Josie, who'd been waiting for them with Hugo, Kara and Jack in the ground floor sitting room of the manor.

"It was lovely - so good to have time alone," replied Zoe, giving Josie a hug. "Thank you both so much."

Zoe noticed that Josie and Hugo looked very tired and hoped that Saffie hadn't kept them awake all night, but she'd find out about that after the meeting when she gave Josie her thank-you present.

Popping Saffie into her baby walker, Ben joined the friends at the big table placed in front of the French windows. Kara passed Ben and Zoe mugs of coffee, and then they all waited to hear why they had called the meeting.

"I'm sure you've all seen the latest disgusting post from the Square Insider?" asked Zoe, and they all nodded. "Well, it looks like the pictures were taken from the same position as previously."

"Yes, we thought so too," said Jack.

"Last week, as you know, Jack, I put an extra camera in Will's bedroom pointing at the south side of the square," said Ben.

"And?" asked Jack.

"The photographer was above Elsie's sitting room," said Ben.

"But why would Elsie... oh, I've been so stupid!" exclaimed Josie.

"What?" asked Hugo, looking mystified.

"We all missed it didn't we?" said Jack. "Elsie only has the ground floor- there is a different resident upstairs."

"Who is it?" asked Kara. "I've never seen anyone else."

"Hang on whilst I get the file," said Jack, getting up and fetching it from the office.

He spread the file on the table and then extracted the latest list of Social Services placements at the square, running his finger down the list until he came to the right property.

"It's a P. Gill, placed under the category of rehabilitation of offenders," he said

"Does it say what they were in for?" asked Hugo.

"No, they can't tell us that, but it would be 'white collar crime', as our rules exclude anything else," replied Jack.

"Is P. Gill a man or a woman?" asked Ben, "Zoe couldn't tell from the images."

"It doesn't say," replied Jack. "I must have a word with Social Services about incomplete information."

Ben had sent the video to Zoe's tablet, and she had been busy extracting the relevant section and selecting the clearest image. Once she had done this, she passed the tablet around for everyone to have a look.

"Still can't tell if it's a man or a woman," said Jack, staring at the image. "They are not very tall, which might suggest a woman, but the figure is quite blocky, which could suggest a man."

"Or a stocky woman?" added Kara.

"Looks like he or she has dark hair – I think blond hair would have caught the light a bit, don't you?" said Josie.

"Yes," said Hugo, peering over her shoulder. "Perhaps shoulder length hair?"

"A woman then?" asked Josie.

"Or a long-haired man?" said Kara.

"Well, only one way to find out," said Jack. "Let's pay he or she a visit."

Not wanting to disturb Elsie by going mob-handed, it was agreed that Jack and Ben should go, and the rest would wait at the manor for news. The two men set off walking down the hill, their friends watching them through the French windows until they were out of sight.

All was quiet in the square when they arrived, Nadia being the only person outside, dead heading her flowers. She waved as they passed, and then watched curiously as they rang the doorbell of the door next to Elsie's - she'd never seen anyone use that door before and wondered if someone must have just moved in. She hoped they were into gardening so she could share her new passion with them.

Will also saw them, and seeing Ben, he hoped he could catch him when he came back out, as he could really do with having someone to talk to. His friends had made sure that he saw yesterday's post, and he was mortified, too embarrassed to show his face in town. He hadn't seen any of the previous posts, but if they had been as bad as that one, it was no wonder that Joy was avoiding him.

Joy noticed them too. After yesterday's awful post, she was keeping Mia inside - it clearly wasn't safe for her to be outside with that pervert Will watching her. She decided that it was time she grew a backbone, and when Jack came back out, she would collar him and demand that Will was evicted from the square. Joy was even more fired up as she was cross at herself, having realised that despite the threat to Mia, when she'd seen the picture, her eyes had lingered on Will's bare chest and his hand on his…

When they got no reply from the doorbell, Ben and Jack hammered on the door. No reply. They hammered some more, and then listened for signs of movements in the eerie silence that followed. Nothing.

"Gill. I know you are in there, come on out!" shouted Jack through the letter box. No reply.

The two friends looked at each other.

"What now, Jack?" asked Ben.

"I think we'll have to try again later. They must be out," replied Jack.

"Don't you have a master key?" asked Ben.

"I do, but this is someone's home, and I can't enter unless it's a matter of life and death," replied Jack.

"Let's ask Elsie to ring us as soon as they come back," suggested Ben.

Jack knocked gently on Elsie's door, and they waited patiently for her to make her slow way to answer it. A sudden commotion behind them made them turn around and they could see Joy and Will on the path just outside their houses. Joy was screaming at Will, thumping him on the chest whilst he just stood there, trying to speak calmly to her.

"Uh-oh," said Ben. "I think I need to meditate."

Leaving Jack to wait to speak to Elsie, Ben set off across the square, separated the young couple, and steered them both to a bench, one arm around each of them to stop them running away. Jack missed what was being said as Elsie had answered the door, and he turned his attention to her to make his request.

"She's probably sleeping it off," said Elsie. "It was a late one last night, about 4am when the last of her guests left."

"Oh, so it's a woman then?" said Jack.

"If you want to call her that. A tart I'd say," she replied.

That was not the first time that Jack had heard someone local being called a tart, and an awful suspicion popped into his head.

"What does she look like, Elsie?" he asked.

"Well, I've not actually met her, but I did catch a glimpse once. Thickset with longish black hair, her chest on display and her skirt too short - as I said, a tart!"

Parts of the description were very familiar to Jack, but not the black hair, but it did match the description given by Adam of his abuser, so Jack would pass the address onto the police to investigate it further. In the meantime, he gave his direct phone number to Elsie to ring him as soon as she heard or saw Ms Gill.

Things had calmed down in the middle of the square; Joy was crying, and Will had his arms around her, stroking her back. Ben patted them both on the shoulder and then walked back to Jack.

"I think those two will be alright now," said Ben, as they walked back up to the manor. "They've both been put under terrible strain by this malicious behaviour. There was so much relief on their faces, Jack, when I explained what had been going on."

"Well done, Ben," said Jack. "I just wish we could have completely resolved the situation, but Elsie will let us know when Ms Gill is back, and I'll try again."

"Oh, so it is a woman then," said Ben.

"Yes, and according to Elsie, a 'tart'," replied Jack.

"Hm, we've heard that before, and the name is very similar," said Ben.

"Yes, but she was blond," replied Jack.

"Ever heard of hair dye...?" said Ben.

Chapter Twenty-Nine

A week went by with no message from Elsie and then another week with no sight or sound of Ms Gill and no more Square Insider posts. Jack, the police and social services all called at Ms Gill's apartment at different times and got no reply. It was beginning to look like she had moved away without giving any notice, and, as the rent hadn't been paid, Jack just had to wait until a full month had passed and then he could let himself into the apartment and remove Ms Gill's belongings.

He didn't have to wait that long, however, as the following week Sandra, the post lady, collared him and told him he needed to check on Ms Gill's apartment. Sandra had been delivering a letter to Ms Gill and when she lifted the letter box flap loads of flies had streamed out, along with an awful stench.

"Fair made me sick," said Sandra. "I hope to God she hasn't left a cat or something in there and it's starved to death."

Jack hoped so too. A few years ago, he'd had to remove several dead cats from the old carriage house, and he could still remember the terrible smell. It seemed to Jack that an 'odious emission' was a good reason for a landlord to enter a property, so after getting no response from the doorbell again, he used his master key and let himself in.

Sandra hadn't been joking about the flies; the air as thick with them as Jack fought his way upstairs. The smell was ten times worse than the smell he remembered in the carriage house that day, and a hundred times worse when he opened the apartment door at the top of the stairs. Pulling his t-shirt up over his mouth, he moved through the kitchen diner, where the mouldy remains of a meal crawling with flies had been left. The kitchen worktop was cluttered with dirty pans, shrivelled vegetables and bottles of booze, mostly empty, and the sink was full of filthy crockery.

Jack gingerly opened the main bedroom door and found it in darkness, blackout blinds covering the windows. The smell and flies were even worse in there, so holding his t-shirt tighter over his mouth and nose he felt with his other hand for the light switch just inside the door. The sudden illumination made the scene in front of him even more shocking, and Jack froze, unable to process for a moment what he was seeing.

On the floor next to the bed was a body, a bloated, putrefied body, crawling with maggots and covered in flies. Body fluids had seeped into the carpet around it, rusty-red around the head. Straggly black hair with lighter roots half covered the face, and Jack made himself take a step closer to see the face better. The discoloured skin on the face had slipped a little, forming darker folds at the hairline and neck, but the face was still recognisable: Poppy, Poppy Gilbert.

The bile rose in Jack's throat, and he turned and ran, down the stairs and out into the blissful fresh air, where he vomited onto the path. Nadia saw him and came running over, took his arm and helped him to a bench. Jack couldn't speak, and Nadia ran and fetched him a glass of water which he spilt more than he drank, his whole-body trembling with shock. Eventually, he took a steadying breath, pulled out his phone and with shaking fingers dialled 999.

When Kara arrived, summoned by Nadia, Jack was still sitting on the bench, a blanket around his shoulders and a mug of tea clutched in his hands. The Square was crawling with police, and CSI officers in white coveralls were coming back and forth to a van in the car park. A small crowd of people had gathered on the other side of the police tape line and Kara had had to fight her way through. She eased the cold cup from Jack's hands and pulled him to her. For a moment he remained rigid, and then he collapsed against her, and she had to hang onto him to stop him falling.

Chapter Thirty

Against Kara's advice, Jack went into work on Monday, needing to keep busy as when he stopped the terrible image of the rotting body filled his mind. He had been assigned to Mia when she'd first started at the school and wasn't talking, but now she was speaking again there was no shutting her up, so Jack had now been allocated to a little boy, Noah, who had recently started having behavioural problems. Although extremely bright, Noah was having difficulty staying on task and occasionally would lose his temper and lash out at anyone who happened to be in his way.

Noah had a wide knowledge of nature and was a wonderful artist, so today, when he was obviously on edge, Jack had asked him to draw a wildlife picture for the cover for a booklet the class was making on local plants and animals. Jack had just started him on the task when the school secretary entered the classroom and caught Jack's eye, miming 'phone call' to him. Jack apologised to the teacher and then hurried after the secretary who handed him the phone before leaving the office to give him some privacy.

"Jack is that you?" asked Joy.

"Yes. Is everything okay, Joy?" asked Jack.

"They've arrested Will. You've got to help him, Jack. He couldn't have done it!" said Joy, sounding a little hysterical.

"What Joy? What has Will been arrested for?" asked Jack, shocked.

"Murder. That awful woman's murder," said Joy.

"What?" exclaimed Jack. "No way!"

"I know. He is the gentlest, kindest man I've ever met, and wouldn't hurt a fly, but they cuffed him and took him away," wailed Joy, clearly crying.

Jack's eyebrows shot up as he struggled to process the two big bits of information. Will and Joy were clearly an item, and Will had been arrested for murder. Poppy's murder.

"Listen Joy, I'll finish work in an hour. If you're okay till then, I'll come straight to you and bring Mia home with me. Then, if I can leave Dottie to play with Mia, I'll go to the police station to try and sort this out," he said, sounding a lot calmer than he felt.

"Please Jack," said Joy.

Just over an hour later, Jack and the two little girls arrived at the square. Leaving the girls to eat some lunch that Joy had kindly prepared for them both, Joy took Jack into the snug to fill him in on what had happened.

"If you remember Jack, Mia was coming to stay with you tonight for a sleepover," said Joy.

"I couldn't forget – Dottie has been so excited!" said Jack.

"Well, Will and I were going away for the night to stay at the Crown Spa Hotel in Scarborough. Separate rooms – we are taking things slow – but our first proper date," said Joy, sadly. "He was just putting our bags in his car when the police arrived, and asked Will if he wouldn't mind coming down to the station to answer some questions. Jack asked if he could do it tomorrow as he had plans for today, and so they cautioned him, and arrested him on suspicion of murder."

"Did they say anything to you Joy?" asked Jack, handing her a tissue as her eyes had filled with tears.

"Nothing. They just drove away, leaving our suitcases in the car park. Then two officers came back and went into Jack's house and came out a while later with his computer and with his bokken in an evidence bag. I asked them what was happening, but they wouldn't speak to me," she replied, tears now spilling down her cheeks.

"There's obviously been a mistake, Joy," said Jack, patting her hand. "I'm going to ring Kara and get her to find a good solicitor - they use an excellent firm for RSPCA prosecutions, so if not them, they will be able to recommend someone. If the girls can stay here for now, Kara will pick them both up when she finishes work, if I'm not back by then, and bring them both up to us for their sleepover as planned, if you are still okay about that?"

Joy nodded.

"Good," said Jack, "I'd never have heard the last of it if the sleepover was cancelled!"

Leaving her to compose herself, Jack went outside to ring Kara, who was as shocked as he was but thought she knew a good solicitor. Jack said a quick goodbye to Joy and the girls and then set off for the police station in Pickering where an incident room had been set up. Going inside the 1960's building, Jack asked to speak to the officer in charge of the murder enquiry. The desk sergeant looked him up and down and told him he would have to wait. Jack sat on a bench for almost an hour being completely ignored, but then, knowing how anxious Joy was, he decided to pull rank.

The desk sergeant looked up from his ledger and glared at Jack.

"I thought I told you to wait," he said.

"You did, and I have been doing so, but you never asked my name to pass onto the officer in charge," said Jack, pleasantly.

"Name then?" asked the sergeant in a bored voice.

"Lord Jack Henry Neville Brown," replied Jack quietly, but with authority.

"What?" exclaimed the sergeant, startled.

"Lord Kirkby is shorter to write down," said Jack with a smile.

"Yes, Lord Kirkby. If you wouldn't mind taking a seat for a moment longer, I'll just go and see if the Detective Chief Inspector is free," said the sergeant, almost saluting Jack before dashing off.

Jack smiled wryly. He hated how a title altered the way people treated you – everyone should be treated with courtesy and respect – but sometimes it was very useful!

A few moments later, Jack was ushered into a small room and immediately joined by Detective Chief Inspector Quinn who shook his hand. DCI Quinn was a lady of middle years, smartly dressed but very tired looking.

"How can I help you, Lord Kirkby," she asked politely. Her accent was not local, and Jack wondered if she had been brought in from a larger force to head up the murder investigation.

"You have arrested one of my tenants, Will Appleby. I'd like to know why, and whether he has a solicitor present," said Jack firmly.

"Mr Appleby is a person of interest in the murder of Ms Gilbert," replied Quinn.

"On what grounds?" asked Jack.

DCI Quinn, narrowed her eyes and looked at Jack for a moment, deciding if she should tell him anything or not. Knowing that he had found the body, Quinn realised she probably wouldn't be telling him anything he didn't know and may get some useful insights in return.

"Ms Gilbert had been posting salacious things about Mr Appleby on the Kirkby Facebook. He is highly trained in martial arts – something that was witnessed by my officers when he single-handedly took down an intruder. He uses a wooden sword, a bokken I understand it's called. As you found the body, Lord Kirkby, you will know that there was a head wound that may or may not have led to Ms Gilbert's death, a head wound that could have been caused by a blow from a bokken. In addition, Mr Appleby has no alibi for what we believe was the night of the murder," replied DCI Quinn.

"All circumstantial," replied Jack, hoping he was right. "Will practices Aikido, a discipline that is about restraint, not violence. If you read your officer's reports relating to his apprehension of the intruder, he achieved that without inflicting a single injury on the man concerned."

DCI Quinn raised her eyebrows: she hadn't read the reports, but she would now.

"Yes, but then there is the question of the images of a young girl on his computer. Ms Gilbert accused him of being a paedophile – maybe there was a grain of truth in her posts after all?" continued DCI Quinn. "Maybe, seeing as he was worming his way into the household of the child concerned, he wanted to shut Ms Gilbert up before she spoiled his chances?

Jack felt sick. He knew in his heart of hearts that Will wasn't a paedophile and hadn't killed Gilbert, but put like that, he couldn't help a seed of doubt creeping in.

"Utter rubbish and supposition, DCI Quinn," he said as scornfully as he could.

"Possibly, but then there is also the fact that Mr Appleby was just about to go away – suspicious in the circumstances, wouldn't you agree?" said the DCI.

Before Jack could explain that Will was only going to Scarborough for the night, there was a knock at the door and a constable informed Quinn that Mr Appleby's solicitor was here.

"Ah, good," said Jack. "Please can you arrange for Mr Appleby to consult with his solicitor. I'll wait in reception, as I expect to see him released without charge very soon."

Quinn's eyebrows shot up, but she ushered Jack out without further comment. The solicitor was waiting in reception, and recognising Jack, shook his hand warmly before following DCI Quinn back to meet his client.

Just over an hour later, the solicitor reappeared accompanied by a whited faced Will. Jack steered them both outside, and the solicitor explained that with absolutely no evidence to link Will to the murder they had no choice but to release him on police bail, pending the autopsy and forensics report from the murder scene. They had taken Will's fingerprints and a DNA swab and had retained his bokken for forensics, but other than that he was free, however, he had to remain at his home address and report to the police station once a week.

Jack thanked the solicitor and then drove Jack home.

"I'm sorry Will," said Jack as he drove, "I know you were supposed to be going away tonight."

Will nodded miserably, too stunned to even speak.

"We have Mia for the night, so you can still spend the evening alone with Joy. Why not order a nice meal to eat in? Not the same as the Crown Spa I know, but better than nothing."

Will's face brightened a little and he nodded again. On arriving at Joy's house, Joy flew into Will's arms, and they held each other tight. Jack gathered up the excited girls who were unaware of the unfolding drama, and ushered them into his car, leaving Joy and Will alone together.

Chapter Thirty-One

Taking Will's hand, Joy led him inside and sat with him on the settee whilst he pulled himself together. He was visibly shaken by the events of the day, and Joy knew exactly what that felt like after years of abuse at the hands of her husband. She did what she wished someone had done for her - just held his hand and stroked his back and was 'there' for him.

When Ben had explained to them both what had been going on, Joy had been ashamed with how she had treated Will: how could she have believed such rubbish when her instinct had always been to trust him? In the last couple of weeks, they had spent a lot of time together, and the fledgling feelings for Will that she had previously suppressed had started to grow.

She knew he thought a lot about her too, but was shy, so asking her to go away for the night had been a big thing for him. He'd made sure that she knew he'd booked separate rooms, but even if he hadn't, she would still have said yes. In fact, she suspected, had the events of the day not intervened, they would have only used one room.

When the police had arrested him on suspicion of murder, not for one second had she believed he was guilty. She had doubted him once and wouldn't make that mistake again; he was a good, kind, gentle man, as different to her husband as it was possible for someone to be.

"When I was at school I was bullied badly," said Will suddenly. "My dad was ill for a long time and died when I was very young, so I had no male role model to teach me to stand up for myself. I was small, slight and into art, not sports, so I was the perfect target for the bullies."

Will paused, thinking back to those awful times and Joy just squeezed his hand and waited to see where he was going with this.

"There was this cartoon I loved, Dragonball Z, all martial arts training and fighting, good always overcoming evil. The main character, Goku, was constantly striving to improve himself and get stronger, and I so wanted to be like him," said Will, shaking his head at the memory.

"I decided to take up martial arts, but a lot of the Dragonball show was fighting for fightings sake, and I didn't want that - that was what the bullies did. I found out about Aikido, which is about defence not attack, turning the opponent's violence back against themselves. Mum wasn't keen - she didn't know about the bullying - so I saved my pocket money to pay for lessons and walked the three miles to the dojo and back every Saturday morning. My body filled out and my mind became calm - I suppose I exuded a sort of 'no go' vibe, and the bullying stopped."

"Wow," said Joy, "that is impressive!" Will smiled at her and shook his head a little, not thinking of himself as impressive in any way.

"What I loved most was being in control - of my body and any situation," he continued. "But today in the police station, that control was taken away, and I felt like that little boy again."

"Oh no, they didn't openly bully me or threaten me," said Will, seeing the shocked look on Joy's face, "but they did their best to intimidate me, pressuring me to say something that would condemn me. I couldn't get up and leave, or take a minute to meditate, or even go to the toilet without being accompanied, and I felt panic rising inside."

"Oh Will," said Joy, putting her arms around him and holding him tight. "It's all circumstantial, Will, they have no forensic or other evidence, so they won't be able to charge you - it will all be over soon."

"I wish that were true, Joy, but they could have some forensic evidence - I was in Ms Gilbert's apartment on the afternoon of the murder," said Will flatly.

"What!" exclaimed Joy, leaping up.

"You were in that woman's apartment - with that whore? How could you, Will!" she cried, her heart breaking. She grabbed her jacket and headed for the door.

"No, no, Joy, it wasn't like that," cried Will, grabbing her hands, trying to stop her flight, to pull her close to him again.

"Get off me," Joy shouted, pulling her hands out of his and pushing him away. "I should have known not to trust a man!"

The door slammed behind her, and once again Will was alone, the sudden silence loud once the echo of the door slam faded.

Chapter Thirty-Two

The post-mortem had been completed and a Coroner's inquest opened. Both Jack and Will were summoned to attend, and after a police officer covered the basic facts, Jack was called to the witness stand. He had been dreading it, but although the coroner cross examined him on exactly what he had seen when he discovered the body, the questioning was gentle, and Jack relaxed a little and tried his best to give clear, concise answers.

Jack was surprised when the coroner questioned him about the remains of the meal on the table, and any evidence of food preparation on the worktops. Jack struggled to remember - the putrid body having blotted everything else from his mind - but the coroner had the statement Jack had given to the police and was able to prompt him on details.

Will was then called to give evidence, and glancing nervously around the room, he was surprised to see Joy sitting with Kara and Josie amongst other members of the public. She avoided Will's eye, and he sighed heavily, prompting the coroner to ask him if he was alright. Will was tempted to say 'no', he wasn't alright, and never would be again unless Joy let him explain, but she had refused to answer the door and had gone to great lengths to avoid him. He didn't have her email address and she had blocked him on social media, so he was stuck in his misery.

With no explanation or apology his computer and bokken had been returned to him and he was no longer required to report to the police every week. He was now permitted to leave Kirkby, and if Joy had been speaking to him, he would have been delighted and rebooked their Scarborough hotel. Without her, there was nowhere he wanted to go.

"Mr Appleby, please can you describe your first encounter with the deceased on the day of her death," asked the coroner, bringing Will back to the present.

There was a sharp intake of breath, which Will knew was from Joy, so he focused on the coroner and tried to block her presence out.

"I had gone for a walk," started Will, "and took a route from the square up through the woods."

"Were you alone, Mr Appleby?" asked the coroner.

"Yes, my friends were engaged in a cricket practice," replied Will, a look of sadness crossing his face as he remembered how he had felt seeing Joy and Mia out in the square laughing with their neighbours, knowing he couldn't join them without spoiling Joy's day. He had decided to go for a long walk to take himself away from the torture of seeing her so close but so unreachable.

"And you came across Ms Gilbert in the woods?" prompted the coroner seeing Will lost in thought.

"Yes, although I didn't know who she was," replied Will.

"Describe your encounter please, Mr Appleby," said the coroner.

"As I walked up the road, I saw a woman knelt down at the side of the road with a carrier bag next to her. As I passed, I muttered a polite 'Good Morning', and she leapt up and said 'Oh it's you! Hello'. I was bemused as I'd never seen the woman before, but she told me she was a neighbour and had seen me lots of times. This surprised me, as I work from home and I've not been out in the garden much, so I'm not very visible in and around the square. She told me she lived directly opposite me, and my morning exercises were the highlight of her day. I found this comment disconcerting - the sides of the square are some distance apart, so either she had exceptional eyesight or used binoculars," said Will.

"Did you raise this concern with her?" asked the coroner.

"No. She had moved to stand a lot closer than is normal and I felt uncomfortable, so I backed away and said that I had to get going and continued along the road," replied Will.

"Did she say anything else to you?" asked the coroner.

"No, but I could hear her laughing as I walked away."

"Can you tell me what she was doing at the side of the road and what was in her bag?" asked the coroner.

"I don't know for certain, but I think she was foraging, putting stuff into her bag as she found it. This would make sense as she later told me she was a cordon bleu chef and liked to use unusual ingredients."

"I'll come back to 'later' in a moment, Mr Appleby, but can you suggest what she might have been collecting in the woods?" asked the coroner.

"It's hard to say. The bluebells were just coming out, but I don't think you can eat them. A little later, when I stopped to sketch the bluebells, I could see and smell that there was a little wild garlic still about, so maybe she was picking wild garlic leaves for a recipe?" Will replied.

"Was the area where you saw her sunny and dry?" asked the coroner.

"I don't think so, it's an ancient woodland and very overgrown and mossy - you notice the dampness in the air as soon as you enter the woods," Jack answered.

"Is it the kind of area that mushrooms would grow in?" asked the coroner.

"Oh yes: I'm working on a series of illustrations for a modern 'Flower Fairies' book, which is why I was sketching the bluebells. I noticed some mushrooms and photographed them in case I wanted to sit a fairy on one in a later illustration," replied Jack, a little bemused at the question, and slightly embarrassed to be talking about fairies in a coroner's court.

"Thank you, Mr Appleby. Now, can you tell me about your second encounter with Ms Gilbert that day?"

"Well, I was out for several hours, sketching initially, and then I continued my walk in a long loop and arrived back at the square at around 3pm. As I crossed the car park to enter the square, I saw Ms Gilbert unloading shopping from her car. The bags looked really heavy, and normally I would have offered to assist, but she'd made me feel so uncomfortable earlier, I tried to sneak by without her seeing me. Unfortunately, she saw me and asked me to carry her bags, saying they were too heavy for her. I could hardly say no, so I picked them up and followed her to her front door," said Will.

"Did you see what was in the bags?" asked the coroner.

"There was a lot of booze, which is why they were so heavy, and a long box of ready-made pastry poking out of one bag, but other than that I don't know," Jack replied.

"Is this when Ms Gilbert told you she was a chef?"

"As I waited whilst she found the key and unlocked the door, she mentioned it and said the shopping was for clients coming for dinner that evening," said Jack.

"Was that the end of your encounter with the deceased?" asked the coroner.

"Not quite," replied Will, his face going red at the memory. "She lived in an upstairs apartment, so I carried the shopping upstairs and through to her kitchen. As I leant over to place the bags carefully on the floor due to the bottles, I felt her hand on my bottom. Well, not just my bottom, she slid it underneath, and cupped my...privates."

There was a gasp in the room, but Will looked down at the floor, not wanting to catch Joy's eye.

"Was this advance welcome, Mr Appleby?" asked the coroner, keeping his voice neutral.

"Not at all!" exclaimed Will. "I have... sorry had, a girlfriend who means the world to me. I almost ran out of the apartment - I couldn't get away from there quick enough."

"Was that the last time you saw Ms Gilbert, Mr Appleby?" ask the coroner.

"Yes," replied Will.

"Thank you, Mr Appleby. You have been most helpful," said the coroner.

As Will sat down he couldn't see how what he had said had helped the coroner in any way, but he fervently hoped it had helped sort out the rift between him and Joy.

The pathologist who undertook the post-mortem was called next and ran through her findings in a very long-winded way.

The coroner stopped her and asked her to go back to the head injury.

"Can you just clarify if the head injury was instrumental in Ms Gilbert's death, please?" he asked.

"Oh no, the head injury occurred after death. From a blood sample taken from the bedside table and from the shape of the wound, I am pretty certain she hit her head on the corner of the table as she fell down dead. If she had been alive when she hit her head, there would have been substantially more blood."

Jack went a bit pale, remembering the small rusty red halo around Gilbert's head.

"Are you certain that she wasn't killed by a blow to the head?"

"Certain," the pathologist confirmed. "She died of a heart attack."

A murmur of surprise rippled around the room.

"So, her death was by natural causes?" asked the coroner.

"Far from it," said the pathologist, "the heart attack was brought on by muscarine poisoning."

A collective gasp was now heard in the room.

"So, someone poisoned her?" asked the coroner.

"I didn't say that!" said the pathologist, a little crossly. "I'm saying that the deceased ate something that contained muscarine, which is a poison."

"An important difference," said the coroner with a wry smile. "Do explain."

"From her stomach contents we know she had eaten a steak and mushroom pie, along with fried potatoes and peas. She had also consumed a large quantity of wine. The mushrooms in the pie she had eaten were of two types: a very small amount of dried Psilocybin mushrooms, commonly known as 'magic mushrooms', and a larger quantity of fresh Ivory Funnel mushrooms. The pie consumed also contained onions, wild garlic, herbs, spices and a commercial gravy mix.

Traces of Agaricus Bisporus mushrooms, better known as button mushrooms, and Psilocybin mushrooms were found on three of the plates left on the table. The fourth plate, positioned at the head of the table, had traces of Psilocybin mushrooms and Ivory Funnel mushrooms but no Agaricus Bisporus mushrooms. Saliva on the cutlery laid across the plate concerned matched the deceased's. As we only have one corpse, I think it safe to say that the plate and cutlery had been used by Ms Gilbert and that she was the only one who ingested Ivory Funnel mushroom."

"And they contain muscarine?" asked the coroner.

"Yes. In high doses they cause death by cardio-vascular failure within hours of consumption. Soon after consumption, there will be pronounced sweating, salivation, nausea, vomiting, diarrhoea, abdominal pain, and myosis. Samples of sweat, vomit and faeces were taken from the bedding as would have been expected."

"Could Ms Gilbert have been forcibly fed the Ivory Funnel mushrooms?"

"I don't think so. The food had been well chewed and there were no injuries to the mouth or throat to suggest that," said the pathologist.

"Was there anything else of relevance from the post-mortem, please?" asked the coroner.

"There were also several samples of semen, from three different men, on the sheets. One of them matched semen in Ms Gilbert's vagina, but there was no evidence of rape or violent sexual assault. The deceased had the beginning of cirrhosis of the liver and some atherosclerotic plaque in the coronary arteries. Neither of these killed her, but the atherosclerotic plaque could have contributed to the cardio-vascular failure."

The coroner considered what he had heard and then thanked the pathologist and summoned the police officer again.

"The pathologist has told us that the pies made by Ms Gilbert for her guests contained a quantity of 'magic mushrooms'. In your investigation were you able to find where they had come from?" he asked.

"Empty packaging recovered from the scene contained traces of dried Psilocybin mushrooms. From her internet history, we believe that the package had been ordered from a supplier based in Brazil where possession and sale of Psilocybin mushrooms is legal. She had recently tried to place another order, but that transaction hadn't been successful as she attempted to pay with a stolen credit card that had had a stop placed on it earlier the same day," replied the officer.

The coroner raised his eyebrows and considered for a moment if a stolen credit card was relevant. He decided to leave that for later, if necessary, and concentrate on the mushrooms.

"So, you cannot purchase Psilocybin mushrooms in the UK?" he asked.

"No. Up until 2005 it was legal to sell Psilocybin mushrooms in the UK, but section 21 of the Drugs Act 2005 made them a Class A drug," confirmed the officer.

The coroner nodded and thought for a moment.

"Was there any packaging from the button mushrooms at the scene?"

"Yes: they were purchased from the local supermarket. However, from the pathologist's report, I understand that there were no button mushrooms in the pie eaten by Ms Gilbert."

"Did you find any other packaging?" the coroner asked.

"Two carrier bags were recovered from the kitchen bin. The top one contained traces of Ivory Funnel mushrooms. The bag that was lower down in the bin had traces of wild garlic but had no traces of any type of mushroom" the officer replied.

"Was there any evidence that these had been gathered locally?" asked the coroner.

"Yes. Forensic analysis of soil recovered from each of the bags concerned found it to be identical to the soil in the local woodland," said the officer.

The coroner paused for a moment again and then changed tack.

"Were you able to identify Ms Gilbert's guests that night and if so, were they questioned on the state of her health before they left her?" he asked.

"We have spoken to two of her guests, a Mr Smythe and a Mr Fernsby, and they both confirm Ms Gilbert was fit and well when they left. There was a third guest whose description matches, er, video footage that we have, but we haven't yet been able to contact him. Mr Smythe and Mr Fernsby only knew his first name, Nigel, but confirmed that he left well before they did. In light of the post-mortem report, we didn't think it was necessary to pursue his identity further at this time."

The coroner nodded in agreement and dismissed the police officer, before calling for a brief recess to consider his verdict. Conversation started around the room immediately, everyone discussing what they had just heard, but it was only five minutes later when the coroner returned, and an immediate hush filled the room.

"In summing up, ladies and gentlemen," said the coroner, "the pathologist found highly toxic Ivory Funnel mushrooms in the deceased's stomach which were the cause of the heart attack that killed her.

We have evidence given by Mr Appleby relating to what I believe was Ms Gilbert foraging for mushrooms and evidence from the police officer's report of traces of Ivory Funnel mushrooms in a bag.

We know the deceased had almost used up her supply of dried Psilocybin mushrooms and had failed in an attempt to buy more, so it is reasonable to assume she was attempting to replace her supply with fresh Psilocybin mushrooms gathered locally.

Sadly, instead of Psilocybin mushrooms, she picked Ivory Funnel mushrooms, which are similar in appearance, and baked them in a pie which she then ate. In light of these facts, I will be recording a verdict of accidental death."

He paused and frowned as surprised whispers spread quickly around the room. A court official asked for silence and the coroner waited until everyone was quiet before continuing.

"It is very sad that a relatively young woman's life has been cut short in this horrible manner, a woman who I understand was a cordon bleu chef. The only consolation is that these tragic events may serve as a warning to others not to eat wild mushrooms. I am releasing her body for cremation: may she rest in peace."

The coroner bowed his head a moment, and everyone else followed suit, expecting maybe a prayer or something to conclude the formalities, but after a few moments' contemplation, the coroner just turned and left. The witnesses and members of the public filed out almost in silence, shocked that what they all thought was a murder was in fact a silly accident.

Outside, Jack and Kara hugged each other and then Kara took Josie's arm and almost dragged her away, deliberately leaving Joy alone to wait for Will.

Chapter Thirty-Three

Considering that no one had known that Poppy Gilbert had been living in the square, after her death there was an almost palpable lightness in the air, a feeling that a great weight had been lifted. Her apartment had been professionally cleaned, but so far no one had moved into it, and Jack wasn't sure if anyone ever would.

Although everyone was glad Poppy's malevolent presence had gone, Josie was greatly saddened that a woman's life had been wasted and that there was no one to mourn her passing. As Poppy had no family or obvious funds, it fell to the council to arrange her funeral – a 'pauper's funeral'. Josie had asked to be informed of the date and, hating to think of a funeral with no one attending, she went along, alone, as Hugo couldn't be persuaded to go with her. He was more in Zoe's camp - let's have a party to celebrate that she won't be troubling us any more - but Josie felt it was wrong to celebrate anyone's death, no matter how awful they had been in life.

The drive to the East Yorkshire Crematorium was a lovely one, through rolling Wolds and tiny villages with duck ponds and ancient churches and Josie took her time, enjoying the view. She arrived eventually at the crematorium which stood alone amongst open fields, its entrance marked by two large stone cairns. She was surprised to see three other cars in the car park and then saw two men chatting outside the door to the chapel. As she got closer, she recognised one of them instantly, even though he looked a lot older than when she had last seen him: Smythe. Both men were laughing at something, and then patted each other on the back before going inside.

Josie followed them in, and saw that the owner of the third car, a woman, was already seated. Josie recognised her as DCI Quinn, and the men seemed to recognise her too, and suddenly moved apart, each sitting on different sides of the chapel several rows back from her. Josie sat down on the opposite side but about level with the second man in order to get a good look at his face. She vaguely recognised him but didn't know where from: she racked her brains, but the name just wouldn't come to her.

Josie turned her attention to the front of the chapel, to the beautiful stained-glass window depicting a boat midway between the sky and sea, the simple white altar and, to one side, the cheap coffin unadorned with flowers. She thought of Poppy's life, the lies she had told and the hurt she had caused and tried to forgive her. Whilst that was a struggle, Josie's anger was replaced with sadness, and she wished she had brought flowers, as if nothing else, Poppy had once been a gardener.

The vicar entered and the service started, but there were no warm words or touching family remembrances, just the bare facts of Pauline Gilbert's life and death. Looking at the sparse congregation, the vicar didn't attempt a hymn, just the standard reading and a few half-hearted prayers.

As soon as the final prayer was said, and even before the curtains had finished closing around the coffin, both men got up, and by the time that Josie got outside, their cars were already roaring away at speed down the long drive. Josie stopped to speak to DCI Quinn who had attended, much as Josie had done, because she thought no one else would. Quinn raised an eyebrow when Josie asked her if she knew who the second man was. Josie thought perhaps she hadn't seen them, but Quinn was a detective and missed nothing, and was able to inform Josie he was a Mr Fernsby, one of Poppy's guests on the fateful night.

On the long drive home, Josie continued to ponder where she knew Mr Fernsby from, but with no luck. Arriving home to a hug and a hot meal prepared by an apologetic Hugo (who said he should have come with her), she put it from her mind.

Chapter Thirty-Four

Spring became summer, and the vegetables and flowers in the square's communal garden were becoming established due to Bert and Nadia's hard work, helped by other residents and the allotment community. The fresh green leaves of carrots, parsnips and leeks filled one bed, wigwams of canes supporting young beans and peas were in another, whilst courgettes and marrows were rapidly filling their own beds with their huge leaves.

After an early disaster when the pigeons ate all the cabbage, beetroot and cauliflower seedlings, a second planting was thriving under netting and the fresh green leaves of potatoes were starting to emerge from their soil mounds. After much deliberation about the possibility of a late frost, tomatoes started off on windowsills had been planted out and tied to canes. Bert checked them religiously for side shoots that needed to be removed or for new growth to be tied up, and the plants were growing fast and strong.

The strawberries were a mass of white flowers giving the promise of a good crop, and the children checked them almost daily: Bert knew that once the first fruits appeared that they wouldn't last long. Bees hummed happily amongst Nadia's colourful mass of flowers and blue tits were nesting in a bird box on one of the trees. Elsie loved to watch the parent birds flying back and forth above her head, completely fearless, and hoped she would be there to see it when the babies eventually fledged.

A raised bed had been set aside just for children to grow what they wanted, and this had a somewhat chaotic mixture of flowers, fruit and vegetables, with sunflower stems just starting to emerge above the other plants. Will and Joy had been encouraged by Mia and Dottie to get more involved and they now regularly helped out, Will doing any heavy work and Joy helping to keep all the beds weed free.

On Sunday mornings, if it wasn't raining, Will was teaching all the children the basics of Aikido on the play area. He was particularly keen to teach Mia simple self-defence, never wanting her to be in the same position that her mother had been. Kara brought Dottie, Lily and Ronan down to join in, and Ronan enjoyed it so much that he had now joined the dojo, going with Will each week. Kara was delighted, as he now spent less time on his phone, and his teenage moodiness was less evident.

Will and Joy were clearly now an item again, but no one knew the details of their reconciliation, although Zoe and Kara had speculated on it endlessly.

"In Will's position, I'm not sure I'd have taken her back after she doubted him a second time," said Zoe when the two friends met for coffee in the Cosy Café one morning.

"Ah, but I'm sure Will understood her mistrust in men, after the years of abuse the poor girl suffered," replied Kara.

"Yes, I suppose so, and I guess 'love conquers all'," said Zoe with a wry smile.

"They really do make a lovely couple, don't they?" said Kara.

"They do," confirmed Zoe. "It's time we had another wedding!"

"Give them a chance! Anyway, her divorce isn't through yet," replied Kara. "Talking of which, I'm not sure if we told you - her husband got eighteen years for her abuse and Dottie's kidnap. Jack and I were in the courtroom with Joy two days ago, and he really is a nasty piece of work, but thankfully he's not going to be bothering anyone for a long time."

"Oh, thank goodness," said Zara, squeezing her hand. "That must be such a relief to her, and to you."

"Yes," replied Kara. "After what he put Dottie through, I could have happily killed him with my bare hands, but justice has been done, and Jack and I are trying to move on."

"Is Dottie fully recovered now?" asked Zara.

"I think so. At first, she was very quiet and not eating much - not like her at all! She was also having nightmares and had to sleep in our bed, but with the help of the school and an excellent counsellor, she does seem to be back to normal, but you never know do you? I think we'll always worry a bit about how it may have affected her," said Kara sadly.

"I'm sure she'll be fine, Kara. She's made of strong stuff and couldn't have better parents than you two - I just hope Ben and I do half as good a job with Saffie," she said, looking down at the little girl fast asleep in her pushchair next to them.

"Don't be daft! You're brilliant parents," replied Kara.

"Thanks, but babies don't come with manuals, do they?"

The friends laughed, and then Zoe remembered her own bit of news.

"Forgot to tell you - when I took Saffie for her last check-up, Nadia was just coming out of the clinic. She looked radiant, so putting two and two together, I think we might soon have the first baby in the square."

Chapter Thirty-Five

Now that they were safely beyond the three-month mark, Nadia and Amir decided it was safe to tell their friends that they were expecting a baby. They also needed to tell their family, but they'd been putting it off, not knowing if they would be happy for them. Neither set of parents had visited their new house yet, so it seemed like a good time to invite them all over, show them the lovely place where they lived and tell them their good news.

"What's the matter, love," asked Amir, seeing Nadia's concerned face when she came off the phone after calling her parents.

"My parents are coming, but Dad's just said he's going to hire a minibus and bring my uncles, aunts and my cousin Rashid too. The last time I spoke to my uncles, they forbade me to marry you, and I won't even tell you the awful things Rashid said, and now they are all coming here! Our location will no longer be a secret!" cried Nadia.

"Darling, we can't hide forever. I'm sure your father wouldn't have invited them if he didn't think it was safe to do so. How about we invite some of our friends and neighbours too - that way our families might be on best behaviour and less likely to cause any trouble?" suggested Amir.

"I think that's an excellent idea, Amir. If we are inviting neighbours, we can have the party outside in the garden as they won't all fit in the house," replied Nadia, smiling now.

"We're having a party now?" asked Amir, raising his eyebrows.

"Well, once the baby comes it will be a long while until we can again, so yes, let's have a party and celebrate in style. Show our family we have friends and a place in the community," said Nadia with a determined look on her face.

"I'd better ask Jack's permission then," said Amir, grinning at his wife.

Jack was more than happy to give permission, and stressed it was their home and they could do what they liked, as long as it didn't inconvenience their neighbours. Amir told him they would be inviting all the neighbours and hoped that Jack and his family could come too. Jack was delighted to be invited, as a multicultural, multi-generational event in the square encapsulated the ethos he had been trying to achieve.

With just a week to the event, Nadia spent every available moment cooking, but she needn't have worried, as her friends and neighbours all brought along dishes and added them to the trestle tables set out in the centre of the square. Kara had borrowed the tables from the town hall and Nadia had draped them in colourful fabric, adding vases of flowers from the garden. On Elsie's instruction, Bert had braved a ladder and hung paper lanterns in the trees, so the whole square had taken on a festival atmosphere.

Amir's parents had arrived in good time and were already in the square chatting to Nadia and Amir's friends and neighbours when the minibus bringing Nadia's family arrived. Nadia waited to greet them nervously, Amir at her side, but relaxed when her mother pulled her into a big hug whilst her father shook Amir's hand warmly. Her two aunts also hugged her, and her uncles greeted them both cordially enough, but her cousin Rashid ignored Amir's outstretched hand and completely blanked Nadia.

Very soon all the guests were mingling as they enjoyed the lovely food and the garden. Out of respect for Nadia family's Islamic beliefs, there was no alcohol, but no one seemed to miss it. Nadia and Amir had told their parents their happy news in private whilst they were showing them around their house, and both sets of parents now sat together outside, chatting about the upcoming happy event. Having told their family, the young couple now felt they could tell their friends, and everyone was delighted, the party now taking on an air of celebration.

Rashid was the only person not celebrating the lovely news, and when Nadia went into the house to top up the fruit punch jug, he followed her inside. Coming up behind her in the kitchen, he grabbed her arm and berated her as a 'whore living in sin'. Nadia tried to pull herself free, but his fingers just dug harder into her arm.

"You should kill yourself rather than give birth to a bastard baby," he said, starting to shake her, his face a mask of rage.

Nadia began to fear for herself and her baby, but Rashid was suddenly pulled away from her, and she fell back against the worktop, unhurt but shaken. She thought it was Amir or Jack who had come to her rescue, but it was her uncle, who was now berating his stunned son.

"How dare you accost your cousin, Rashid!" he said. "Did not the Prophet Muhammad (praise be upon him) say, 'Observe your duty to Allah in respect to the women, and treat them well'?"

"Yes, but father..." started Rashid.

"No 'buts', Rashid," interrupted his father. "I have spoken to Amir's father, and the marriage was properly conducted with the correct witnesses. Nadia is married in the eyes of Allah and the law and Allah has smiled on her with a child. The Prophet (praise be upon him) said that 'paradise lies at the feet of Mothers': it is your duty to honour and respect your cousin."

"I'm sorry father," said Rashid looking shamefaced.

"It's not me you should be apologising to, Rashid, but Nadia," said her uncle sternly.

Rashid muttered an apology and dashed outside, leaving a shocked Nadia and her uncle alone in the kitchen. Nadia started to thank her uncle, but he stopped her.

"Niece, do not thank me. I too should apologise to you for not showing you the regard you deserve. You have married a good man and been a faithful wife and now carry his child. You both work hard and have the love and respect of your community. You have honoured Allah by creating a garden, a paradise on earth to reflect his paradise in heaven. I am proud of you child."

Nadia was too shocked to say anything, so her uncle just kissed her forehead and left her. It took her a moment to compose herself, and then she filled the fruit punch jug and went out into the sunshine, feeling like a weight had been lifted from her shoulders.

Amir saw her and came and took the jug off her, joking about her being in a delicate condition. Nadia just smiled and said nothing: she would tell him later what had just happened. They sat together in the sunshine and watched their family and friends mingle. Rashid had been dragged into an impromptu game of cricket, a sport he loved, and he was now smiling for the first time all day. Bert was discussing vegetable gardening with Nadia's uncles, and Nadia's Aunts were wandering around the flower garden with Kara, stopping and smelling various flowers as they passed. Jack was in what appeared to be a deep discussion with Nadia's parents and Amir's parents were assisting Elsie to sample new dishes.

"It seems this place has worked its magic," said Amir, kissing his wife on the cheek and pulling her close.

Nadia leaned against him and turned her face to the sun. For the first time in ages, tonight she would raise a prayer of thanks to Allah.

Chapter Thirty-Six

Something about Poppy's death was puzzling Josie but she couldn't quite put her finger on what it was. The familiarity of the man who she now knew was Mr Fernsby was one thing, another was the elusive Nigel – who was he and how did he fit into things? At the inquest, the officer had said something about video footage of Nigel, and the way he had said it had sounded a bit off to Josie.

She couldn't work out what was bothering her, but a good starting point would be to speak to Ben about the video aspect. Ben confirmed that he had handed a copy of the external security footage to the police, and well, he might just have kept a copy. Josie grinned, knowing that Ben would be embarrassed at her catching him out in something slightly illegal - not for the first time!

Ben brought his laptop over and sat next to Josie at her kitchen table whilst the footage of the square in the last hours of Poppy's life played out in fast forward. They saw Will carrying Poppy's bags in for her, and then saw him come out again very soon afterwards, almost at a run. They saw the residents of the square coming and going as the afternoon became evening, saw lights coming on and curtains being drawn.

Poppy came out her front door, went to the archway, and a few seconds later came back with a man - presumably she had opened the gate for him to come in. Nothing much happened for quite a while, then two more men arrived together, rang Poppy's bell and were admitted. At Josie's request, Ben wound the video back and ran it slowly, zooming in as much as possible.

"Okay, I'm pretty sure that's Smythe," said Josie, pointing at the taller of the two men who had arrived together, but I've no idea who the other man is with him."

"Me neither," said Ben, "but I think I know who the man is who arrived much earlier."

He wound the recording back further and then ran it slowly and zoomed in as the first man arrived.

"Oh, it's Mr Fernsby," said Josie, squinting at the screen. "It's been driving me mad trying to work out where I know him from."

"Julian Fernsby? Yes, it is him," said Ben.

"You know him?" asked Josie,

"Yes and no. I know him as much as you do," he replied.

"I know him?" asked Josie, confused.

"Do you remember when we were trying to stop Smythe selling off the allotments and Jack and Kara went to Leeds to 'accidentally' meet with the property developer that Smythe was taking a backhander from?" asked Ben.

"Yes," said Josie.

"Well, that was Julian Fernsby," said Ben. "If you remember, Jack thought he recognised him in a video of him and Poppy, and I had to enlarge and clean up the image so he could be sure. I spent quite a long time looking at his face, so I recognised him instantly"

"Oh yes. I knew I'd seen him somewhere before," exclaimed Josie. "How could I forget! That video was a bit X-rated, wasn't it?"

"Interesting that the three conspirators from way back then were all together the night Poppy died, though," said Ben.

"Isn't it!" replied Josie. "I'm surprised they stayed friends, seeing as their past relationship ended in prison for Smythe and Gilbert and a large fine for Fernsby."

Josie pondered for a moment.

"Actually, I think I've also seen Mr Fernsby in a local café recently, so that will also be why he was so familiar."

Ben wound the video forward again and they watched as several hours later Nigel left, and then, about half an hour later, Fernsby and Smythe left together, staggering a little, Poppy coming with them through the garden to unlock the gate. She was much more unsteady than they had been, and on the way back home she stopped partway and retched into the flower beds. Knowing what came next, it was obvious the poison was starting to take effect - she wasn't 'fit and well' as Smythe and Fernsby were reported to have said at her inquest. It was eerie – almost like seeing a ghost, and Josie shivered.

"That's strange," said Ben. "Poppy had to come down to let those two out, but Nigel, whoever he is, let himself out."

"So he did," said Josie, "and when he arrived with Smythe, Poppy didn't come down and let them in either. That must mean that Nigel had his own key."

"That's not possible, is it?" asked Ben. "Aren't they all restricted keys?

"I thought so. I'll ask Jack about it," replied Josie.

"Is that your mystery solved now?" asked Ben, closing his laptop.

"Well, you've identified Julian Fernsby for me, but maybe this video footage was all the police officer was referring to in relation to Nigel, but something still doesn't feel right to me," Josie replied.

"You and your mysteries, Miss Marple," said Ben, shaking his head. "Whatever they were up to, it doesn't change the fact that Poppy mistakenly picked poisonous mushrooms and baked them in a pie - accidental death, not murder, Josie."

After Ben had left, Josie made a cup of tea and took it into the garden. She watched her cat, Lucky, trying and failing to stalk the birds that came to the bird table, and pondered over what she had just seen. Ben had solved one mystery, but had given her two others to think about: how and why did Nigel have a key, and, something that had not occurred to her before, how come the poisonous mushrooms only ended up in Poppy's pie?

Josie remembered Fernsby and Smyth laughing outside the funeral chapel, slapping each other on the back as if in congratulations. Accidental death had been the coroner's verdict, but could it have been murder? A perfect murder? If so, she might not be able to work out how, but maybe she could try and work out who and why.

Chapter Thirty-Seven

"Good morning, Mrs Greenwood," said the locksmith as Josie entered his shop.

"Hello Philip," said Josie, smiling at him warmly.

"What can I do for you, Mrs Greenwood?" asked Philip. She'd been his teacher many years ago, and his children had also attended her school when she was the headmistress, so he held her in high regard.

"Well, I'm hoping you can throw some light on a bit of a puzzle, please, Philip," she said.

"I'll try," he said with a smile, knowing how much Josie liked to solve mysteries.

"Well, if you can't, nobody can, because it's about keys," said Josie, smiling back. "You supplied the keys to the new gates into Lady Kirkby Square, didn't you?"

"Yes," replied Philip. "They are part of the suit of keys we supplied for the whole of the Square, which means that one master key can open any lock, but all the other keys only open specific locks."

"That's what I thought," replied Josie, nodding. "So, if someone wanted a spare key the same as one they already had, can they just bring it in, and you'd cut an extra one for them?

"Oh no," replied Philip, horrified. "I can only cut more suited keys for Lord Kirkby himself, or for a trustee such as yourself, Mrs Greenwood, but only if you have a letter of authorisation signed by Lord Kirkby."

Philip turned to a rack of key blanks behind him and selected one, and then held it out towards Josie.

"See here, Mrs Greenwood," said Philip, pointing to some tiny writing inscribed on the head of the key. "It says 'do not duplicate', so even if a key is taken to another company for cutting, they wouldn't do it."

Josie nodded, and then thought for a moment.

"How do you know which suit of keys a key belongs to?" she asked.

"Each has the master key reference number and then the key number inscribed on the head," said Philip. "We keep a register of all restricted keys, so we know which belongs to which set and can ask for the appropriate authorisation.

"Is there anyone else locally who has restricted keys, Philip?" Josie asked.

"Only one other person, Mr Blakemore," replied Philip. "He owns a lot of holiday cottages across the region and the locks are all suited so that Mr Blakemore only needs to carry the master key when checking his properties. It's also handy if a guest forgets to return the key – the housekeeping team can still get in whilst we cut a replacement."

"Can you tell me the last time Mr Blakemore had a new key cut, please Philip?" asked Josie.

Philip hesitated a moment, not sure if there was an issue of confidentiality or not, but couldn't see one, and besides, it was Mrs Greenwood who was asking...

"Let me see," he said, opening up a hardback notebook and running his finger down a page.

Looking at it upside down from her side of the counter, Josie could see the page was headed up with a name and then there were three columns. The first one was a date, the next a number and the last a signature. All the signatures looked the same, apart from the last one, which was where Philip's finger stopped.

"The last key was issued to Mr Blakemore at the end of March," he said, looking up from the book.

"Is the second column the key number?" asked Josie, pointing to the column.

"That's right, Mrs Greenwood," said Philip looking down at the numbers. "Hmm... that's not right," he murmured to himself, frowning at the last entry.

"Is the key number this one?" asked Josie, handing him the gate key that Jack had issued to her as a trustee.

Philip looked at the number on the key head and then at the entry, before nodding slowly, his face going a little pale.

"Yes, it is. I'm so sorry Mrs Greenwood, this key was cut by my apprentice, and he obviously didn't check properly. I'll be having strong words with him," said Philip crossly.

"Oh, please don't Philip, no harm done," said Josie. The photograph of Poppy's bloated body shown in the Coroner's Court flashed into her mind, and she fervently hoped that the apprentice's mistake hadn't been a factor in her death. "You've been very helpful – thank you."

She turned to go, and then stopped.

"Just one more thing please Philip. What is Mr Blakemore's first name?" she asked.

"Oh, Nigel, I believe," he replied.

Chapter Thirty-Eight

Joy and Will walked hand in hand along the promenade, giddy with happiness at escaping at last for their postponed seaside 'date'. Mia was having a sleep-over with Dottie, and was probably even more excited than they were, but Joy did feel a little guilty when she saw families on the beach building sandcastles together. Will must have read her mind as he squeezed her hand and suggested that they book a caravan to have a week at the seaside with Mia in the upcoming summer holidays. Joy knew in that moment that she loved him and was glad she had changed their hotel booking to a king-sized double rather than two singles - something that Will didn't know yet.

Joy's heart started to beat very fast at the thought of having sex with a new man and she didn't know if it was excitement or fear. There had only ever been her husband, and he had taken his pleasure whenever he wanted, regardless of whether she wanted to or was ready for him. She knew it would be very different with Will, but she just hoped he'd be gentle with her, and if she changed her mind, he would respect that and stop.

Joy didn't want to think of her soon to be ex-husband just now and focused instead on the brightly coloured boats dancing on diamond strewn waves in the harbour. Will put his arm around her shoulder and pulled her close as they watched two fishermen loading orange and green lobster pots onto their boat from the quayside. The little boat laden with pots set off and puttered slowly out to sea and they watched it until it was out of sight.

Crossing the road, they ventured into the John Bull gift shop and bought rock lollipops for Mia and Dottie, laughing at the ridiculous things you could get made from rock. Hand in hand they strolled a bit further along the promenade before stopping at a shop selling ice cream through an open window. Will bought them both ice creams with chocolate flakes, coloured sprinkles and strawberry sauce, and licking them quickly to stop the melting ice cream and sauce from running down their arms, they headed for the pier.

They walked along the pier, over a little swing bridge and on to the lighthouse, its walls glowing bright white in the sunshine. They stopped to admire the 'Bathing Belle', a graceful statue of a lady in a swimming costume poised on tiptoes ready to dive into the waves. At the very end of the pier, they stopped and stood with their arms around each other, looking out to sea, watching the fishing boats and the be-flagged tourist boats coming in and out of the harbour as seagulls wheeled and called above.

Will turned her face to his and looked into her eyes.

"I know it's ridiculous to say this so soon, Joy, but I love you," he said, before kissing her tenderly.

Tears sprung into her eyes and Will started to apologise, thinking he had upset her, but she silenced him with another kiss before telling him that she loved him too. Under the steady gaze of the Bathing Belle, they held each other tight for a long time, before Joy took Will's hand and led him away, back to their hotel, no longer concerned about what the night would bring.

Chapter Thirty-Nine

Poppy's flat had remained empty, no one wanting to live in a place where a dead body had lain undiscovered for weeks, but now there were tenants waiting to move into it, so Jack needed to clear it out. The surprise request had come from Nadia's parents, having fallen in love with the area, and wanting to be near Nadia now that there was a baby on the way. They didn't fit the criteria for an apartment, not being local and not being in urgent need of housing, but rather than the apartment remaining empty, the trustees had agreed that they could have it.

Knowing that Jack must dread going back in there, Ben had volunteered to help him, and armed with rolls of black bags and a pile of flat-packed boxes, the two friends set to work. The trustees had decided that anything of value would be saved for a year, in case any family came forward, and if not, sold and the money given to charity. Clothes and everything else not worth keeping would go to the local charity shop straight away. Poppy, however, had had surprisingly few possessions, and nothing that said anything about her personality, just bland, mismatched furniture, beige curtains, grubby off-white towels and a mess of half used toiletries.

The bedroom was the only room that appeared to have had any thought put into it, with dark red walls and a king-sized four-poster bed swathed in gauzy, glittery fabric. There were matching curtains at the window, draped over a black-out blind that had been left down, giving the room a twilight feel even with the light on. Bedside tables matched two black lacquered wardrobes, and a large mirror in a thick gold frame almost filled the wall opposite the bed. The bed had been stripped by the clean-up team, but Jack got a flash-back to the vomit and shit-stained red silk sheets and the bloated, fly covered body on the floor next to the bed, and for a moment he stood rooted to the spot, staring at the apparition only he could see.

Seeing his distress, Ben sent him into the lounge to see if he could find anything that hinted at Poppy having family, as the police had been unable to find anyone. Jack painstakingly went through a box of papers stuck in the corner of the room but found no address book or any personal correspondence. There were unpaid bills and several bank statements, and Jack wondered if he ought to speak to the bank about settling the bills from the account, but realised he had no authority to do so.

Someone should contact the bank and the creditors he thought, though, and with no one else he supposed it would have to be him as he didn't want creditors troubling the new tenants. There was a pile of post in the hall, mainly red notice bills and another bank statement, so he scooped those up to take home and sort things out later.

On a low table under the window was an expensive SLR camera and a pair of binoculars which Jack placed into the 'to keep' box, but then removed the camera and extracted the memory card from it, putting it inside one of the envelopes he was taking home. Jack could tell from the traces of fingerprint powder on the camera that the police had already looked at the camera and probably checked the photos on the memory card, but if there were more of Poppy's voyeuristic photos on it, he didn't want anyone else to see them.

The police had taken Poppy's laptop away but had since returned it, leaving it on the kitchen worktop still in a sealed evidence bag. Jack knew that if there was anything of interest on the laptop, the police would have found it, but he added it to the pile of post he was taking home, just in case.

Jack then started to pack up the contents of the kitchen cupboards. A lot of the pots and pans were good quality and went into the boxes for the charity shop, along with a smart dining set and crystal glasses. The everyday crockery was cheap and cracked so that all went into the junk bags, and Jack found it very sad that there was a solitary coffee mug bearing the slogan 'Today is a good day'.

Ben called him from the bedroom and as Jack went in, he could see that Ben had made good progress and had finished emptying one wardrobe into black bags ready for the charity shop. Ben was standing in front of the other wardrobe just staring into it with a shocked expression. On the inside of both doors were rows of hooks from which were hung whips of different sizes and viciousness, gimp masks, a range of dildos displayed in size order along with other dominatrix accessories whose purpose Jack could only guess at. Inside the wardrobe were costumes mainly in red or black leather or PVC, featuring chains, belt and buckles, but there were also a few skimpy maid's, nurse's and similar fantasy uniforms.

The two men looked at each other but were lost for words; by unspoken agreement, they put on rubber gloves and emptied the contents straight into bin bags.

"We'll have to make sure we don't get the bags mixed up and take these to the charity shop instead of the tip," said Ben, and the two men laughed, lightening the mood.

Ben and Jack now manoeuvred the items of furniture downstairs ready for the charity shop van to pick them up. The chairs and table were easy enough, but the settee was a struggle to get past the turn in the stairs. They had to stand it on end and then angle the back of it over the banister, but even then, it was a struggle as it snagged on the newel post. Poor Ben was at the lower end, taking most of the weight, and stumbled and nearly fell when it eventually jerked free.

The sudden movement caused something to be released from the depths of the settee and crash onto the hall floor below. When they eventually got down the stairs, Jack saw it was a mobile phone, its screen smashed from when it hit the floor. Once the settee was outside, he took the phone back upstairs and added it to the laptop and pile of papers he was taking home before continuing to take full bin bags outside whilst Ben began to remove the large mirror from the wall.

The mirror was fixed in several places and after he had removed most of the screws, Ben asked Jack to help him by holding the mirror steady whilst he removed the last ones. As they carefully lifted it down and propped it against the wall, a small video camera was revealed secured to the wall behind the mirror. Ben tilted the mirror away from the wall and bent down to peer at the back and found he could see clear through it.

"It's a two-way mirror," said Ben. "Looks like Gilbert was filming her antics in bed!"

They removed the camera and Jack added it to the pile he was taking home. He didn't want to see what was on the camera, but he didn't want anyone else to do so either.

Chapter Forty

Much to everyone's surprise and delight, Will was moving in with Joy and Mia. He had very few possessions to move next door, but his finished portrait of Joy was carried carefully next door and hung in pride of place on the sitting room wall. In addition to several new commissions for book illustrations, his happiness had freed him to paint again, and his pictures were selling well at the local gallery. The couple now had more income which allowed them to spoil Mia and have the occasional family treat.

As there was a waiting list for a house in the square, it was only a week or so later when Evelyn, an attractive lady in her late sixties, moved into Will's empty house. She soon became friendly with Bert and Elsie, joining them in the garden most days when the weather was fine. Unlike Elsie, however, Evelyn was young enough to help in the garden, bringing her pink kneeler and matching gloves to work alongside Bert.

At first Elsie watched the 'youngsters' indulgently, sitting contentedly stroking Blue, but as they moved further away and she could hear their laughter but not join in their conversation, she began to feel left out. She wondered if Bert would notice if she wasn't there, but as he still brought her bits of shopping and joined her for tea most days, so she told herself not to be so silly.

Elise always invited Evelyn to join them for tea, but she seldom joined them, saying, with a laugh, that she was watching her figure. Elsie was glad, as she found Evelyn's constant stream of chatter about celebrities and other trivia exhausting and preferred the comfortable calm of just her and Bert. On more and more occasions, however, Bert went to Evelyn's for his tea, but as Elsie wasn't sure if she was invited too, she didn't join them. Bert would tell Elsie afterwards what a wonderful baker Evelyn was and describe the lovely cakes and pies they had shared. This didn't sound like someone on a diet to Elsie, but she shrugged and told herself it was none of her business.

The first couple of times that Elsie didn't come into the garden on a fine gardening day, Bert called round to see if she was alright. She always said she was fine and 'there was just a bit of a cold wind today' or she 'had some correspondence to catch up on', and Bert just told her to shout if she needed anything and went on his way. A few of the times when Bert called round Elsie just didn't open the door, and maybe he thought she was out or resting, so he didn't persist. In truth, Elsie was watching from behind the curtain, watching as he and Evelyn carried on happily without her.

Elsie wasn't exactly jealous, but she did feel displaced. She had been so happy having a friend, a male friend, after years of loneliness, and the loss of that almost exclusive relationship felt a bit like a bereavement. She knew she was being silly, denying herself fresh air and company, but she wanted to see if Bert missed her and the close friendship they had shared. Bert, however, seemed to be oblivious, chatting away to her as if nothing was different whenever they did meet.

It was Nadia that first realised that no one had seen Elsie for a couple of days and rang her doorbell. On getting no reply, she peered through the windows, but the nets made it impossible to see inside. She mentioned it to Amir, but with the excitement of going for their first baby scan that day they both forgot about it. Later the same morning, Sandra, the post lady, brought Elsie a parcel, but on getting no reply, she popped a card through the letter box and carried on with her round. However, guessing that the parcel contained the new sandals with good arch supports that Elsie and mentioned she was waiting for, Sandra decided to try again before she finished for the day. Getting no reply, she bent down to peer through the letterbox but couldn't see anything.

Worried that Elsie might have had another fall, Sandra phoned Jack but unfortunately only got his answering machine. Seeing Will and Joy coming through the arch from the car park, Sandra called them over and explained her concerns. Will and Joy looked at each other and then shook their heads to confirm that they hadn't seen Elsie recently either. Will knelt down and peered through the letter box, but he couldn't see anything either. He cupped his caps around his mouth and called 'Elsie' through the letter box and then listened, but the only sound he could pick up inside was a slowly dripping tap.

"Should we call the police?" asked Joy.

"We could, but with no information of what exactly the emergency is, it's likely we would be low priority and it could be hours until they arrived," replied Sandra.

"Okay. Stand back," said Will.

Joy gasped as Will took aim and kicked the door with all his might just below the lock. On the second kick the door flew open, and they rushed inside, calling out to Elsie. A quick look around showed that she wasn't in the open plan kitchen / lounge, so they went straight to the bedroom and knocked on the door. There was no reply. Joy and Sandra went in whilst Will waited outside, not wanting to embarrass Elsie if she wasn't dressed.

"Come in Will," called Joy. "She's not here."

The room was indeed empty, so they checked the bathroom and then rechecked the lounge, but there was no trace of Elsie.

"Blue's not here," said Sandra suddenly. "Elsie never goes anywhere without him, so she must have gone away."

"But surely, she'd have told someone?" said Will, feeling a bit foolish for kicking in the door if Elsie had just gone away for a few days.

"Bert!" said Joy. "She'd have told Bert."

Bert wasn't in the garden, so they knocked on his door and got no reply.

"Maybe they've gone away together?" suggested Will as they stood uncertainly outside Bert's door.

"Are you looking for me?" asked Bert, coming up behind them unseen.

They whirled around and saw Bert and Evelyn coming up the path behind them. Both were smartly dressed, Bert in a sports jacket and cravat, and Evelyn in a floaty blue dress. They looked relaxed and happy, but Bert's face immediately changed when they told him they couldn't find Elsie.

"But she can barely walk – how can she have gone anywhere?" he said, concerned.

"Now Bert, don't you fret," said Evelyn, patting his arm. "I'm sure she'll turn up soon."

"When did you last see her?" asked Will.

"Oh, let me see," replied Evelyn, although Will had been aiming the question at Bert. "I think it was Tuesday, Bert. Elsie was sitting on the bench and waved at us, but I wanted to show you the cruise brochure, so we didn't have time to go over and chat with her."

"You two going on a cruise?" asked Sandra.

"Oh no!" exclaimed Evelyn with a tinkling laugh. "I'm going with my new man - we met online you know - I'm expecting a proposal before the cruise is finished! Bert and I have just been out for lunch with him to wish us bon voyage!

"Have you checked her house?" asked Bert, cutting across Evelyn's excited chatter.

"Yes - I'm afraid I broke down the door," said Will.

"Good for you, lad," said Bert, patting Will's shoulder.

"Any idea where she could have gone?" asked Joy.

"No. She'd have told me if she was going away. Well, maybe she hasn't had the chance recently..." replied Bert, glancing at Evelyn and looking guilty.

"Listen Bert, I'm going to have to run - packing to finish," said Evelyn, kissing him on the cheek. "Give my love to Elsie when you find her. Bye everyone - see you in a month!"

"Bye," muttered Bert, distractedly.

Sandra had to go on her way too but made them promise to tell her the moment they heard anything. Seeing how shaken Bert looked, Joy steered him into her house. Will made them all a cup of tea and they sat in silence whilst they drank it, racking their brains as to Elsie's whereabouts.

"She's have had to get a taxi," said Bert suddenly.

"Good thinking, Bert," said Will, scrolling through his phone to find the local taxi company.

It didn't take the taxi company long to find a record of the pick-up from the square the previous day, but there was no record of the destination. The dispatcher promised to speak to the driver and get back to them as soon as he could, and they waited anxiously, jumping when the phone eventually rang. However, it was Jack ringing for news, having just returned Sandra's call. He said he'd be there as soon as possible, and in the meantime, he'd arrange for someone to come round to fix the door.

The next call was from the taxi driver who confirmed picking Elsie up.

"I drove her out to an old farmhouse in the middle of nowhere," he said.

"And left her there?" asked Will.

"Well, yes. I was a bit concerned as the house looked like a building site, but she insisted it was the right place, and said she'd call when she wanted picking up again," replied the taxi driver, sounding a bit defensive.

"And did she?" asked Will.

"I don't know as I was off shift shortly after that," said the driver.

"Can you give me the address you dropped her off at, please?" asked Will.

"I'm not sure I can do that," replied the driver, "data protection and all that."

Bert had been listening into the conversation as much as possible but had had enough now.

"Give it here," he said, taking the phone out of Will's hand.

"Listen here young man," said Bert. "You left a frail, disabled old lady in the middle of nowhere and didn't make sure someone picked her up again? You give us the address right now and just pray she is still alive!"

The driver spluttered for a moment, and then thought better of it and gave Bert the address.

"Let me know she's okay, will you please?" said the driver, but then realised the caller had already gone.

Thirty minutes later Bert and Will pulled up in a cloud of dust outside the former farmhouse. The driver had been right - it was in the middle of nowhere, with spectacular views in all directions. The stone farmhouse was shrouded in scaffolding, but from what they could see it was very old, hunkered down in the landscape as if it had grown there. It looked like it was in the process of being re-roofed, with the traditional stone slates being reused, about half the roof done, and the rest covered in a blue tarpaulin. However, no one was working today, and the only sound was a curlew's rising call somewhere in the distance.

Bert and Will looked at each other, not sure what to do next, before Bert strode purposely towards the house, calling Elsie's name. Will followed him and then walked the opposite way around the building to Bert, also calling out to Elsie. Several of the windows were being replaced and the holes were covered in thick plastic, secured by batons. Will was considering pulling the covering off from one window to get inside, when he saw that the plastic sheet that was covering what would eventually be huge patio doors was flapping in the breeze. Bert then arrived, so without saying a word, Will pulled back the plastic and gestured to Bert to enter before following him inside.

The diffuse light through the plastic covered windows and doors gave the inside of the farmhouse an eerie feel, and it took a moment for their eyes to get accustomed to the change of light after the bright light outside. They were standing in a huge open space; from the newly installed red metal girders across the top of two walls it was obvious that walls had been knocked down to open up the room. The door-less carcasses of new kitchen units lined one wall and the skeleton of a massive kitchen island dominated the middle of the room.

The only original feature was a large black cooking range, and in front of this was a couple of folding chairs and an upside-down crate covered in mugs, newspapers and takeaway packaging. A movement caught their eye as Blue straightened up from where he had been curled up beside one of the chairs. As they hurried towards him, he remained there, still and silent, standing guard on his mistress whose eyes were closed, a peaceful expression on her pale face.

Chapter Forty-One

Jack was concerned about Noah as he was absent from school and no message had been left with the school office to explain why. Jack knew Noah's parents had recently separated, which he believed was the reason for Noah's recent poor behaviour, but surely one of them would have phoned the school if Noah was ill? Jack had plenty to do helping other pupils as needed, but without a specific task to do the morning seemed to drag. Joy was picking up Dottie for a play date with Mia, so as soon as the lunch bell rang Jack grabbed his coat and left, needing to get out into the fresh air.

He decided to walk home through the woods, enjoying the cool greenness and the lilting birdsong which raised his spirits. The bluebells had finished, meadowsweet now frothing alongside the track and under the trees giving the woods a bridal feel. Jack looked for the orchid markers, noting that the Common Spotted Orchid had replaced the Early Purple Orchid, and was doing well. Since Poppy's death, he kept an eye out for poisonous mushrooms, but saw no mushrooms at all, which wasn't unusual for the time of year.

It was such a lovely day so rather than take the turning that would take him to the top of the allotments and from there to the manor, Jack continued on through the woods, making it a longer walk before he doubled back. As he emerged from the cool woods, he passed a few large, detached houses each with fantastic views over the woods and across the whole valley. Jack remembered that Noah lived in one of these exclusive houses and wondered if perhaps, subliminally, that was why he had come this way.

However, he didn't know which one was Noah's house, so he continued walking, heading for the footpath that he needed to take to turn back towards the manor. Jack suddenly heard his name being called and spun round to see Noah shouting and waving at him from the front door of one of the houses.

"Mr Brown, help!" Noah called.

Jack ran towards the distressed boy.

"What is it, Noah?" he asked.

"My dad! Something's wrong with my dad," said Noah, grabbing Jack's arm and pulling him inside.

The hall was spacious with gleaming marble floor tiles and antique furniture, but Jack didn't have the chance to admire it as he was pulled upstairs by Noah. The double doors to the master bedroom were open, and Jack could see Noah's father lying on the bed. He was dressed in a suit and what would have been a smart shirt if it hadn't been splashed with vomit. He was struggling to breath, his eyes closed, his face deathly pale and covered with sweat.

"What's your dad's name, Noah, asked Jack.

"Nigel. Please help him, Mr Brown!" said Noah.

"Nigel, can you hear me?" asked Jack.

There was no reply, so Jack shook him gently and asked again. Nigel gave a groan but didn't otherwise respond. Jack lifted one eyelid and noted that the pupil was very small and unresponsive. Quickly turning him onto his side in case he was sick again, Jack picked up the bedside phone and dialled 999. Once the call taker had run through all the checks and the ambulance was on its way, Jack sent Noah downstairs to look out for the ambulance whilst he stayed with Nigel. Reaching across the bedside table for a tissue to wipe sick off his hands, Jack noticed next to the tissue box a half-drunk cup of coffee and a plate with the last bite of a breakfast muffin on it. Jack wondered if Nigel had suffered an allergic reaction and wrapped the bit of bun in a tissue to give to the ambulance crew in case it helped with a diagnosis.

The wait seemed interminable, and Jack was scared that Nigel would die before they got there, but it was probably less than ten minutes later when Noah thundered up the stairs, followed, not quite as quickly, by the ambulance crew. Having told them the little he knew, Jack took Noah downstairs out of the way to give them room to work. Noah showed him the way to the kitchen and Jack washed his hands and then grabbed a couple of glasses off the drainer and poured them both some water. A superman bowl in the sink showed Jack that Noah had had cereal for breakfast, and looking around, he saw a Ziplock bag on the kitchen island containing a solitary blueberry muffin.

"Is this what your dad had for his breakfast, Noah?" Jack asked, pointing to the bag.

Noah nodded.

"Didn't you want one?" asked Jack

Noah nodded and then shook his head.

"But you didn't have one?" Jack prompted.

"Dad said they were 'special' and not for children," said Noah.

"Oh? Did your mum bake them for him?" asked Jack, and then he could have kicked himself when he saw tears appear in Noah's eyes.

"My mum doesn't live here any more," said Noah, sadly. "A man on a motorbike brought them this morning."

Jack's eyebrows shot up. A courier to deliver two muffins: they must be very special then.

"Were they in a box or anything Noah?" Jack asked. He didn't know why he was so interested in the muffins, but something didn't feel right.

Noah nodded and pointed to the bin, and feeling a bit foolish, Jack peered inside. The box was right at the top with a few coffee grounds staining it, so he pulled it out and put it on the worktop. It was just a plain cardboard book, not bearing the name of any bakery or other information, but inside were some small pieces of torn-up paper with writing on them. Jack laid them on the worktop and moved the pieces around until he could read the handwritten note – 'In case you were missing P's special recipe' was all it said.

Just then the ambulance men could be heard coming down the stairs, so Jack quickly scooped the pieces of paper up and put them into his pocket before grabbing the bag containing the remaining blueberry muffin. Jack took Noah's hand, and they went into the hall to see Nigel being carried past on a stretcher. The ambulance crew assured them that Nigel was stable and not in any immediate danger, but they couldn't say what was wrong with him. After they had loaded the stretcher into the ambulance, Jack gave them the muffin, and they made a note of Jack's contact details before driving off, siren blaring, leaving Jack and a tearful Noah behind in the driveway.

Jack knew he couldn't just take Noah home with him but didn't know what else to do - he couldn't leave him alone in an empty house. He rang social services and asked for the officer he normally liaised with when finding places for people who needed housing. Jack explained the situation and knowing that Jack was DBS checked due to working in a school, they agreed it was best for Noah to stay with someone he knew, pending his mother or another relative being traced.

Jack asked Noah if he knew his mother's phone number and address, but Noah shook his head but did tell Jack that mummy's number was in a book in his dad's desk drawer. The office was just down the corridor from the kitchen, a very male room in greys and browns with a large, dark wood desk with drawers either side. Jack opened the drawers gingerly to look for an address book which thankfully he found in the second drawer. He quickly located the number and sat at the desk to ring it, but it just rang and rang.

As Jack waited for an answering machine to click in so that he could leave a message, he noticed a piece of paper on the floor that he must have pulled out along with the book, so he picked it up. He glanced at it as he put it back into the drawer and realised it was a bank statement and couldn't help noticing that Nigel earned a significant amount each month, but large sums went out each week and by the end of the month he was down to just a few pounds. 'Not just me then' he thought as he shoved the document guiltily back into the drawer.

Unable to leave a message, Jack saved the number into his phone, and then sent Noah to pack his pyjamas, toothbrush and a few toys, whilst he wrote a detailed note for Nigel telling him where Noah was staying. Realising he couldn't leave the house unlocked, and not sure if Nigel would have a key with him, Jack wrote a second short note simply telling him to ring the number given to find his son, and then, finding a roll of sticky tape, stuck the note to the outside of the door before locking up with a key he'd found in a bowl on the hall table.

Chapter Forty-Two

Kara had picked Dottie up from her play date on her way home from work, and the little girl came running in, eager to tell her daddy about the fun she'd had. She stopped short when she saw Noah sitting at the kitchen table drawing and stood with her thumb in her mouth in the doorway, not sure how to handle the situation. Noah had been very naughty at school recently, and Dottie wasn't sure she wanted him in her house.

Jack looked up from cooking tea, and seeing Dottie standing uncertainly, he swept her up in a big hug and tickled her tummy. He carried her upside down and squealing through to the lounge before dumping her on the settee, then sat next to her and explained that Noah's daddy was very poorly so Noah would be staying with them for a little while. Kara, who had followed them in, knew she'd get the details shortly, so for now she just sat the other side of Dottie and asked if she could be a very kind girl and look after Noah who must be very sad.

Dottie nodded solemnly, and then went to join Noah in the kitchen. Kara remained with Jack in the lounge so that he could explain briefly what had happened.

"Thank goodness you were passing Jack!" exclaimed Kara.

"Yes, and I don't know why I was really – I told myself I just fancied a longer walk, but I'd had a nagging concern about Noah all day, so I think subconsciously I was deliberately heading towards where he lived," said Jack.

"Well, thank goodness for your sixth sense, or whatever it was, Jack, otherwise Noah's father might have died," replied Kara.

"I'm not sure he would have died, but he was certainly very poorly, and terrifying for Noah to have to try to deal with it alone," said Jack.

"Terrifying for you too, Jack, I suspect," said Kara, giving him a hug.

"It was a bit," admitted Jack. "Something about it reminded me of finding Gilbert's body, and I just wanted to run out of there, but my first aid training kicked in and I was suddenly very calm."

"Well, I think you're a hero," said Kara, kissing his cheek, "but you'll be my hero if tea is almost ready - I'm starving!"

Jack laughed and took her hand and they walked into the kitchen to find Dottie and Noah drawing together happily. Before long, Jack was serving up home-made shepherd's pie and vegetables and Kara called Ronan and Lily from their rooms to join them. Despite the trauma of the day, everyone ate hungrily and afterwards the family played Pictionary together, something that Noah excelled at.

Jack rang the hospital but was told nothing apart from that Nigel was 'comfortable', so it looked like Noah would be staying the night. Kara made a bed up for him in Ronan's room, but it was a long time before all the children were settled and Jack and Kara could cuddle up together on the settee and properly discuss the events of the day.

"There's something not right about Nigel's illness," said Jack, and then explained to Kara about the muffins and the note.

"I think you're right, Jack," said Kara. "It sounds to me like he was poisoned."

Jack nodded – he'd had the same thought.

"If 'P' in the note was Poppy who died of mushroom poisoning," said Kara thoughtfully, "and if Nigel has also been poisoned by mushrooms, then Poppy's death might not have been an accident, after all."

The couple stared at each other, not sure what to say or do in the circumstances. Eventually Jack stood up and held out his hands to Kara.

"Let's have an early night, and see what the morning brings," he said.

-o-o-o-o-

There was no more news the next morning, so the family and their guest got up, washed and dressed, had breakfast and then went off to school and work as normal. Jack explained to the class teacher and the headmaster what had happened, and asked permission to keep his phone on in class in case Nigel rang. It was almost midday when his phone did ring, and all the children turned to stare at him and tut, knowing that phones weren't allowed in class. Jack went outside into the playground to take the call, not wanting Noah to hear if it was bad news.

"Is he alright?" demanded Nigel, before Jack could even say hello.

"Noah? He's fine. But how are you?" asked Jack

"As if you care!" replied Nigel, bitterly.

"Excuse me?" said Jack, surprised.

"Just tell me how much you want to get my son back," said Nigel, resignedly.

"How much?" echoed Jack, confused.

"Yes. I thought it was all over, but I was wrong, wasn't I?" said Nigel.

"Nigel - can I stop you? My name is Jack Brown, and I work at Noah's school. I don't know what you are talking about, but Noah is fine, so if you are out of hospital, I'll bring him home to you after school."

There was a stunned silence, and then Nigel started to apologise.

"Mr Brown, I'm so sorry. I think I'm a bit delirious still. Ignore me. Yes, I'm home, but I don't think I'm up to driving just yet, so I would be very grateful if you could bring Noah home, please."

"Certainly, Nigel. We'll pick up his stuff on the way, so we'll be there in about an hour."

"Thank you, Mr Brown. See you soon," said Nigel, ringing off.

Jack stood for a moment, trying to process the strange conversation, before going to tell Noah the good news that his dad was okay and home.

Chapter Forty-Three

Elsie was loving the fuss that Bert was making of her, checking if she was okay and if she needed anything each morning, and watching television or playing cards with her in the evenings. Having repaired her front door, Jack had got a spare key cut for Bert at her request, and he seemed to spend more time in her house now than his own. It was almost like being an old married couple, and Elsie smiled at the thought, enjoying their new closeness.

Bert had told her with a tear in his eye that he had thought she was dead, not asleep, when they had found her at the farm. She had laughed and said it would take more than a night in a chair to kill her off, even though the stiffness in her old body continued to remind her of her foolishness. She explained to Bert that she had not 'gone home to die' as he had feared but had just wanted to see her old home again, to look at the fields and hills that she had gazed at everyday of her life before she moved into her new home in the square. She didn't mention that this melancholy had been brought on by feeling lonely since Evelyn had arrived, but he knew, and some of his attentiveness came from guilt at having let a new friendship make him neglect an old one.

When the taxi driver had dropped her off, she had been so overcome with memories that for a moment she forgot that it was no longer her old home. It never occurred to her that the old black Bakelite telephone might not still be on the oak dresser just inside the back door. It had been a shock to see that the back door was no longer there, and half the back wall was also missing, covered by a plastic sheet that flapped in the wind that was always blowing up here on the exposed hilltop. She remembered the buyers had said something about 'opening up' the back of the house to enjoy the views, and wished that she had had the vision, time and money to have done it when she lived there, as the views would be spectacular. Mind you, it would cost a fortune to keep the place heated - houses on the moor were built with thick walls and small openings for a very good reason.

She had peered through the plastic, almost expecting the kitchen to look the same as it always had; a clutter of heavy old furniture, home-made rag rugs, chipped blue patterned crockery and a pile of farming papers on the old dresser, and the big old range throwing out heat. It had been a shock to see the vast, almost empty, space, no trace of her former life remaining: no old dresser and no old telephone. Elsie realised how foolish we had been - she hadn't told anyone where she was going, didn't possess a mobile and as it was Saturday, the builders were not there.

There was only one thing for it - she'd have to wait there until Monday. A section of the plastic had not been nailed closed in order to give the builders access, and with some difficulty, not helped by Blue darting excitedly back and forth, she managed to lift up the corner and manoeuvre the rollator she now used to help her walk through the gap to get inside to wait. Thankfully there were at least some chairs, and as the afternoon bled into night, she was also relieved to find that the electricity had been left on and that there was still a downstairs toilet in the old scullery.

The builders had left behind half a packet of biscuits which she had shared with Blue, and then, with the familiar sounds of the moors all around her, she had slept deeply. She had woken with the light, but her old body having stiffened up overnight she found that she couldn't get herself out of the spindly folding chair. Exhausted with her efforts she drifted back into sleep, dozing and waking and then dozing again. In her more lucid moments, she thought perhaps that this was what dying was like, and when she heard her name being called, she wondered if it was her father, waiting to guide her across to the other side.

It had taken her a moment to return to herself and focus on Bert's living, breathing, lovely old face, but when his arms came around her and he held her tight, she thought this was as close to heaven as she was ever likely to be.

Chapter Forty-Four

"Welcome home, John," said Josie, rushing up to give him a hug.

Much to her surprise, he hugged her back, something he had never done before in the twenty plus years she'd known him. She bent down and hugged Sarah too, and then whilst everyone else welcomed them home, she stood back and appraised them both.

John looked ten years younger than when she had last seen him almost nine months ago, fit and tanned, his hair whiter and longer, looking like what some would call a 'silver fox'. Gone were the checked shirts, beige cords and green body-warmer, replaced by loose cream chinos and an open necked blue linen shirt. Sarah looked much the same as she always had, a sparkle in her eyes and radiating joie de vivre. Her long hair had perhaps more white than previously amongst the blond, but still hung in a heavy plait over her shoulder.

The welcome home party was being held in the ground floor apartment of the manor as it was more accessible for Sarah's wheelchair, and a large table had been set in front of the French windows so that they could look out over the allotments to the square below and watch the sun set as they ate. They all took their places around the table, Zoe and Ben, Kara and Jack, Josie and Hugo and John and Sarah – the friends and trustees of the square all reunited at last.

Jack raised a toast to the returning wanderers, and then they tucked into roast beef with golden Yorkshire puddings and piles of fresh vegetables from the allotment. Everyone wanted to know about John and Sarah's travels, where they had been and what they had seen, but John and Sarah just wanted to know about the allotments and the square, so at first there was chaos as everyone tried to speak at once.

John and Sarah were urged to tell them about their travels first, and with so much to tell, they started with the highlights - the sun coming up behind the pyramids, taking part in Holi (the Indian festival of colour), joining a picnic in the park in Japan to observe the cherry blossom, or the act of 'hanami' as the Japanese called it, and the scent of spring flowers in Crete as they sat outside a beachside bar, tipsy on the local ouzo.

Josie listened in amazement, not just at the stories, the incredible experiences that John and Sarah had shared, but at the changes in John who was transformed from the, frankly, slightly stuffy allotment treasurer who had been stuck in a dark place after the death of his beloved wife, Mary. Previously he had always liked order and certainty, his rows of vegetables perfectly straight and the exact distance from each other, and he'd never wanted to be anywhere other than in 'God's own country'. But now, his unlikely friendship with Sarah had taken him a long way from home and from his comfort zone, and it looked to have done him good.

Reading between the lines, however, Josie suspected that it was John's attention to detail and organisational ability that had made the trip so successful. Sarah was a wheelchair user who didn't let that fact stop her living life to the full, but Josie suspected that without John, her endless enthusiasm for life and her devil-may-care attitude would have quickly got her into trouble on their travels. Not for the first time, Josie wondered about the nature of their relationship - it was obviously very close, as they shared jokes and finished each other's sentences, but if it was more than that there were no clues.

At Hugo's urging, they also told them of the lowlights – being mugged on one occasion and almost shot on another, as well as the insects, noise, heat and occasionally downright dangerous transport that made them glad to be back in the UK. Their friends now filled them in on what they had missed whilst they were away, and John and Sarah were shocked to hear of Dottie's kidnap and Poppy's death.

"There was us thinking nothing much would have happened here!" said Sarah.

"Accidental death?" queried John, who'd been thinking about what they'd told them. "Are you sure?"

"Well, that's what the coroner said," replied Josie, "but no, I'm not sure."

"What?" exclaimed Ben. "What on earth makes you think the coroner was wrong?"

"Lots of little things that don't just add up, but the main one is how come the poisonous mushrooms only ended up in Poppy's pie?" said Josie.

Jack and Kara exchanged looks but said nothing.

"Onions," said John.

"Pardon?" asked Josie.

"Onions," repeated John. "Ms Gilbert didn't like onions. Years ago, I was putting some onions on the swaps bench when I had too many to store, and she was there, loading up her wheelbarrow with everything that was going free as usual, but turned her nose up at my onions. Said they upset her stomach."

"So, you think she baked her pie separately to ensure there were no onions in it?" asked Zoe, cottoning on to what John was saying.

"It's one possible explanation," said John.

"It's a very possible explanation," replied Josie, nodding her head. "Thank you, John, that's a great help."

"Help?" asked Hugo, raising a quizzical eyebrow at his wife. "What are you up to Josie?"

"She's trying to solve a mystery as usual," said Zoe with a grin.

"Do Magic Mushrooms and Ivory Funnel mushrooms look the same?" asked Kara.

"Similar, but not the same," replied Josie.

"Well, I suppose it's an easy mistake to make then," said Sarah and the conversation then moved on, but Josie didn't join in, too busy pondering if a separate pie took away her niggles about 'The Case of the Poisoned Pie' as she mentally referred to it.

If Poppy had made her own pie at the same time as she was making her pies for her guests, surely, she would have shared what she thought were fresh magic mushrooms amongst all the pies, not just put fresh in hers and dried in the others, Josie wondered. She also pondered why Poppy, a supposedly experienced gardener, could have picked the wrong mushrooms. Josie remembered that she'd recently bought a book on the local flora and fauna and decided to consult it later, to see if that gave her any further clues as to how Poppy had made the fatal mistake.

Josie tuned back into the conversation just as John was thanking them all for looking after his and Sarah's allotment. Josie smiled, as she could have predicted that John would have visited their allotment as soon as they were home. The old John would have been perturbed if the veg rows weren't perfectly straight, but the new John didn't seem to care, which was a relief, as Dottie had 'helped' and a certain amount of chaos had ensued, with carrot and parsnip rows becoming intermingled.

They finished their meal with apple pie, made with allotment apples that they had frozen the previous autumn, and eventually the evening drew to a close. As everyone was finding jackets and saying their goodbyes, Jack, who'd been fairly quiet all evening, took Josie aside, and asked if they could meet up to discuss something that was worrying him. Josie readily agreed, and Jack arranged to call at her cottage after work the next day.

Chapter Forty-Five

"Come through - she's in the garden" said Hugo, opening the door to Jack.

Jack followed him through the old cottage, emerging from its cool dimness to the sunshine and riot of colour that was Josie's garden. Foxgloves, delphiniums, alliums and many more cottage garden flowers jostled for space and the air was full of their scent and the hum of bees. Josie's little cat, Lucky, was curled up in a patch of sunshine, one eye open to watch the bees but too lazy to chase them.

Josie was sitting at a small table in the dappled shade of her apple tree, a book open in front of her, but her eyes closed. Jack hesitated, not wanting to disturb her, but Hugo reassured him that she was just thinking, and urged him to go and join her whilst he made them both some tea. Jack sat down quietly, and Josie's eye remained closed, giving Jack the chance to study her. He thought she looked very well - marriage clearly suited her, and although she had filled out a little from the gaunt Josie of a few years ago, she was trim and lightly tanned from spending so much time gardening.

Hugo brought the tray of tea, and Josie's eyes flew open when he plonked it down. She greeted Jack warmly, before accepting a kiss goodbye on the cheek from Hugo who was going up to their allotment to leave them in peace.

"I think he's really going to get some peace himself," said Josie with a fond smile as Hugo left. "I'm afraid I've been bending his ear incessantly about 'The Case of the Poisoned Pie'."

"Well, that's what I wanted to speak to you about," said Jack, accepting the cup of tea Josie had poured him.

"Oh good – someone who doesn't think I'm going mad!" said Josie.

"Well, if you are, so am I. Something is definitely off about all this," replied Jack. "There's something I haven't told anyone about, apart from Kara, as it involves one of my pupils and I don't like to gossip, but I'm very concerned."

Josie was a bit confused, thinking that Jack must want to talk to her, as a former Headmistress, about a child safeguarding issues, not about Poppy's death, but she soon realised that was not the case when Jack outlined what had happened to Noah's father.

"The two things that worry me most," concluded Jack, "are the note that come with the muffins and the strong impression I got that Nigel thought I'd kidnapped his son!"

"Nigel?" exclaimed Josie.

"Yes, Nigel Blakemore, Noah's father."

"Well, well, well," said Josie, "the plot thickens!"

"What do you mean?" asked Jack.

"Well, at the inquest, a third guest of Poppy's that fateful night was someone named Nigel, but no one knew his last name."

"And you think that's this Nigel?" asked Jack.

"Yes," replied Josie.

"But there could be more than one Nigel, surely?" asked Jack.

"Yes, but only one, a Nigel Blakemore, who had a key cut for the gate into the square," said Josie.

"What!" exclaimed Jack. "That's not possible: the keys are restricted and only me or one of the trustees can get new keys cut."

"In theory, yes, but unfortunately the locksmith's apprentice got a bit mixed up between us and another client who also has restricted keys," explained Josie.

"And that client was Nigel," stated Jack, with an air of resignation.

"Yes Jack, it was. Philip the locksmith sends his profound apologies, but I suspect the apprentice was in for a roasting," said Josie.

"So," said Jack, slowly, "if Nigel had his own key, that suggests he was a regular visitor."

"Yes, and not one that wanted to hang around and wait to be admitted," said Josie. "Someone who wanted to pop in and out unnoticed. Someone who was having an affair perhaps?"

"Nigel's wife left him recently," replied Jack, "so an affair could be the reason for that split."

"Yes. She could have left him because he was seeing Poppy, or, alternatively, he could have been seeing Poppy because his wife had left him and he needed some female company," said Josie.

"He'd have had to have been pretty desperate," said Jack with a shudder.

They both thought for a moment.

"Poppy was a dominatrix, wasn't she?" asked Josie.

"She certainly was. You should have seen the stuff she had – a whole wardrobe full of whips, masks and... other stuff," replied Jack, a little embarrassed to describe to the retired headmistress everything they had found.

"Well maybe Nigel is that way inclined, and his wife isn't?" suggested Josie.

"Or maybe, being a businessman and always in control at work, he found it relaxing for someone else to be in charge occasionally?" replied Jack.

Josie looked at him sharply, and Jack laughed.

"Oh no Josie, I know who the boss is in our household, and I'm very lucky to have her!" he said.

"I wasn't suggesting anything else, Lord Kirkby," replied Josie, enjoying teasing him.

They sat for a moment, enjoying the sunshine and reflecting on how lucky they were that fate had found them their partners.

"But maybe that wasn't the whole reason Nigel was visiting her," said Josie. "What was it that the note said, Jack?"

"It was 'in case you were missing P's special recipe' if I remember correctly," said Jack.

"Well, I think we know what the 'special recipe' ingredient was, don't we - magic mushrooms. Zoe did an internet search for me, and Poppy was running a business called Dinner+, and there was a reference to 'foraged ingredients' and also 'magic meals'," replied Poppy.

"Really?" said Jack, raising an eyebrow. "Are Psilocybin mushrooms addictive?"

"I don't think so – there's nothing about that in my book," replied Josie, tapping the book on the table.

"Maybe Nigel just enjoyed the relaxing effect of them, a release from a high-powered job?" suggested Jack.

"Possibly, the same as letting Poppy take over in the bedroom - an escape perhaps?" agreed Josie.

Jack nodded in agreement and then once again they both lapsed into thought.

"What we really need to know is who sent Nigel the muffins," said Josie, suddenly.

"They were delivered by a motorbike courier," replied Jack, "and there can't be too many of them around here."

"You're right. Leave that one with me and I'll make some calls," said Josie, and Jack grinned, knowing how much Josie liked to get her teeth into solving a mystery.

"We also need to know what was in them," continued Josie.

"Ah. I might be able to help there," replied Jack.

"Oh? How?" asked Josie.

"When I found Nigel there was a bit of muffin left on a plate next to his bed. I wrapped it in a tissue to give to the ambulance crew and then I found a whole muffin and gave them that instead. I forgot all about it and I only found it in my pocket a few days later - starting to go mouldy I'm afraid. I was going to throw it away, seeing as Nigel was recovering, but for some reason I kept it – it's in a Ziplock bag in the freezer," Jack replied. "I'll see if Kara can get it analysed at the lab the RSPCA uses in animal poisoning cases."

"Oh well done, Jack – we'll make a detective of you yet!" said Josie with a grin.

"One thing we also need to know is why they were sent – as a kind 'pick-me-up' that went wrong, or a deliberate attempt to kill him?" said Jack.

"If Poppy's death was accidental, as the coroner ruled, could Nigel's poisoned muffins have been an accident as well?" asked Josie.

"A bit of a coincidence, don't you think?" replied Jack.

Josie nodded - she didn't really believe in coincidences.

"And if this was attempted murder, was Poppy's death murder too?" pondered Josie.

"That's what we need to find out," replied Jack.

Chapter Forty-Six

When Hugo returned home with a bag full of fresh salad leaves, bright green pods of peas, luscious strawberries and fragrant sweet peas, Josie was on the phone speaking to a motorbike courier company. Hugo raised an eyebrow, but knowing his wife, left her to it and took his haul through to the kitchen before putting the kettle on to make a fresh pot of tea.

"Oh, good afternoon," Josie was saying into the phone when he placed a cup of tea next to her a few minutes later. "Yes, I can hold, no problem."

Josie smiled her thanks at Hugo and took a much-needed sip of tea. From the crossings out on the list in her hand, Hugo thought she must have already made a few calls, but this looked like the last on the list, so he sat down with his own tea and waited for her to fill him in on what she was up to.

"Yes, this is Mr Blakemore's secretary," Josie said, casting Hugo a guilty look.

Hugo's eyebrows shot up in surprise. Josie was always scrupulously honest, so if she was lying to someone, it must be for a very good reason.

"You delivered a package to Mr Blackmore on the date I just gave your colleague, but there was no sender's address. Mr Blackmore really enjoyed the muffins you delivered, and wanted to put a regular order in, support a local business like your own," said Josie grimacing as she laid it on thick, and then listened to the reply.

"Oh, I quite understand you can't give me the name and address of the person who sent the muffins. It's a long shot, but can you tell me the nearest bakery to where the sender lives so I can speak to them and see if it was them that made the delicious muffins, please? Oh, that's lovely - many thanks, I'll give them a call. I'll tell Mr Blakemore how helpful you've been, and we'll certainly bear you in mind when he next needs a courier. Thank you again - goodbye."

Josie hung up and scribbled a quick note before looking at her husband guiltily, her face quite pink.

"Josie? What *are* you up to?" asked Hugo.

"I'm putting two and two together, and hopefully not making five," said Josie, before picking the phone up again.

To Hugo's surprise, she didn't ring the bakery whose details she'd noted down, but rung Zoe, gave her the bakery name and address and then hung up, confusing Hugo further. Whilst she waited for Zoe to ring back, she filled Hugo in on what Jack had told her, and what she was trying to do.

"How does knowing the address of the nearest bakery help you, though?" asked Hugo, still confused. "Surely a commercial bakery wouldn't bake poisonous mushrooms into a muffin at a customer's request?"

"Of course not!" replied Josie, with a laugh. "I knew the courier wouldn't give me the name of the sender but if I knew the name of the nearest bakery, it would give the rough area where the sender lived. Zoe is getting the addresses of my two suspects from the electoral rolls, and then pinpointing them and the bakery on a Google map to see who lives nearest to the bakery."

"My clever girl!" said Hugo, giving her a hug. He was constantly surprised by his wife's ingenuity and knew there would never be a dull day in their life together.

Five minutes later, Zoe rang back and gave Josie a name.

"Well, well, well," said Josie, "I think I may know the name of the murder. All I have to do now is prove it!"

Chapter Forty-Seven

It was all change again at the square. Fiona and her three boys had moved out, reconciled with the boy's father, and had returned to the family home in Leeds. Lily was heartbroken, but Felix assured her they would keep in touch and Jack convinced her that a long-distance relationship was very romantic. Between theatrical sighs, Lily texted and Face Timed Felix several times a day but wasn't as distraught as she pretended to be. Kara cosseted her, remembering how painful young love could be, but she had the wisdom not to say to Lily that this infatuation would pale into insignificance when she met someone that she loved with all her heart, as she did Jack.

Nadia and Amir had just found out they were expecting twins, so wasted no time in moving into the three-bedroom house that Fiona had vacated. Everyone helped with the move, not letting Nadia move a finger. She sat on Hope's bench, stroking her gently rounded stomach, and watched as their possessions were carried from one house to another. Once everything was done, Nadia just walked into the house, stuck the baby scan picture onto the fridge, and she was home.

Her parents then moved into Poppy's old apartment a week or so later, and with twins on the way Nadia was so glad that she would have them close at hand. Whilst neighbours helped them move in, Nadia's mother was busy cooking and then served a mountain of delicious food up to all the helpers. They brought heaped plates to sit around in the square, relaxing, enjoying the evening sun, the wonderful food and the scent of flowers. Jack sat with Ben and Will, the three young men having been the muscle to move the bed and other heavy items.

Jack and Ben were quietly discussing the poisonings and Will listened with astonishment. Jack had just told Ben that the muffin piece that Kara had got tested had also contained Ivory Funnel mushroom traces, so it was pretty certain the two cases were linked. Jack had spoken to the police, but unless Nigel reported a 'crime', as the coroner had already ruled on Poppy's case, the police just weren't interested. Ben told them that Zoe and Josie had a main suspect in mind but weren't saying who it was until they could prove it, as they didn't want to put anything out there and be sued for slander if they had got it all wrong.

Will had really disliked Poppy Gilbert, and she had caused him a lot of pain, but if it really was murder, then even she deserved justice to be done. The thought that there could still be a murderer out there in their little community was chilling, and Will wondered what he could do to help solve 'The Case of the Poisoned Pie and Muffins', as they were now calling it. Will listened to Ben and Jack chatting, his mind running over the details, and when the other two ran out of steam and tucked into their food, he spoke up.

"I think you might be approaching this from the wrong angle: what we should be asking ourselves is 'why'. What was the motive?"

Jack and Ben stared at Will in astonishment.

"You're absolutely right!" exclaimed Jack. "If we work out 'why', 'who' should be obvious!"

"From what you've told me I think the motives in each case are different, although they are of course linked, but I think that it's probably the same murderer," said Will

"I think you're right that the motives are different," said Ben, nodding. "Nigel thought Jack was holding Noah until he paid up to get his son back, so maybe Nigel knows who Poppy's murderer was and was being blackmailed?"

"Yes, it does sound like that, doesn't it," agreed Jack.

"On the other hand, maybe he was Poppy's murderer and that was why he was being blackmailed?" suggested Will. "He had his own key and could come and go as he wanted, so he may have had the opportunity to slip the mushrooms into her pie."

"Yes... but if he was the murderer, why was he poisoned too? Seems like someone wanted to shut him up – permanently," said Ben.

"Revenge perhaps? Someone that loved Poppy and wanted revenge for her death?" asked Will.

Jack and Ben looked at each other and then burst out laughing. Will stared at them for a moment perplexed and then joined in.

"Yeah, you're right: I can't imagine anyone having feelings for Ms Gilbert, apart from contempt," he conceded.

"I really can't imagine Nigel as a murderer," said Jack. "Everything about this feels like he's the victim here, however, I think he could know who the murderer is."

"Can we ask him what's going on and offer to help him - he must be terrified they'll try again?" said Will.

"I'd love to talk to him," replied Jack, "but the day after he came out of hospital, he took Noah out of school two weeks ahead of the holidays and they've gone abroad. The headmaster was furious, as there was no reason given in the email and we don't allow pupils to go on holiday in term time, apart from in exceptional circumstances."

"Well, I suppose someone trying to kill you is exceptional circumstances, but if he's gone into hiding, he can hardly tell the headmaster that!" said Ben.

"Sounds like we can't solve that one just now, but who would want Poppy murdered?" asked Will.

"I think we'll need a big piece of paper to write down that list!" said Jack, attempting a little humour.

"Okay. Different question," said Ben. "Who would want Poppy dead, and was prepared to carry it out?"

"Good question," said Will. "She deliberately hurt a lot of people, including me and Joy, but I think that whilst most of those people hated her and would never forgive her, I really don't think that any of the people who I know and who she hurt could have killed her - they just don't have whatever it is that murders have."

"So, it's a very short list then. And one with no names on it currently," said Jack.

The three men stared morosely into the distance, frustrated at being unable to get anywhere.

"I think we need to bring in cleverer minds than ours," said Ben at last. "We need Kara, Josie and especially Zoe's devious mind."

Jack and Will nodded in agreement, and with no other ideas, they all got up and went to fetch more curry. Whilst Jack was helping himself to a little more of the aromatic food, Nadia mentioned that her parents had just had a bank statement addressed to Poppy delivered. Jack apologised and said he'd take it and sort it out - he had tried to get in touch with Poppy's bank once, but after hanging on the phone for ages being played annoying music, he'd given up and had forgotten to try again.

Jack had paid Poppy's outstanding utilities bills out of the deposit she'd paid when she'd moved in, but he did need to pay the remaining balance of the deposit into her account, and then leave it up to the bank to decide what to do with her money. He didn't imagine there would be much as she'd had so few possessions and no obvious signs of wealth, but if there was no next of kin, he assumed it would go to a charity eventually and then at least some good would come out of her miserable life.

Chapter Forty-Eight

The trustees met in Lady Dorothy's apartment, summoned not to a board meeting, but to solve a murder, for Jack was now convinced that was the case. Jack had set up a flip chart, Josie had brought a book and a folder of notes, Zoe had brought her tablet, and Ben brought along a couple of bottles of wine. Will and Joy had also joined them, but Joy was very kindly babysitting Dottie, Mia and Saffie up in Jack and Kara's apartment, so that the 'detectives' could concentrate without distractions.

"I thought it might help to establish what we all know," said Jack, picking up a marker pen. "From the CCTV, we know that Julian Fernsby arrived a few hours before the others, not long after Will helped Gilbert in with her shopping."

"That's right," said Zoe, referring to her tablet. "The time stamp on the video was just after 3pm when Fernsby arrived."

"Thank Zoe," said Jack writing '3pm Fernsby arrives' on the flip-chart.

"Hang on," said Will, "should we start a bit sooner - perhaps when I saw her foraging in the woods?"

"Good idea - roughly what time was that?"

"Mid-morning - around 10:30 I think," replied Will.

Jack squeezed '10:30 PG foraging in woods' above his first note.

"Did you see if she picked any mushrooms, Will?" asked Josie.

"No, I didn't see what she had in her bag, and I didn't see any mushrooms where she was, but then, she could have just picked them all, couldn't she?" Will replied.

"Did you see any mushrooms anywhere, Will?" asked Josie.

"Yes, I photographed some as reference for my Flower Fairy drawings," Will replied, scrolling through his phone.

"Can I see please?" asked Josie.

Will handed her the phone, and she stared at the image and then opened a bookmarked page in her book on local flora and fauna.

"Yes, that makes sense. Those are definitely Ivory Funnel mushrooms, as I expected at that time of year," said Josie, holding up her book so that the others could see the illustration. The mushrooms were clearly the same, but there was a yellow skull-and-crossbones next to the picture of them in the book, so that no one could be in any doubt that they were poisonous.

"When do Psilocybin mushrooms grow then Josie?" asked Kara.

"Not until the autumn," replied Josie.

"So, anyone that knew anything about our native flora and fauna would have known that?" asked Ben.

"Yes, or anyone that had a book like this," replied Josie.

"Hang on a minute, darling," said Hugo suddenly. "Didn't that chap have a copy of that book?"

"What chap, Hugo?" asked Josie, puzzled.

"The one you were ogling in the Walled Garden café," replied Hugo.

"Ogling?" asked Josie, glaring at her husband. "What are you talking about?"

"You know, the spivvy looking chap you were staring at. The one you thought you knew, but then decided you didn't. He had a copy of that book," replied Hugo.

"So he did, and actually I did know him. I'd forgotten all about that, but that was why he was so familiar when I saw him at Poppy's funeral," said Josie, almost to herself.

"Who is he, Josie," asked Jack.

"Julian... Julien Fernsby," she replied.

There was a stunned silence as Josie and Zoe exchanged looks.

"So," said Jack slowly, "Fernsby arrived well before the others and may have had knowledge of poisonous mushrooms."

"Was he carrying anything when he arrived, Zoe?" asked Kara.

Zoe whizzed through the CCTV footage on her tablet.

"Yes, he was," she said, excitedly. "He has a carrier bag."

They all looked at each other and then Ben let out a low whistle.

"Do you think Fernsby is our murder?"

"Well, looks like he had opportunity and possibly knowledge, but did he have a motive?" asked Kara.

"Four years ago, he was fined heavily for trying to bribe a councillor, so maybe he bore a grudge against Poppy who ensnared him into the deal?" suggested Jack.

"Possibly - but is that a strong enough motive for murder?" asked Hugo.

"It doesn't feel a strong enough reason to kill someone, but then, I couldn't think of any reason good enough to take someone else's life," said Will.

"If it was him, what would be his motive for trying to kill Nigel?" asked Josie.

"Do we know that was him?" asked Will.

"No, but we do know that he had knowledge, and may still have had some of the mushrooms in his possession," replied Kara.

"We also know that the package containing the muffins was picked up from, or very near, Fernsby's house," said Josie.

"What! How on earth did you find that out?" asked Jack.

"There's no end to my wife's talents," replied Hugo and they all laughed, lightening the mood.

Kara went around and topped up their wine glasses whilst Josie explained how she and Zoe had worked out where the muffins had been sent from. Jack left them for a short while, saying he was just going up to their apartment to check that Joy was okay, and that the children were in bed and not playing her up. He soon came back carrying some envelopes, the video camera and the phone he had found at Poppy's apartment.

"I've been thinking about motive," said Jack, as he placed the items on the table, sat down and picked up his wine glass. "I think Poppy was blackmailing the three men."

"What about, do you think?" asked Hugo.

"I think I know," said Ben, reaching over and picking up the video camera. "We found this behind a two-way mirror in Gilbert's bedroom. I think she was recording the men having kinky sex with her, and then was blackmailing them if they wanted her to keep quiet."

Ben opened the screen on the tiny video recorder and pushed a few buttons. Even without the sound of heavy breathing and moaning filling the room the group would have known from the expression on Ben's face that he was right. Zoe craned her neck to see the screen too, but her expression was more of amusement than shock.

"Well, I never knew that was possible!" she said. "Ms Gilbert was much more flexible than she looked!"

Ben laughed and shut off the playback.

"Okay, I think it's pretty clear that she was recording her 'performances', and I'll go through the rest of the video later and check who she has on film. However, this alone doesn't prove she was blackmailing anyone – the recordings may have been for her personal enjoyment or her CV!"

"Payments into her account might though," said Jack, looking through the bank statements in front of him that he had just opened. He gave a low whistle.

"There is a great deal of money in her account. Three payments of £1,000 had been coming in every week, each from different accounts."

"Does it say who they are from?" asked Josie.

"No, just from an account number with no payment reference."

"That doesn't prove anything then," replied Josie. "Even if we went to the police and they got bank details for the payees, without other evidence it could just be payment for 'services rendered', as evidenced by the video."

"Phew - for that sort of money, she must have been good!" said Ben, earning him a slap from Zoe.

"Well, maybe I ought to watch the video too and make notes," said Zoe, fluttering her eyelashes at her husband.

"Behave yourselves," said Kara with a laugh, and the couple grinned at each other and then refocused, Zoe leaning across the table and picking up the phone.

"The evidence could be on here," she said. "Pity the screen is smashed, but I'll plug it into the computer and see if I can get in. If you have the camera memory card, I'll take a look at that too, Jack. Jack?"

Jack was miles away, and took a second to tune back in.

"Sorry Zoe, I was just trying to remember something," said Jack. "When Nigel was ill, I was looking for his address book to phone his wife and a bank statement fell to the floor. I couldn't help noticing that a large sum went out each month, and by the end of the month his account was almost empty. I'm trying to visualise the page and read the amount - £1,000 certainly feels familiar as it's a nice round figure."

"Well, the Police will be able to check all those details, Jack, but we need more than theories and vague memories before we go to them," said Josie.

"You're right Josie. Let's finish off this timeline and see if it highlights anything else," replied Jack.

Referring to the copy of the square's CCTV on Zoe's tablet, they added the time that Smythe had arrived along with Nigel. The next time noted was much later when Nigel left, and then, a while later, Smythe and Fernsby, accompanied by Poppy to unlock the gate for them. Poppy then returned to the apartment, but no one else came or went for the remainder of the night. Zoe fast-forwarded the next few weeks, but until Jack discovered her body, apart from the postie, no one else came to Poppy's door.

"She was clearly alive when everyone else left, although obviously not very well," said Kara. "We have no evidence that anyone else entered the apartment after they left, so one, or all of them must have poisoned her that night."

"Unless of course she poisoned herself, as the coroner ruled?" replied Hugo, always the voice of reason.

"I don't think it could have been Nigel," said Josie, ignoring her husband as she knew in her heart that this had been murder. "Whoever sent him the poisoned muffins wanted to shut him up, which leads me to think he knew the identity of the killer."

"He has his own gate key, suggesting he visited Poppy regularly, yet he never visits her again after that night. Does that suggest he knew she was dead, so there was no point visiting her?" asked Josie.

"The same could be said about the other two," said Hugo, "so do we think they were all in it together?"

"Well, if they were all being blackmailed by Poppy, they could have planned the murder together to kill her off and stop the blackmail? suggested Ben.

"Does the fact Nigel left early suggest that he didn't want to hang around once the deed was done?" asked Zoe.

"Why would Nigel think that Jack had kidnapped his son?" asked Kara. "That doesn't seem to fit with anything."

"Maybe Nigel did kill her, and the others were blackmailing him?" asked Will.

"Okay, I think we're going round in circles now," said Jack, rubbing his temple. "My brain hurts - let's leave it for tonight, and see what Ben and Zoe uncover from the phone etcetera."

There were murmurs of agreement and then the friends finished their drinks and said their goodbyes. Those with children went upstairs with Jack and Kara to collect them, gently carrying their sleeping children out to their cars. Josie and Hugo walked arm in arm down the hill towards their home, passing the square bathed in soft light from carefully placed spotlights. The gates were locked, and it looked so calm and safe that it was difficult to imagine that a murder had taken place within the wall's warm embrace.

Chapter Forty-Nine

The school summer holidays arrived at last, and the Kirkby streets and playground were full of the sounds of children playing outside through the long hot days. The allotments and the gardens of the square were brimming over with ripe vegetables and vibrant flowers. Nadia, with the growing twins swelling her tummy, was finding it difficult to bend to weed the flower garden, but Evelyn, now returned from her cruise, was out there helping most days with her pink kneeler and matching gloves. Her cruise hadn't ended in an engagement, but she'd had fun, and had moved on to another man she'd met online. Bert continued to tend the vegetable beds, helped often by Will who had come to realise that gardening was a form of mindfulness, and that an hour in the garden was just as good as his former early morning meditation, especially as he'd rather spend early mornings cuddled up with Joy in bed.

Elsie would sit and watch the gardeners working and the children playing, and she realised that she was happier now than at any point in her life previously. Bert was attentive to her every need, making sure she had cushions and cold drinks and setting up a parasol for her when the sun was hot. They still had their tea together most days, but were often joined by Will, Joy and Mia, at one or other of their houses, as Mia had adopted Elsie as her Granny. On the rare occasions when she felt the need to see the green fields of the farm, Bert would drive her there and together they would look at the view for a while before going for a pub lunch. Theirs wasn't a romance, but a deep friendship that meant a lot to them both.

All across the allotments and the square gardeners were coaxing and protecting their best specimens ready for the autumn Allotment Association's Annual Produce Show. Jack was always amused how seriously people took this, but rivalry was fierce, and even John who had been away for most of the year was trying to make up for lost time by feeding up his marrows in the hope of retaining his 'biggest marrow' trophy. In the last ten years, he'd only lost the trophy once, and he was determined not to lose it ever again. Sarah teased him mercilessly of course, but had caught the competitive gardening bug, and secretly hoped that her dahlias would do well, regularly checking the National Dahlia Society website for advice.

With the twins on the way Nadia had decided to wait a few years before taking a RHS gardening qualification but in the meantime, she had been attending a few local flower arranging classes instead. With Evelyn picking flowers for her she practised regularly, in the hope of entering the flower arranging class at the show. As well as Evelyn and Nadia's parents, Elsie was often the lucky recipient of the vases of flowers, each arrangement being more accomplished than the last. Josie asked Nadia to join the church flower rota, and the vicar was delighted to welcome a Muslim lady to her church. Mentored by Josie, Nadia soon learnt how to do really large arrangements - first creating a strong background of greenery before adding a few bright flowers as highlights.

Nadia was fascinated to find that in the Christian church women were permitted to attend alongside men, very different to the mosque where women were encouraged to pray at home and had to sit separately if they did want to attend the mosque. Although Nadia never attended a church service out of deference to her own religion, she grew to love the calm, cool interior of the church, the way the sunlight through stained glass danced with colour across the ancient stone floor and made the waxed wood of the old pews glow. On hot days, when the weight of the babies exhausted her and she grew anxious about the birth, she would stop at the church on her way home from her shift at the Co-op and just sit in the silence for a while, letting her heart slow and her mind wander until she felt at peace.

Jack had little time for his own allotment as he was busy working on other peoples' gardens through most of the school holiday. At this time of year Brown's Green Gardening were in demand, mainly cutting grass and weeding, but a couple of complete garden overhauls were putting extra pressure on the little business. On the bigger jobs Jack worked alongside Todd, Alex and Adam, enjoying the camaraderie of his team and the way that their different skills complemented each other's.

Adam had got over his confusion from Gilbert's sexual assault on him earlier that year, and now had a girlfriend, Rosie, a cheerful young lady who had Down's syndrome. They were very happy together, and Rosie would often come and help Adam at work. She came to be near to her boyfriend, but Jack insisted on paying her as she worked hard and could spot a weed a mile off. If Alex was jealous, he didn't show it, laughing and joking with Rosie as they all worked side by side. The boys and Rosie adored Dottie and made a real fuss of her when Kara popped onto site with her. Jack couldn't decide which they enjoyed most - seeing Dottie or eating the sandwiches and home-made cakes that Kara always brought with her.

Investigations into the 'Case of the Poisoned Pie and Muffins' had hit a brick wall and were put on hold as one by one the trustees and the residents of the square went on their summer holidays. People came and went, going away pale and jaded, returning tanned and relaxed, before taking their turn to keep an eye on neighbour's empty houses, watering plants and feeding cats as their friends or family had done for them.

The first to go away were Josie and Hugo who had rented a cottage in Cornwall for two weeks. They wandered around tiny seaside villages, ate fish or lobster caught that morning by local fishermen and swam in the sea whenever the waves weren't too wild. A couple of days it rained, so they had a long lunch in the local pub one wet day and visited the Tate at St Ives on another. Hugo said he preferred the wonderful views of Porthmeor Beach from the windows to the modern art inside, but Josie liked a lot of it, the freshness and simplicity appealing to her. They lunched in the rooftop café, and as the rain had eased off, at Josie's insistence, afterwards visited the nearby Barbara Hepworth sculpture garden. Hugo enjoyed the garden and said that the sculptures were 'alright', but later in the car he talked about perhaps getting a small sculpture for their own garden.

On the next sunny day Hugo chose their destination and they drove east to the Lost Gardens of Heligan. For both of them it was the highlight of the holiday, wandering slowly around the two thousand acre restored site, admiring the beauty of the Pleasure Grounds and the wide range of vegetables grown in the Productive Gardens. Hugo chatted animatedly to the gardeners about vegetable varieties and was delighted to find he could buy heritage seeds in the estate's shop. Josie loved the sleeping Mud Maid sculpture in the woods, the body clothed in living plants - it was an idea she would take home and try and recreate on a much smaller scale in the children's garden at the allotments.

Will and Joy had a week in a caravan at Scarborough with Mia, just as Will had promised, enjoying the beach, donkey rides and too much fish and chips and ice cream. One calm day they took a boat trip out to see the seabirds at Bempton cliffs, astonished at the noise and clamour that around half a million seabirds make. Their guide helped them to identify the gannets, guillemots, razorbills, kittiwakes and fulmars that crowded the ledges of the chalk cliff, but it was the puffins that Mia loved most. She monopolised the binoculars, watching the clumsy puffins, or 'parrots' as she kept calling them, dive off the ledges and fly down to the sea below.

The highlight for Will was when Mia suddenly called him 'daddy' as they built a giant sandcastle together. Mia was oblivious to the tide of emotions this caused, but Joy caught his eye and nodded, understanding the enormity of that one word. That evening, once Mia was asleep, Will proposed to Joy and she immediately said yes. As soon as her divorce was final, they would be married, and Will would officially adopt Mia and then, legitimately, he'd be her daddy.

Zoe and Ben flew to Crete with Saffie for three long weeks, spending their days mostly lazing on the beach, soaking up the sun, or swimming in the warm turquoise sea. They tried to keep Saffie out of the sun under a large brolly, but now that she was toddling, she'd have none of it, so they just resorted to frequent applications of factor fifty sun cream. Likewise, they soon realised that a visit to the historic Knossos Palace or to the spectacular Samaria Gorge was pointless with the youngster, and resigned themselves to the fact they might have to wait at least ten years before they could enjoy the kind of holidays they had enjoyed pre-Saffie.

However, it wasn't all bad as the Greek hoteliers and restaurant owners all adored their little girl and made a fuss of her wherever they went. Each evening as they watched the sun set over the sea from one of the beachside tavernas, dishes of ice-cream (for Saffie) and glasses of raki, the local moonshine, regularly appeared free of charge.

With a four-year-old, a pre-teen and a teenager, Jack and Kara had great difficulty deciding on a suitable location for their holiday, and it was almost the end of the school holidays when, in desperation, a frazzled Kara managed to get a late cancellation for Center Parcs in the Lake District. Jack reckoned if the park was awful, they could always explore the Lakes, and at least it would be a change of scene.

Holidays had been few and far between for Jack as he was growing up, and he had expected Center Parcs to be a bit like Butlins but was pleasantly surprised at the wonderful woodland setting and the luxury Scandinavian style lakeside lodges. Cars had to be left at the park perimeter, so moving around the site was on foot or by bike only. Jack hired them all bikes, one of which had a trailer attached so that Dottie could be carried around in style if her little legs got too tired to peddle her own small bike. It had been many years since Kara had ridden a bike and after the first day she could barely walk, but after a couple of hours in the on-site spa she felt much better.

All the family loved the subtropical swimming pool complex, spending hours in its warm water. The older children enjoyed the rides, slides and rapids and Dottie loved the children's water play area with its little slides, spray fountains and splashing pool. Another highlight was watching red squirrels in the forest, and from that day onward, Pink Rabbit was relegated, and Dottie carried her own cuddly squirrel, 'Red' with her everywhere. Jack, Lily and Ronan went on the exciting treetop adventure which culminated in an exhilarating zip-wire over the lake. Watching them from the safety of the ground, Kara, who wasn't particularly fond of heights, was glad she had needed to stay on the ground with Dottie.

Although Jack really enjoyed the holiday with his family, his mind kept returning to the poisoning cases. One evening as he sat outside their Lodge, drinking a beer and looking at the stars reflected in the lake, something suddenly occurred to him: if he was right, they may just be able to prove that it had been murder. When they arrived home a couple of days later, Jack just dumped their bags and went straight to check on some papers in his office. Two minutes later he was on the phone to Josie, and thirty minutes later he made a call to DCI Quinn.

The inspector listened carefully, mindful that she was speaking to Lord Kirkby, but then politely told Jack that unless Nigel returned to the UK and made a complaint, or other, more tangible evidence emerged, she was not inclined to reopen Ms Gilbert's case. Jack tried not to show his frustration but until Zoe and Ben returned from their holiday and cracked the phone code, there was nothing else he could do but wait.

Chapter Fifty

The school holiday eventually came to an end, and the children and Jack returned to school. Jack was delighted to see that Noah had returned to class, and even more delighted when Noah told him his mummy was back home with him and his daddy. Noah was a much happier child with no more bad behaviour, and as Jack no longer needed to support him, he was assigned to a new child with learning difficulties. Jack would have loved to talk to Nigel about his relationship with Poppy, but now that his wife had returned, Jack thought it was probably best not to say anything in case Mrs Blakemore knew nothing about her husband's extramarital relationship.

Ben and Zoe had returned from their holiday but, so far, hadn't been able to crack the phone code. The camera's memory card had been full of photos of Will, most of them taken with a telephoto lens when he was exercising bare chested. Zoe could understand Poppy's preoccupation - Will really did have an attractive gently muscled torso, but then Zoe looked at Ben, who was taller and broader with even more impressive pecs, and was very pleased with her lot. She wondered whether to offer Joy the photos, but then thought better of it and just deleted them all – better Joy didn't know the full extent of Poppy's obsession with her fiancée.

Ben downloaded the footage from the video camera and found it went back months. Ben got so sick of seeing Poppy's, frankly, ridiculous antics, he took to fast forwarding it, just noting down names and dates. Nigel tended to visit in the afternoons when Poppy would be dressed in full dominatrix mode, whereas Smythe and Fernsby visited in the evenings when Poppy interspersed the leather and whips with maids and nurses outfits. The only straight forward sex was on Poppy's last afternoon on this earth, when Fernsby was remarkably gentle with her, leaving her sated and sleeping when he left the bed.

As the video would have been hard to access behind the mirror, Ben assumed that Poppy had been able to download it remotely and wondered if any of it was on her laptop. He collected the laptop, still in its evidence bag, from Jack, and found that it was also password protected. However, he knew that the police had accessed it, so he didn't think the password would be too hard. It wasn't - just Dinner+, Poppy's 'catering' business name.

Looking in the video folder he found three short clips, one of each of the three men, their faces clearly captured but Poppy's out of shot. All three clips had been emailed from the laptop to Poppy's own email address, but there were no emails that had been sent out with them as attachments. He took a quick look through other emails and documents on the laptop but didn't see anything else of interest.

The trustees met for supper again and agreed they could do no more if the police weren't interested. As Poppy's place at the square had been arranged by Social Services, Josie had been liaising with them to identify if there was any next of kin that needed informing of her death, or who would inherit her 'estate'. Through their records, and Josie's own sleuthing, she had found out about Poppy Gilbert's (aka. Pauline Gilbert, aka. P. Gill) sad upbringing – a non-existent father and a mother who died of a drug overdose when Pauline was only eleven years old.

She had been placed in care, fostered for a couple of short periods, but each time she was returned to a council run children's home. She ran away at fifteen, was found and returned to the home, but at sixteen moved into her own accommodation but still with council support whilst she attended a Youth Training Scheme.

"Now here's where it gets interesting," said Josie. "Poppy did two youth training courses during that period – one in catering, and one in gardening."

"So that was the basis of her previous claim to be a 'qualified chef' – cordon bleu no less?" asked Kara.

"It seems so - I can't find any record of her attending catering college, and Le Cordon Bleu has no records of her attaining any of their qualifications" replied Josie.

"Any record of her becoming RHS qualified or working at Kew as she boasted when she first came to Kirkby?" asked Jack.

"None whatsoever, Jack," replied Josie, "I checked with them too.

"Looks like that was just another of her fantasies," said Kara.

"It seems to me she had a sad upbringing, and her fantasies were a way of coping, reinventing herself regularly," said Hugo, being unusually perceptive.

They sat in silence for a moment, understanding, perhaps, a little of how Pauline Gilbert had ended up the opportunist, vindictive, morally deficient individual that had blighted their lives.

"It's a decision to be bad," says Josie suddenly. "I know Poppy had a terrible upbringing and we can all understand why she became the unpleasant person that she was, but lots of people had similar, or much worse, upbringings, and still choose to be kind, honest and caring. I'm always deeply saddened when someone actively decides to be nasty when it's just as easy to be nice."

They all nodded in agreement and Zoe patted Josie's hand. In doing so she glanced at Josie's notes, and saw they were very detailed, with the name of the Poppy's mother and the details of the children's home she had lived in.

"Can I borrow this for a moment please Josie," said Zoe, pointing to Josie's notes.

Josie handed it over without a word, knowing that Zoe's amazing mind would be whirling away. Zoe pulled out her tablet and took a quick scan of the notes before handing them back. Ben raised an enquiring eyebrow and wasn't surprised when a few minutes later Zoe made their excuses and got up to leave. Once home, Zoe stared at the scan and then started to play with Poppy's phone. Five minutes later, using the name of one of the children's homes as a password, she was in.

Chapter Fifty-One

The arrests were made at dawn, Smythe and Fernsby woken up and taken away in handcuffs, both protesting loudly and threatening to sue the police for wrongful arrest. They treated Nigel differently, asking him politely to come to the station to answer some questions later that day. Smythe and Fernsby were photographed, had fingerprints taken and the inside of their mouths swabbed for DNA before being placed in separate cells and left to stew.

Before long it was obvious that their individual solicitors had arrived, both were interchangeable 'Hooray Henrys', with sharp suits and loud plummy voices that echoed down the corridors of the custody suite. After giving them time to consult with their clients, DCI Quinn commenced interviews, starting with Julian Fernsby. She set the recorder going, stated the date and time and the names of the people present, but before she could ask her first question, Fernsby's solicitor barrelled in, demanding that his client was released immediately. Quinn let him rant until he ran out of steam and then turned to Fernsby.

"Mr Fernsby, can you tell me when the last time was that you saw Ms Pauline Gilbert, who you may have known as Poppy?" she asked pleasantly.

Before answering Fernsby looked at his solicitor who gave a slight nod.

"I can't remember the exact date, but the middle of May," replied Fernsby.

"Would that have been the 15th of May, Mr Fernsby?" asked Quinn.

"Possibly," said Fernsby with a nonchalant shoulder shrug.

"About what time did you arrive at Ms Gilbert's apartment on that date?" asked Quinn.

"You expect me to remember three months later?" asked Fernsby disdainfully.

"Just roughly will do Mr Fernsby," replied DCI Quinn, still in a pleasant tone.

"About 7:30, I imagine," replied Fernsby.

"Would you have a diary note or electronic appointment reminder that could confirm that, Mr Fernsby?" asked Quinn.

"No, it wasn't that kind of appointment," said Fernsby, causing his solicitor to give him a stern look to which Fernsby just shrugged.

"What kind of appointment was it?" asked Quinn.

"A dinner," replied Fernsby.

"Oh, was Ms Gilbert a friend of yours then?" asked Quinn.

"No. More a service provider," replied Fernsby archly, earning another glare from his solicitor.

"And what kind of service would that be?" asked Quinn.

Before Fernsby could answer, his Solicitor intervened.

"Ms Gilbert ran a company called Dinner + and hosted dinners. Business dinners. My client is a property developer and used her services to talk to prospective clients in a relaxed atmosphere," he said.

"Strange that a business dinner wouldn't be in your diary, Mr Fernsby?" remarked DCI Quinn mildly.

"Well, they were always at the same time, so no need to write it down," replied Fernsby, nonchalantly.

"Always at 7:30?" asked Quinn.

Fernsby nodded.

"For the tape please, Mr Fernsby," instructed Quinn.

"Yes," snapped Fernsby.

"And you wouldn't arrive early to assist Ms Gilbert with preparations?" Quinn asked.

"Why would I do that when I was paying for her services? replied Fernsby in an irritated voice.

"And what services would that be?" asked Quinn.

"Catering, of course!" replied Fernsby, scowling.

"Nothing else?" asked Quinn nonchalantly.

"What are you implying?" interrupted the solicitor.

"Nothing. But as you know we took a DNA sample from your client earlier. We also have a semen sample recovered from the body of Ms Gilbert," replied DCI Quinn, leaving them to draw their own conclusions.

Quinn said nothing further and let the silence stretch, knowing from experience that people were uncomfortable with silence and would often speak out to fill the void. Fernsby looked at his solicitor who gave a tiny shake of his head.

Quinn extracted a document from the folder in front of her and passed it across the table towards Fernsby. It was a still shot taken from the square's CCTV footage showing a back view of Fernsby walking towards Poppy's door.

"Can you confirm this is you, Mr Fernsby?" she asked.

"Could be anyone," Fernsby replied disdainfully, barely glancing at the picture.

"And this one?" asked Quinn, pushing another photo across the table. This one was taken from the other side of the square, footage from the secret camera in Will's apartment. Fernsby was right outside Poppy's door and was looking over his shoulder furtively – straight into the camera.

Fernsby went a little pale, and even more so when DCI pointed to the date and time stamp on the photo, 15 05 15:05.

"Nice, neat date and time that, don't you think?" said Quinn conversationally, making sure that Fernsby was in no doubt that the time was different to the time he'd said.

"For the tape" she said, "the pictures both show Mr Fernsby arriving at Ms Gilbert's apartment at 15:05 on 15th May. Would you care to comment on the time discrepancy Mr Fernsby?

"I was mistaken," Fernsby said nonchalantly.

Quinn raised her eyebrows and waited, but he said nothing further, Julian Fernsby also being familiar with using silence as a negotiating tool.

"And would you care to tell me how you filled the afternoon?" asked Quinn.

"I think you already know," snapped Fernsby, well aware that his DNA sample would match the semen sample and cursing himself for being so sentimental and stupid.

"You had sex with Ms Gilbert?"

Fernsby nodded, looking down at his hands.

"For the tape, Mr Fernsby just nodded," said Quinn. "So, not just a business relationship then Mr Fernsby. Was Ms Gilbert a friend?"

Fernsby's head snapped up. "No. Absolutely not."

"But friendly enough to have sex with her though," commented Quinn, pleased she had riled him. "Or was sex part of the 'service' that Dinner+ provided – perhaps the 'plus' part of the name?

"DCI Quinn, I don't like this line of questioning," interrupted the solicitor.

"Well, it might just be an accounting issue," said Quinn sweetly. "I'm just trying to work out what was so special about Ms Gilbert's cooking."

"Poppy was a Michelin starred cordon bleu chef, I understand," said the solicitor, "so she was understandably more expensive than a less qualified chef."

Quinn raised an eyebrow, interested that the solicitor called Gilbert by her first name: perhaps he had been a 'client' of hers too.

"Really? Pie, chips and peas hardly sounds like the work of a Michelin starred chef, but then, what would I know – I certainly couldn't afford to pay £1,000 for a meal," she said.

The solicitor was just taking a sip of water, and nearly choked.

"£1,000! You must be mistaken!" he exclaimed.

"Well, not according to Mr Fernsby's bank account," replied Quinn, passing an itemised bank statement across the table. "It's especially interesting that this is Mr Fernsby's personal, not business, account."

"I need to consult with my client," demanded the solicitor, standing up to indicate that the interview was at an end.

"Certainly. It will give me a chance to speak to Mr Smythe," replied Quinn.

"Smythe! You have Smythe here too?" exclaimed Fernsby.

Quinn nodded, very interested in his discomfort.

"Oh, just one thing before we finish, if I may? Can you tell me what is in your carrier bag, please, Mr Fernsby? You can see it clearly in the photo I just gave you."

"No comment," said the solicitor, almost pulling Julian to his feet.

Chapter Fifty-Two

Quinn took a break before interviewing Smythe and reviewed the case so far with her colleagues, so it was early afternoon before a very cross Smythe was brought into the interview room.

"How dare you keep me here and make me wait. Don't you know who I am?" Smythe exploded as soon as Quinn entered the room.

"An ex-convict you mean?" asked Quinn innocently.

"No! That was all a mistake – I was framed and will clear my name one day. My good name as a former Lord Mayor!" shouted Smythe, his face turning beetroot red.

"Perhaps you would like to clear your name now, at least in regard to the matter in hand," said Quinn.

"No comment," replied Smythe, folding his arms.

"What, you don't want to clear your name?" asked Quinn, innocently.

Smythe just looked down his long nose disdainfully at her.

Quinn passed a photo of Smythe arriving at Poppy's across the desk.

"Is this you, Mr Smythe?"

"No comment," said Smythe.

"Well, it certainly looks like you, Mr Smythe, but we can run it through face recognition software, if you want, just to be sure," said Quinn sweetly.

Smythe just glared at her.

"I'll just draw your attention to the date and time stamp on the picture, Mr Smythe - 15 05 19:35. Did you go to dinner at Ms Gilbert's apartment on that date?" asked Quinn.

"No comment," replied Smythe.

"Well, your presence there was confirmed at the inquest into Ms Gilbert death, so I think we can take that as read, can't we?" said Quinn.

"That inquest ruled that Gilbert's death was accidental," interjected the solicitor. "So, unless you have any evidence that my client was involved in a crime, you need to release him."

Quinn pushed a copy of Smythe's bank account across the desk, an account that was seriously overdrawn.

"Can you tell me what you were paying Ms Gilbert £1000 a week for, Mr Smythe? With due respect, money you could ill afford," said Quinn.

"No comment," said Smythe, glaring at her.

"You're not being very helpful are you, Mr Smythe? Mr Fernsby was a lot more forthcoming. Pity, as with your record, you could get a full life sentence for Ms Gilbert's murder. At your age, that's probably the rest of your life," said Quinn, conversationally.

Smythe spluttered but said nothing, but his pale face told DCI Quinn that she had hit home.

"I need to consult with my client," said the solicitor.

"Certainly, said Quinn. "That will give me time to interview Mr Blakemore."

Mr Smythe's face went even paler, and Quinn had a job to keep a smile from her own face until after they had been taken out of the interview room.

Chapter Fifty-Three

Nigel Blakemore waived his right to a solicitor and followed DCI Quinn into the interview room. He had come clean to his wife about his obsession with Poppy and they were now reconciled, but on the condition that there were no more lies.

Nigel told Quinn about how a business acquaintance of his, Julian Fernsby, had invited him to a dinner at Ms Gilbert's apartment in the spring. He knew that Fernsby wanted him to commission him to build a holiday complex, an idea he'd been toying with to extend his holiday lets portfolio, but he wasn't confident that Fernsby's was the right company to do it. Knowing that Fernsby could be very persuasive, he was careful not to drink too much, but there must have been something in the food as he found himself losing his inhibitions.

Next thing he knew, he was in bed with Gilbert, and she was very much in charge. This was something he hadn't experienced before, and it thrilled him.

"I became obsessed with her – all I could think about was the enormous release of someone else being in control," Nigel confessed shamefaced. "Running a business, being the 'big boss' and constantly having to make decisions is exhausting, so when I was subservient to Poppy, I could finally relax and release all that tension. She got me my own gate key so I could come and go discreetly, and I thought no one would know. Then I got a blackmail email with bits of graphic video attached - pay up or my wife would be told."

"So, what did you do?" asked DCI Quinn.

"I paid. I've a successful business, but it was an eye watering amount to pay - I was going to struggle to make ends meet," replied Nigel.

"£1,000 a week?" said Quinn, passing him a bank statement.

"Yes," replied Nigel quietly, not needing to read it to know what it showed.

"But still you kept seeing her?" asked Quinn.

"Yes," replied Nigel almost in a whisper.

"Then what happened?" asked Quinn

"My wife found out and challenged me. It was perhaps Poppy's cloying perfume that I couldn't seem to shower off, or my late-night unexplained disappearance or the economies I had to introduce to the household – or possibly just a wife's instinct. I tried to deny it, but she could see from my face it was true."

Nigel paused to wipe his eyes and DCI Quinn waited quietly for him to carry on.

"She left me, and I missed her so much – I'd been taking her for granted and never realised how much she made a house a home. Those brief periods of excitement with Poppy were not worth the loneliness without my wife. Noah missed her even more and started to have behavioural issues at school, and I could see the damage my stupid behaviour had caused."

"So, what did you do?" asked Quinn.

"Poppy was hosting a dinner and I decided that I would go to it in order to finish things with her once and for all. I thought it would be easier with Fernsby and Smythe there – I was a bit scared of Poppy to be honest – it was possibly just her dominatrix persona, but she seemed to really enjoy hurting people."

"How did she react?" asked Quinn.

"Well, I don't know if she was drunk or high, but she barely made a comment. I knew by then that she regularly put magic mushrooms into her pies, so I'd pushed mine around the plate and hardly touched it, but Smythe and Fernsby ate theirs and were very giggly. Poppy was fairly well out of it and just laughed when I told her, but I made sure she was clear that I wouldn't be seeing her again. And then I left," replied Nigel.

"If you look at the bank statements I've just given you, Mr Blakemore, the payments from your account continued after her death: why did you keep paying?"

"I didn't know she was dead until it was in the paper three or four weeks later. Not long after I left on the night of the dinner, I got a text telling me that even though I wasn't going to see her again, if I didn't want all my customers and friends to know what we'd been up to, I had to keep paying, otherwise she's send the video to them all," replied Nigel.

"This text?" asked Quinn, pushing another piece of paper across the desk.

"Yes," replied Nigel.

"I note that this text gives a different sort code and account to pay into," said Quinn.

"Yes, I had to set it up again – I don't know why," he replied.

"Did you happen to notice that the text had come from a different number than previously?" asked Quinn.

"No," said Nigel, "I didn't! I was so shaken up with everything I never even noticed that!"

"What happened when you found out that Ms Gilbert was dead?" asked Quinn before Nigel could ask her whose number the text had come from.

"I cancelled the payments. It's a terrible thing to say but Poppy's death was such a relief - emotionally as well as financially. It gave me the chance to start again, to come clean to my wife and try and patch things up," Nigel replied.

"But?" asked DCI Quinn sensing an unspoken 'but'.

"I was poisoned. I don't know if they were trying to scare me into continuing to pay, or they wanted me dead in case I came to you about what had been going on. Whatever their intention, without Jack Brown's miraculous help, I think I would have died, and poor Noah would have been left all alone," said Nigel, tears filling his eyes again.

"They?" asked Quinn.

"I can only think it was Smythe and Fernsby, as they knew about the affair - I have a horrible feeling that very first night with Poppy when I was well out of it, that they were watching: an absolutely mortifying thought."

"So, you went into hiding?" Quinn asked.

"Yes, I went to France, and I persuaded my wife to join us. We talked for a long time and now that Noah is in school full time, she is going to join me in the business - share the burden. We returned to the UK just a few days ago and I was going to come to you to explain everything today - one of the conditions of my wife returning with me. It was so strange when I got the call to come in - almost like you knew!" said Nigel.

"Coincidence," said Quinn with a grin. "But I'm not a believer in coincidences, generally, and you may have just helped me unravel another unlikely coincidence. I'm going to leave you with my sergeant to make a detailed statement, especially about the poisoning, and then you are free to go. Thank you for your time."

Quinn stood up and shook Nigel's hand. He was a foolish, weak man who didn't deserve the love of a good woman, but he wasn't a criminal.

Chapter Fifty-Four

Smythe's solicitor informed DCI Quinn that he was ready to cooperate, if his assistance would be taken into consideration should any charges be made. Quinn agreed and the interview resumed in the same room as previously.

"It was Julian's idea," said Smythe as soon as DCI Quinn had set the recording going.

"What was?" asked Quinn, keeping her voice neutral.

"Poisoning Poppy. I had nothing to do with it."

"Why would he want to poison Ms Gilbert?" asked Quinn, trying to keep the excitement out of her voice and avoiding asking the more obvious question of whether they had planned it together.

"She was blackmailing us," Smythe spat out. "After everything I'd done for her, that filthy whore was blackmailing me. I'm trying to get myself back onto the council, boast my pathetic pension, run for mayor again – she knew all this but still threatened to send a video of us having sex to everyone at the council."

DCI Quinn knew that Smythe hadn't a hope in hell of getting his old job back, but said nothing, instead just turned her laptop toward him.

"This video, Mr Smythe?" she asked.

The short clip that the police had previously recovered from Poppy's laptop showed Smythe naked apart from his black socks, his wrists and ankles tied to the bed frame with red silk scarves, his pale, skinny body almost glowing in the dim light.

Ms Gilbert had her back to the camera, her fat thighs overspilling her thigh-length spike-heeled boots, her flabby bottom ballooning out from under a black leather basque. She was careful that her face was never in the shot, but the long leather wipe she was flicking at Smythe's limp penis was very much in evidence.

"Turn it off!" shouted Smythe, his face red with rage, and Quinn was happy to oblige, not wanting to see the video ever again.

"You said 'us', Mr Smythe - who else was she blackmailing?"

"Fernsby and Blakemore. All of us were paying her £1,000 a week - they could afford it, but she knew that I couldn't," Smythe said angrily.

"You think she should have offered you a discount, 'mates rates', for old times' sake?" asked Quinn pleasantly, deliberately trying to rile him.

"I shouldn't have been paying anything! It's that cow's fault I went to prison before, well, hers and that do-gooder Jack Brown. I brought Julian to her parties, and he brought Blakemore - she was making enough from those two without putting the screws on me too - it wasn't fair!"

"So you killed her?" asked Quinn.

"What! No - I didn't kill her. Julian killed her!" exclaimed Smythe.

Quinn's pulse quickened but she kept her face neutral.

"How did Julian kill her?" she asked calmly.

"He made sure that the mushrooms in her pie were poisonous," Smythe replied.

"How did he do that – weren't you concerned that some might accidentally get into your food?"

"He said he'd be very careful," said Smythe, looking petulant.

"I need a word with my client - now," said the solicitor, glaring at Quinn.

Despite her frustration at the interruption just when she was getting somewhere, she allowed the solicitor five minutes with his client before she recommenced the interview.

"My client wishes to withdraw his last statement," said the solicitor immediately.

"The one where he admitted he knew of the attempt to poison Ms Gilbert?" asked Quinn.

"No. I never said that!" exploded Smythe.

"You had no knowledge of Fernsby's plan to kill Ms Gilbert?" asked Quinn, attempting to look him in the eye.

"No," replied Smythe, avoiding her gaze.

"So, you didn't know she died that night?"

"Of course I didn't - how would I, if I knew nothing about the plan?" said Smythe defiantly.

Quinn noted with interest that Smythe said 'the plan', not Julian's plan. The solicitor noticed the same and glared at Smythe.

"I called on her a few times over the next three weeks but got no reply, so I assumed she had gone away," Smythe improvised badly, his cheeks flushing a little at the lie.

"I'm sure we can confirm that with CCTV," said Quinn smoothly, knowing full well that the CCTV only showed Jack, the police, someone from social services and the post lady ringing her doorbell during the period between the party and Jack discovering her body.

"So, for clarification, please confirm that you had no knowledge that Ms Gilbert was deceased until her body was discovered nearly three weeks later," requested Quinn.

Speaking slowly, as if to a child, Smythe confirmed that to be the case. Quinn looked at him steadily for a moment and then represented the bank statement she had shown him earlier.

"Mr Smythe, can I ask you why, if you didn't know she was dead, that on the very same night as her death, you cancelled your standing order to pay the blackmail money into her account?" she asked equally slowly.

"No comment," interjected the solicitor. "My client has nothing to say on this point."

"Does your client also have no comment on the fact that he texted Mr Blakemore, once again the very same night, and instructed him to change the account he was paying his blackmail money into?" Quinn asked, her voice hard. She pointed to several entries on Smythe's bank account, weekly payments into his account of £1,000 commencing immediately after the weekly payments of £1,000 out of his account ceased.

"No comment," said Smythe.

"Mr Smythe," said DCI Quinn, "I believe we have enough evidence to charge you in connection with the murder of Ms Pauline Gilbert. I am referring your case to the Crown

Prosecution Service. In the meantime, you will be returned to your cell."

As Quinn left the room, she could hear Smythe protesting loudly to the sergeant who was handcuffing him that he didn't kill Poppy. Quinn was fairly certain that actually was the case, but that didn't mean he wasn't guilty of joint enterprise murder, and she smiled as she walked away, hoping that she could be instrumental in putting that nasty, arrogant excuse for a man in prison.

Chapter Fifty-Five

Mindful that she had only 24 hours to either charge her prisoners or apply for an extension, after a quick cup of tea and a short discussion with her superiors, DCI Quinn had Julian Fernsby brought back to the interview room.

"I have a statement to read out on behalf of my client," stated Fernsby's solicitor before Quinn had a chance to speak.

"Mr Fernsby is greatly saddened by the death of Ms Gilbert and deeply regrets that he was unaware of her condition on the evening of 15th May, and so unable to intervene and get her the medical assistance she needed. As witnessed by Mr Appleby at the coroner's inquest, Ms Gilbert had foraged for ingredients for her pies on the morning of her death. It appears that she mistakenly picked Ivory Funnel mushrooms, not the 'magic' mushrooms she sought. Mr Fernsby cannot throw any light on why Ms Gilbert only put the freshly picked mushrooms in her own, separate, pie."

The solicitor paused for breath and then continued.

"In relation to sums of money paid to Ms Gilbert by my client, Mr Fernsby has confirmed that he paid Ms Gilbert a retainer to entertain clients he wished to pursue for business reasons. Part of the amount paid covered 'personal services' my client received from Ms Gilbert, hence the higher-than-normal fee involved. In light of what I have just explained, I demand that you release my client immediately."

The solicitor looked at Quinn expectantly, but she ignored him, and pushed a new bank statement across the desk to Fernsby.

"Mr Fernsby, this is a bank statement from earlier in the year. Please look at the entry for £24.99 that I have underlined. Can you tell me what that payment was for?"

"Of course I can't – you can't expect me to remember every piddling amount that leaves my account!" Fernsby snapped.

"Well, let me enlighten you then," said Quinn. "This was a payment to the Walled Garden shop for a book. A book on the local flora and fauna. I wouldn't have pegged you as a gardener, Mr Fernsby – can you tell me why you bought this book?"

"A present, Quinn. The book was a present for, er, my mother!" Fernsby replied, stammering a bit.

"Your mother Mr Fernsby? I happen to know your mother passed away several years ago - left you the company I understand – amazing what you can find out online. Do you want another guess?" Quinn asked pleasantly.

"My aunt, I meant to say," said Fernsby, flustered.

"Well, I can soon check if your second guess is correct Mr Fernsby, but I put it to you that you bought this book for your own use."

Whilst Fernsby spluttered out a denial, Quinn extracted another piece of paper from her file and passed it across the desk.

It was an enlargement of a text with a photo attachment, a text sent by Fernsby and recovered from Poppy's phone. The photo was a close up of Ivory Funnel mushrooms, and the accompanying words explained that these magic mushrooms could be found in Kirkby woods. Fernsby's face went white, and paler still, if that were possible, when DCI Quinn took a copy of the book Fernsby had purchased from her briefcase. She opened it at a book-marked page.

"You can see here, Mr Fernsby, that the image sent from your phone to Ms Gilbert's on the morning of 15th May, was a photograph of this page in the book you purchased. The photographer was very careful to frame the picture so that it omitted the text under the photo which clearly says these are Ivory Funnel, not Psilocybin mushrooms, and that they are highly toxic."

"If Ms Gilbert picked the mushrooms herself and put them into a pie that she knew only she would eat, whatever you are trying to pin on me, Quinn, won't stick," said Fernsby, more panic than conviction in his voice.

Quinn smiled and extracted another piece of paper from her file.

"This, Mr Fernsby, is Ms Gilbert's reply to your text: shall I read it to you?" asked Quinn pleasantly. Fernsby looked wildly at his solicitor, but neither said anything.

"Piss off Julian – you trying to kill us all?" read DCI Quinn. "Them's not magic mushrooms – they R not around until autumn!"

Quinn paused to let the words sink in, which gave the solicitor the chance to leapt in.

"Whether my client texted that picture or not makes no difference: Ms Gilbert didn't pick any of the mushrooms pictured, so my client's error is not responsible for her somehow obtaining some and putting them into her own meal. Accidental death, just as the coroner ruled."

"Ah, but here is where it gets interesting," said Quinn, really starting to enjoy herself. "Mr Fernsby was at his office in Leeds at the time he sent that text and had meetings scheduled all afternoon. Immediately after he got Ms Gilbert's reply, those meetings were cancelled and he left the office, to quote your secretary, Mr Fernsby, 'in a tearing hurry'. Speed cameras then recorded him doing 95mph on the A1 heading north, for which he later received six points and a large fine - I'm surprised you weren't disqualified actually."

"So, I was in a hurry?" said Fernsby with a shrug. "I was looking forward to a bit of rumpy-pumpy with Poppy before the others arrived.

"But you still found time to stop and shop along the way?" asked Quinn.

She extracted another photo, this one taken from the CCTV footage, showing Fernsby outside Poppy's door with a carrier bag.

"I was bringing a bottle, as is polite," said Fernsby arrogantly.

"I don't think so," replied Quinn, passing him yet another photo, this time a close up showing a logo on the bag. "We carefully analysed the video footage and from the way the bag hangs and moves as you walk, it's obvious that the contents are extremely light – mushroom perhaps?"

"You can't prove that," growled Fernsby.

"Oh, but we can. I have the transcript from the coroner's inquest that records that traces of Psilocybin mushrooms were found in a bag in the bin, along with traces of soil that matched the local woodland's soil. The pathologist who undertook that analysis photographed the bag before commencing his investigations, and the logo we can see in the photograph I've just given you matches the logo on the bag in his photograph. The logo is of a small independent shop, local to you Mr Fernsby, a shop that sells high end toiletries, not fruit and veg."

Quinn paused, and then held up her hand as Fernsby started to speak.

"This morning I obtained a warrant to search your house. We found a Ziplock bag in your freezer containing Ivory Funnel mushrooms. I'm confident that the lab will match traces of soil on those mushrooms to the soil in Kirkby woods."

"You can't prove I picked them," spat Fernsby.

"Oh, but I think I can," said Quinn, really enjoying herself now. "I can certainly prove you were in the woods before you went to Ms Gilbert's. A discreet appeal on the local Facebook brought forward an eyewitness who saw you in the woods that day. She remembers you clearly, Fernsby, because you kicked her dog when he came up to say hello to you whilst you were picking mushrooms. She took the dog to the vet as it was limping afterwards - just bruising you'll be pleased to know - and the vet has a record of the date of that appointment - 15th May."

The solicitor (who was a dog lover) gave Fernsby a filthy look but neither said anything, unable to come up with any further excuses. DCI Quinn knew that she still couldn't prove that Fernsby had actually put the mushrooms into Poppy's pie, but she hoped she had enough to charge him with murder on the evidence she did have.

Quinn decided to change tack whilst Fernsby was unnerved.

"I understand that you're a bit of a baker, Mr Fernsby. A fan of 'Bake-off' are you?" she asked conversationally.

"What?" replied Fernsby, confused.

"Baking. You know, cakes, buns, or in your case, muffins. Muffins baked to your own recipe. Muffins you sent to Nigel Blakemore."

"I don't know what you are talking about," said Fernsby in a voice lacking conviction.

"Why did you try to poison Nigel Blakemore?" Quinn asked.

"What!" exclaimed the solicitor. "If you are considering bringing additional allegations, I will need to speak to my client."

"Certainly, however, just to let you know that we have evidence from the courier concerned that the poisoned muffins were collected from Mr Fernsby's residence. We already have the 'extra ingredient' from Mr Fernsby's freezer, as you know, and the team who are currently searching his house have specific instructions to bag up and take away for forensic analysis any food mixer, mixing bowl or muffin tins. It's pretty nailed on that your client was responsible for the attempted murder of Mr Blakemore – I just wondered why?" replied Quinn.

Fernsby said nothing, just slumped further down in his chair. Quinn imagined he was pondering why he'd been so stupid, leaving a trail that came straight back to him. Quinn sighed, suddenly feeling very weary.

"Mr Fernsby, I am referring your case to the Crown Prosecution Service as I believe we have enough evidence to charge you with the murder of Ms Pauline Gilbert. I will also ask them to consider an additional charge of the attempted murder of Mr Nigel Blakemore."

Quinn looked hard at Fernsby hoping to see a small flicker of something - fear, guilt, regret - but there was nothing. She sighed again.

"Sergeant – please take Mr Fernsby away."

Chapter Fifty-Six

DCI Quinn rang Jack to apologise for not taking his concerns seriously initially, and to let him know that the CPS had given permission to charge both men with Poppy's murder. Smythe was also being charged with blackmail and Fernsby was being charged with the attempted murder of Nigel Blakemore. Traces of the contaminated muffin mix had been found on the blades of a food mixture in his house, as well as some Ivory Funnel mushrooms in his freezer and a copy of the book on local flora and fauna in his office, so that charge was pretty nailed on.

Both men had appeared in the Magistrates Court where they had pleaded 'not guilty' to all charges: they had been indicted to the Crown Court for the trial before being released on a substantial bail. Quinn explained that they had been required to surrender their passports and must report to their local police station every week until the trial took place.

"It's likely to be late spring next year before it comes to court," said Quinn. "I'm pretty sure we will get convictions on all counts; however, Fernsby's murder charge would be much more straight forward if we just had the proof that Fernsby actually put the mushrooms in Gilbert's pie."

Jack agreed but couldn't think of any way that could be proved. It was strange that although Poppy Gilbert had blighted all their lives, he still wanted justice for her. He and his great grandma had worked so hard to create The Square, a community where everyone was safe and happy, and he found it deeply upsetting to have that dream blighted by the murder. Getting some justice for the victim might help him come to terms with it.

"Please pass on my thanks to your team, Jack, especially Zoe who cracked the phone code and recovered the deleted files – if she ever wants a job, let me know!" said DCI Quinn as she said goodbye.

Jack updated his friends on what Quinn had told him. Zoe was on a bit of a high that she and Ben had helped prove the case and was chuffed at Quinn's comments, but Ben was uncharacteristically quiet, not teasing her about the 'job offer' as she would have expected. They would both be called to give evidence in court as 'electronic communications experts', and Zoe wondered if Ben was worried about that, although it would be out of character if he was, as very little in life worried him.

With the trial being several months away, life returned to normal, and the 'Case of the Poisoned Pie and Muffins' began to feel like a dream, or rather a nightmare that was fading with the daylight. Mr Blakemore sent Jack a case of champagne as a thank you for saving his life, and over the next few months he and his wife often invited Dottie on a play date with Noah as the two children had become firm friends.

Zoe, as the Chair of the Allotment Association, was busy organising the annual produce show. Josie and Kara, as old hands, helped her as much as possible and the event went smoothly, despite the usual fierce rivalry.

John lost out on the 'biggest marrow' trophy, Bert beating him by one measly centimetre. In previous years John would have been very disappointed, but he clapped Bert on the back and handed over 'his' trophy cheerfully, teasing Bert that it was 'beginner's luck'. John applauded loudly when Sarah got a first prize for her dahlias, her success more than making up for him being pipped at the post.

Nadia was absolutely delighted to come second in the flower arranging class, even though her bump had been getting seriously in the way and her arrangement wasn't as perfect as she would have liked. Jack, as a professional gardener now, didn't enter anything, but Kara won a highly commended for her courgettes and got a first in the cake baking category.

John had entered a jar of pear chutney made by Josie without her knowing and was delighted when it came second in the preserves category. Josie made jars of it for him every year using his late wife's recipe, so this was his way of saying thank you to her. Josie also got third place for her carrots, much to her surprise as they weren't particularly large, but for once she'd managed to avoid the dreaded carrot fly when many others hadn't been so lucky.

Hugo did well with his green beans and his strawberries came second. Bert would have liked to have entered some strawberries, but they'd all been eaten as soon as they'd ripened.

In the children's categories, Mia, coached by Will, got a first-place rosette for a painting she had done of the vibrant flower garden at the square, and Lily got a highly commended for a photograph of the sunrise over Kirkby, taken from her bedroom window in the manor.

Jack's school class won a rosette for their broad beans and were placed second in the handicraft section for their bird boxes, which they had been making and selling all year to raise funds towards next year's school trip to Disneyland Paris.

Elsie had been invited to present the awards, an honour that used to be Lady Dorothy's, and after her the Lord Mayor's, but with so little joy in her life until recently, Zoe wanted Elsie to have the privilege. She proved a very popular choice, resplendent in a new hat that Lady Dorothy would have been proud of, and with a kind and knowledgeable word for each of the prize winners. Bert was at her side wearing his best suit for the occasion and helped her by passing her the right trophy, certificate or money envelope for the right winner at the right time and regularly fetching her tea and cake.

It was a happy occasion, one where all of Kirkby came together, a chance to celebrate the joy of growing and of being creative, a chance to celebrate being a close community. The annual show over, and with Halloween and then Bonfire Night on their way, the year continued its well-worn path and the stress of the events earlier in the year began to fade.

Chapter Fifty-Seven

The annual bonfire was held on a field just outside the town, and for weeks Jack's gardening team had been piling up tree and hedge branches as they cut them down in the course of their work. Residents had added to this pile over the last week or so with redundant furniture and anything else that would burn.

The highlight of the evening was to be a short fireworks display, paid for by a local landowner. The Scout Master was in charge of the firework display, and he and the scouts had been busy all day setting it up. True to the scout's 'be prepared' motto, he had a first aid bag, a bucket of water and a fire extinguisher positioned close by, just in case.

The farmer who owned the bonfire field had donated a crate of potatoes for baking, and a smaller bonfire had been lit earlier in preparation for the potatoes which had been wrapped in foil and placed in the glowing embers. Jack was responsible for raking them out safely, and a table with slabs of butter and piles of grated cheese were ready nearby. There was also soft, spicy parkin baked by Kara, and the pub had donated a barrel of locally brewed beer. Soft drinks had been provided by the Co-op, and they had also donated paper napkins, plates and cups and wooden forks, all of which could be burnt on the bonfire afterwards.

Everyone from the square was there apart from Elsie and Nadia. Elsie had stayed at home with Blue who hated the bangs of fireworks, and Nadia, with only a week until the birth of her twins by planned caesarean section, was resting with her feet up on the settee. Amir was on a late shift so she was alone, but unconcerned as she knew she could just ring her parents if she needed anything. However, unaware that

Amir was working, Nadia's parents had gone to the bonfire, taking a big pot of curry as a thank you to the community who had made them feel so welcome.

At first Nadia dismissed the pains as Braxton Hicks, something she had been suffering from on and off for days. She must have dozed off, but a much sharper pain woke her with a start; when another one soon followed, and then another, she realised she was in labour. Reaching for her mobile she found it was dead - she thought she had plugged it in to charge but must have forgotten or not plugged it in properly, as the cable was just dangling. Without Amir to pull her up, getting off the low settee was the first hurdle. As she hefted herself upright, she felt warm liquid run down her legs - her waters had broken, and she knew she needed to get help fast.

Getting to the front door felt like a marathon, each contraction more painful than the last. Nadia looked across the square towards her parent's upstairs apartment and her heart sank when she saw that there were no lights on. There were lights in Elsie's apartment below theirs and knowing that Elsie was on an emergency call system, Nadia slowly, painfully, made her way there, stopping and leaning against the house walls as each contraction ripped through her.

Elsie had been watching the fireworks light up the sky when she saw a strange, rounded figure creeping around the walls towards her. For a moment she was terrified, imagining it was a boggart, an evil hobgoblin of Yorkshire folklore that she had been terrified off as a child after her dad had told her it would take her away if she wasn't good. In the pitch-black nights of the moorland farm her imagination had run wild, but here in the softly lit square with colourful fireworks overhead, she knew that it couldn't be. Someone needed help, so leaning on her rollator, unafraid, she made her way to open her door.

Nadia almost fell inside as the door opened and she grabbed the other side of the rollator to steady herself. She hung on as another contraction left her helpless. Elsie, unable to move whilst they both held onto the mobility device, calmly pressed the emergency button on the pendant around her neck. A disembodied voice asked her what the emergency was and there was a stunned silence when she told them that twins were about to be born; with an elderly lady registered to the service they expected a fall or a stroke, not childbirth.

Nadia had now sunk to her knees in the hallway and was breathing fast.

"I need to push!" she screamed in a panic.

Reassuring the girl as much as she could, Elsie pulled a throw off the settee and dropped it onto the floor in front of Nadia. With great difficulty, Elsie slowly lowered herself to the floor, not sure how she would ever get up again. The responder on the emergency line could be heard alternately asking for updates and reassuring them that the ambulance was on its way. If Elsie replied, it was probably drowned out by Nadia's screams, as nature inexorably took its course, and the first baby continued its unstoppable journey into the world.

Blue lights flashing, the ambulance pulled up at the gate to the square and found it locked. In issuing keys after Dottie's abduction, Jack hadn't given any thought to emergency access and that oversight could now prove to be disastrous. The ambulance crew phoned the police and the police phoned Jack, but above the noise of the fireworks he didn't hear his phone. Thankfully, not long afterwards Will and Joy returned home, Mia having been frightened by the loud bangs of the fireworks. Will opened the gate and ran across the square to Elsie's, the ambulance crew at his heels.

They found Elsie and Nadia on the floor of the hallway, blood pooled on a blue throw on the floor and two beautiful wide-eyed babies, one in Nadia's arms and one in Elsie's. One was wrapped in Elsie's cardigan and the other in Nadia's hijab and seeing Nadia's long hair uncovered added to the surreal quality of the scene.

"The afterbirth is yet to be delivered," said Elsie calmly.

Before long mother and babies were on the way to hospital and Will lifted Elsie to her feet and helped her to a chair as she had completely seized up. Whilst Joy made Elsie tea with a drop of whisky in it (at Elsie's request), Will started to clear up the mess in the hall. A few minutes later, Jack, having eventually picked up the messages on his phone, raced in, followed closely behind by an out of breath Bert who had seen the ambulance pulling away.

Bert saw the blood on the hall floor and went pale.

"Elsie - is she alright? Did she have a fall?" he cried.

"She's fine Bert. More than fine - she just delivered twins," Will replied with a laugh.

Jack and Bert gawked at Will in disbelief and then opened the door to the lounge and stared at Elsie.

"How did you know what to do Elsie," asked Bert, taking her hand.

"I've helped deliver lambs for over seventy years, Bert," replied Elsie calmly. "I reckoned it wouldn't be much different."

"You never cease to amaze me Elsie," said Bert, giving her a kiss on the cheek.

Chapter Fifty-Eight

Throughout November, Bert and his band of helpers planted hundreds of tulips and daffodil bulbs in the square's gardens to give them all something to look forward to through the dark, cold winter months. Throughout the allotments, gardeners tidied up their plots, compost heaps piled-up with raked-up leaves and discarded vegetation. Parsnips, red cabbage and knobbly stalks of Brussel sprouts were left in the ground for Christmas dinners, but otherwise most plots were cleared, dug over and left ready for spring planting.

Early snow towards the end of November put an end to gardening and although it didn't last, near freezing temperatures and high winds continued for a couple of weeks, keeping most people indoors. Then Christmas lights began to appear everywhere, cheering up the gloom. They started with a few in shop windows and houses and then the owner of a local stately home gifted thousands of pounds worth of stunning decorations to the town, his team of gardeners installing them through the town centre so that Kirkby became the best dressed town in the area.

Little Christmas trees adorned with multi-coloured fairy lights were fitted into special brackets on the walls of houses forming a necklace of lights through the town that continued up the hill towards the allotments. Jack, Ben and Will manoeuvred a giant Christmas tree into the centre of the square, covered it in white lights and then slung ropes of coloured lights across the front of all the houses. The residents of the square came together to decorate the tree, the children hanging home-made decorations on the lower branches, the adults standing on step ladders to decorate the higher branches. Glasses of hot fruit punch and mulled wine were handed around and the Christmassy feel was almost palpable.

Nadia and Amir sat on Lady Dorothy's bench each holding a well wrapped-up baby in their arms. Their little boy they had named Mikail and their little girl, Alayna, and everyone adored the smiley babies and thought of them as part of their own family. Both babies looked extra cute in miniature Santa's hats, their heads having been shaved at a week old as per Muslim tradition to keep Nadia's family happy. After handing Alayna to Elsie who had joined them on the bench, Nadia hung two large filigree gold stars on the tree, one for each of the babies.

As Christmas approached Jack and Kara were delighted when Will came to see them and asked if they would be witnesses to their wedding on Christmas Eve. Jack and Kara looked at each other and smiled - Christmas Eve would be their 5th Wedding Anniversary and attending a wedding would be a lovely way to celebrate. It was to be a quiet wedding at York Registry Office with just Jack and Kara and the children as guests, Mia and Dottie being bridesmaids.

On the wedding day Jack borrowed the school's minibus and parked it in a car park near the River Ouse which sparkled with the reflection of the hundreds of Christmas lights throughout the city. Christmas songs could be heard from the many buskers and the smell of chestnuts, sausages and mulled wine reached them from the St Nicholas street fair. Jack's family, Mia and Will walked to the registry office, skirting the ancient city wall and Bootham Bar splendid in a net of white fairy lights.

The registry office was looking festive with a beautifully decorated Christmas tree and strings of white fairy lights. They took of their coats, and Kara's eyes filled with tears when she turned and saw her little girl holding tight to Mia's hand, both of them in sparkly white dresses with fairy wings and tinsel headbands, like twin angels.

After giving Dottie and Mia strict instructions on their duties, Will, Jack, Kara, Lily and Ronan took their places in the lovely Georgian ceremony room to await the bride who was arriving by chauffeur driven car. Kara held Jack's hand and her other hand caressed a lovely carved wooden heart in her pocket that Jack had made her to commemorate their fifth or 'wood' anniversary. He had carved on it the words that were on the inside of Lady Dorothy's engagement ring, 'My one and only love', and Kara felt her eyes tear up again just thinking about it.

The registrar asked them to stand, and then Tom Odell's gentle rendition of The Beatles 'Real Love' started as the doors opened and Joy entered on the arm of Will's mother. Joy looked radiant in a simple long white velvet dress, its neck and hem trimmed with soft white fur. Will's mother was wearing a smart dress with a jacket in the same dark green tartan as the groom's kilt, and she had a smile as bright as the bride's.

Behind them the two little bridesmaids walked beautifully, their faces serious as they concentrated on not stepping on the small train of Joy's dress. Kara's tears now fell in earnest, and Jack passed her a clean white linen handkerchief and smiled at her, his own eyes full of tears too as he remembered their own wedding day.

The bridal couple travelled back in the wedding car, giving them some time alone before joining their friends and neighbours at Kirkby Manor, where Jack and Kara were holding a Christmas party which would double as their wedding reception. Josie had borrowed trestle tables from the town hall, and these were covered in white tablecloths and swags of greenery and were laden with food and drink. The tables were arranged around the walls of the large entrance hall and Jack smiled to see them, remembering a similar arrangement for his great-grandmother's hundredth birthday party.

The doors into Lady Dorothy's former apartment had been flung open and guests wandered back and forth with champagne flutes, helping themselves to food, chatting and laughing. Children and dogs ran around between people and through legs and it was a good job that Jack had invited all the residents of the manor (as well as all those of the square) so that they wouldn't complain about the chaos.

No one had been told about the wedding, but when Will and Joy arrived, flushed and happy and resplendent in their wedding clothes a ripple of applause started and spread quickly throughout the apartment. The penny dropped for anyone who hadn't worked it out when Kara brought out a magnificent wedding cake that she had made, and Jack proposed a toast to the happy couple.

Much, much later when everyone had gone home, carrots were put out for Rudolf, a mince pie and glass of sherry for Santa and the excited children put to bed. Jack stood at the window cradling a drink, looking down over the dark allotments to the square below lit up with Christmas lights. As he waited for the children to be fast asleep so that Santa could tiptoe in and fill their stockings, he thought about the people who lived in the square who would soon be waking up on Christmas morning safe and happy in the homes he had made for them.

He thought about Will and Joy sharing their first Christmas as an official family and about little Mikail and Alayna who had brought everyone so much joy. He thought about Poppy who'd been a cuckoo in the nest and hoped she was at peace and would soon have justice, and lastly, he thought about Lady Dorothy who had changed his life. "Happy Christmas, great-grandma," he whispered before finishing his drink and turning out the lights.

Chapter Fifty-Nine

January and February brought snow and ice, cold dark days when everyone just felt like hibernating. Then ice turned to constant rain with flooding in many low-lying areas, but thankfully none in Kirkby. Slowly, so slowly, the days got longer, a few snowdrops appeared, followed by the sunshine of daffodils so that no one could deny that spring was at last on its way. Brown's Green Gardening won the contract to cut back all the hedges on the rural roads ahead of birds nesting, so they were busy again after a winter of very little work. Across the allotments gardeners started to plant their first crops, and in the square, one by one the glorious tulips opened making the gardens a bright tapestry of many colours.

The date of the trial was announced at last, and Jack, Will, Ben and Zoe were summoned to attend. As it was likely to go on for several days, Jack worried how the school would manage in his absence, but Bert and Elsie stepped into the breach, Elsie to hear the new readers and Bert to take the gardening classes at the children's allotment. Elsie arranged for the farmer who had bought her land to bring some new-born lambs into school one day, so Jack didn't think the pupils were going to miss him one little bit.

The trial at York Crown Court attracted a lot of media attention and the friends had to fight through the crowds to report to the Witness Waiting Room. Fortunately, no one knew who they were, so they didn't have to suffer the paparazzi as Smythe and Fernsby did when they arrived to stand trial for Poppy's murder and the blackmail and attempted murder of Nigel Blakemore.

The cameras were also turned on Nigel when he arrived holding tight to his wife's hand, but he calmly ignored the questions thrown at him.

The morning of day one was mostly taken up with opening statements by the prosecution and defence, followed by the pathologist's report. Jack wasn't called to the witness box until early in the afternoon, and after being sworn in, he was questioned about finding Poppy's body. Having previously gone through this in the Coroner's Court, Jack had hoped not to have to relive it again. He tried his best to calmly answer the barrage of questions from both sides, but the Fernsby's arrogant barrister took great delight in trying to make him look stupid.

Will, and the dog walker who had seen Fernsby in the woods, were both questioned and released, but Jack had to remain in the witness room as he would be recalled in relation to finding the hidden video camera and Poppy's phone. Just before the end of the day he was summoned and questioned briefly before being released. Ben and Zoe hadn't been called but were told that they would be giving evidence first thing the following day. Having been confined to the witness room all day, Zoe was like a caged tiger, eager to get on with it, but Jack was just glad to get his part over with.

Day two, and Jack took a day's holiday in order to attend, driving in with Josie who was keen to watch the proceedings. Ben was the first witness called and he explained how he had downloaded the video footage from the hidden camera and catalogued its contents. He confirmed that he had found three short clips taken from the overall footage in the deleted files on Poppy's laptop and that she had emailed these to herself. Ben was asked if there was any evidence of her emailing these clips to anyone, and he confirmed that there wasn't. Fernsby's barrister suggested that these clips had been kept by Ms Gilbert for her own enjoyment and were not evidence of any blackmail.

Zoe was then called and questioned about Poppy's phone, and she explained about recovering deleted blackmail texts each with the individual video clips attached and then sent to the three men. The prosecution lawyer asked if these were the same clips that Ms Gilbert had emailed to herself, and Zoe confirmed that they were. Fernsby's barrister sat sour faced but didn't question her.

Zoe went on to describe the text from Fernsby's which had a picture of Ivory Funnel mushrooms attached, and then read out Poppy's dismissive response to it. The prosecution asked a few questions but then Fernsby's barrister suggested that his client, who was a property developer, not a mycologist, had sent the picture in good faith to assist Ms Gilbert, and would not have known of his error. Zoe had to bite her lip not to respond to this ridiculous assertion and fought to keep her face impartial.

The Judge may also have been struggling to remain impartial as he asked for the book from which the picture had been taken to be shown to the court; it was immediately obvious that Fernsby had cropped the image very carefully to exclude the skull-and-crossbones and the dire warning that ingestion could prove fatal. Fernsby's barrister had scored a home goal.

Ben and Zoe were returned to the witness room and the trial continued with DCI Quinn giving details from bank statements, phone records and transcripts from the police interviews. Smythe's statement stating that it was Fernsby who had killed Gilbert elicited a gasp from the courtroom and those close to him could hear Fernsby swearing under his breath at Smythe.

As the day went on it became clear to Jack that the case against Smythe and Fernsby for conspiracy to kill Poppy Gilbert was cut and dried, but Fernsby's barrister argued that was just a fantasy to stop her blackmail but was never enacted. Jack began to worry that they would, literally, get away with murder, although Smythe's blackmail charge and Fernsby's attempted murder charge against Blakemore seemed pretty watertight.

The difficulty was lack of proof that either of the men on trial had actually put the poisonous mushrooms into Poppy's pie; the defence barrister suggested that she could have done it herself by mistake. He then contradicted himself by arguing that she clearly knew which mushrooms were which, and that maybe she was attempting to kill off her guests, not the other way round. This gave Jack pause for thought - she had been a pretty despicable character - could this actually be the case? The looks on the faces of the jury told Jack that the barrister had successfully seeded that idea in their minds too.

The prosecution lawyer then recalled Ben to the witness box and asked him about the work he had done on the video clip from Poppy's last day alive. Ben explained that he had used AI technology to identify and remove from the recording the smoochy music that had been playing in the bedroom and then identify and amplify the voices of Poppy and Fernsby so that they could be clearly heard. He'd also isolated and amplified background sounds so that they became clearer.

The video clip was first played to the court in its original muffled version, starting at the point when Fernsby got out of bed, said something to Poppy and then Poppy turned over and appeared to be sleeping. The video ran on with nothing much happening, until Poppy turned over to face the doorway, opened her eyes and appeared to be speaking before closing her eyes again and going back to sleep.

The clip was then replayed with the background music removed and the voices enhanced. Fernsby words could now clearly be heard as he told Poppy to get some sleep and he would make tonight's pies for her. After a pause, Fernsby's voice came from the kitchen asking her where the beef was; Poppy opened her eyes for a moment and told him it was in the slow cooker so that it would be tender. Just before she went back to sleep, she could be heard reminding him not to put any onions in her pie, and he said, 'I know - I'll mark yours with a pastry P'.

The recording was then played again with all sounds removed apart from the kitchen sounds: the clang of the slow cooker lid being taken off, the rustling of a plastic bag, and the sound of a knife on a chopping board.

At the end of the recording, you could have heard pin drop in the courtroom; there was muttering amongst the spectators and a couple of the press reporters left the courtroom, presumably to catch that evening's headlines. Fernsby's barrister tried half-heartedly to question Ben, but you could tell from his face that he knew he was beaten. Smythe's lawyer asked if there was anything on the recording to suggest that his client had been involved in baking the poisoned pie and Ben confirmed that Smythe's voice was not found on the recording that afternoon. Ben and Zoe were then released to sit in the court and Jack had to restrain himself from giving them both a 'high five'.

Nigel Blakemore was then called and questioned about his relationship with Poppy. Jack watched him with sympathy, knowing that Blakemore's wife was in the courtroom, but when Jack glanced at her, he was relieved to see her face was serene, and she was giving her husband nods of encouragement whenever he looked her way. He told the court that on the night Poppy died he had told her he wasn't going to see her again and had then left, leaving Smythe and Fernsby behind.

"In hindsight, I know now that the poison was already taking effect, but I just thought she was drunk or high," said Nigel. "She wasn't a very nice person, but I still feel terribly guilty that I did nothing to save her. Also, with the benefit of hindsight, I can't help thinking that Smythe and Fernsby were laughing at her dying, not just giggly due to eating magic mushrooms as I thought at the time. It makes me feel sick to think about it."

Nigel was lost in his thoughts a moment and missed the next question, catching up when asked for the second time when he first knew of Poppy's death.

"I heard it on the radio. I was driving and nearly crashed. I pulled into a lay-by and called Smythe and said that we needed to go to the police, but he warned me off and made veiled threats against my son," said Nigel. "I heard nothing more from him for a short while but then when the box of muffins arrived, I thought I must have misunderstood things and that Smythe had sent them as an apology."

"Can you tell me what the note meant in the box of muffins - 'In case you were missing P's special recipe'?" asked the lawyer

"I realised it referred to 'magic mushrooms', something Poppy sprinkled liberally into her cooking," replied Nigel, shamefacedly.

"So why did you eat them?" asked the lawyer.

"I hadn't been sleeping as I was so stressed about my wife leaving, the blackmail and Poppy's death. I was exhausted and not thinking straight and decided a few bites wouldn't hurt if it helped me to relax. Sadly, I was very wrong, and they nearly killed me!" Nigel said wryly.

Nigel was then cross examined by the defence barrister who appeared to be inferring that Nigel could just as easily be Gilbert's killer as his client. The Judge reminded him that Nigel was not the one on trial and shortly afterwards he was dismissed and joined his wife in the courtroom. Smythe's lawyer asked if there was any evidence that the muffins had been baked by, or sent by, his client, and it was confirmed that there was no evidence of his direct involvement.

A handwriting expert was called next, and he confirmed that the writing on the note sent with the muffins matched Mr Fernsby's writing. It was obvious to anyone looking at the stuck-together note side by side with a sample of Mr Fernsby' handwriting, that that was the case, and the defence asked no questions.

The prosecution lawyer then asked for DCI Quinn to be recalled, and once she was back in the witness box, asked her if there was anything on Smythe's phone that linked him to Fernsby sending the muffins to Blakemore.

"We recovered from Fernsby's iCloud storage a deleted text to Smythe where he asked for Blakemore's address; Smythe replied with the address," replied Quinn.

"What is the date of those texts?" asked the lawyer.

"The day before the courier delivered the muffins," replied Quinn.

Smythe's lawyer asked DCI Quinn if anything in Fernsby's text, or Smythe's responses, indicated that his client knew anything about the poisoned muffins or Fernsby's intention to send them to Blakemore. Quinn confirmed that there was nothing other than the address sent as requested.

The final witness called was one of the pallbearers from the Funeral Directors who had handled Poppy's funeral. The man was dressed in what was obviously his best suit and was nervously twisting his cap in his hands.

"This is new," whispered Zoe to Jack.

Jack nodded his agreement and listened with interest to the man's account as he explained that after helping to carry the coffin in, he was having a cigarette out of sight around the side of the crematorium's entrance porch.

"Two men were outside the crematorium talking loudly and laughing, and I was surprised as it's usually hushed voices and tears at funerals," he said. "I moved a bit closer to see who they were but kept out of sight as I'm not supposed to smoke on duty."

"Are the men present today?" asked the lawyer?

"Yes, it's the two men in the dock," the man replied, nodding in that direction.

"What happened next?" asked the lawyer.

"I heard the tall one say, 'the whore won't be troubling us any more', and then the other one said 'yes, we made a good job of it, didn't we?" and then they laughed and slapped each other on the back. The first then said 'hey, we should have picked the funeral music – I've got the perfect song' and the other one asked 'what' and he replied, 'Ding-dong the witch is dead' and they howled with laughter. A lady was then coming towards them, so they put on serious faces and went soberly into the chapel."

A shocked whisper went round the courtroom, and Jack glanced at Smythe's lawyer, and saw he had put his head in his hands. Fernsby's barrister tried to discredit the witness, saying that he couldn't possibly have remembered the conversation word for word, but the witness stuck to his account.

"It was when I saw Fernsby and Smythe laughing outside the chapel that I first began to doubt if Poppy's death had been accidental," Josie whispered in Jack's ear.

Once the last witness had been dismissed, the Judge called on the prosecution lawyer to present his closing arguments. The lawyer took a moment to get his notes in order, and then turned to the jury.

"Ladies and Gentlemen of the Jury, you have heard from the pathologist that Ms Pauline Gilbert died from a heart attack brought on by ingesting a lethal amount of muscarine which is found in Ivory Funnel mushrooms that had been baked in a pie.

You have seen the text and videos that Ms Gilbert was using to blackmail the defendants Smythe and Fernsby, and also another man, Mr Blakemore. In addition to all three men being clearly recognisable from the videos, samples of semen on Ms Gilbert's bed sheets matched all three men's DNA. Mr Fernsby's semen was also recovered from inside Ms Gilbert's vagina.

We know from the photo taken of a page in a book belonging to Mr Fernsby and texted to Ms Gilbert that he tried to get her to pick the poisonous mushrooms, and when she didn't, he cancelled his appointments and rushed to the woods to pick them himself - in such a hurry that he got a speeding ticket on the way. An eyewitness in the woods has confirmed he was picking mushrooms that afternoon. We know he placed these mushrooms in a bag that had previously contained gentleman's hair products - an exclusive brand only available from a shop near Mr Fernsby's home in Leeds.

We know from the enhanced sound on the video of that fateful afternoon that Fernsby left Ms Gilbert in bed and that he prepared the pies for the dinner that evening, marking one pie with her initial, 'P', to ensure that only she ate that particular pie.

We know that Fernsby retained a small amount of the poisonous mushrooms and baked these into muffins which he sent to Mr Blakemore, either as a warning to keep quiet or to ensure that he wasn't able to ever speak up about what went on in Ms Gilbert's apartment. Fortunately, Mr Blakemore didn't eat both muffins and thanks to his five-year-old son seeking help, he survived. There was nothing to stop the said child from helping himself to the remaining muffin, and if he had, he would certainly not have survived."

The lawyer paused and took a sip of water, and Jack shuddered at the thought that little Noah could so easily have been another victim of the evil pair.

"Mr Fernsby's barrister will argue that Ms Gilbert picked the poisonous mushrooms herself and baked them into a pie which unfortunately only she ate. From her response to Fernsby's text, we know that Ms Gilbert knew those mushrooms were poisonous and so not only would she not have picked them in the first place, but she certainly would not have put them into her own separate pie. Consider, if she had picked them by mistake thinking that they were actually Psilocybin mushrooms, as she only had a small supply of dried Psilocybin mushrooms left for everyone, wouldn't she have shared them amongst all of her guest's pies?

Consider if Mr Fernsby was sick of the hold Ms Gilbert had over him, especially the video evidence that could ruin his reputation and therefore his business, a business that partly due to Ms Gilbert's actions, he had nearly lost a few years earlier. Remember that he was also paying her a considerable amount of money each month to keep her quiet, payments he cancelled on the same night as the fateful party, even though when he left her apartment, she was still alive. That is clear evidence that he knew she was dying, and even though that afternoon they had been lovers, he left her to die a painful death - alone.

You may believe that Mr Smythe is innocent in the murder of Ms Gilbert, but I suggest they planned it together, as confirmed by the conversation overheard at the crematorium. Mr Smythe clearly also knew that when he left her apartment Ms Gilbert was dying, as he didn't even wait until he got home to cancel the weekly blackmail payments, he used a banking app on his phone in the car park of Ms Gilbert's apartment. He also didn't waste any time redirecting Mr Blakemore's blackmail payments into his own account either, sending a text to Mr Blakemore a few seconds after he'd stopped his own payments.

Whether Mr Fernsby was party to Smythe's little side scheme we don't know, but we do know that when Mr Blakemore heard of Ms Gilbert's death and contacted Smythe, he must have told Mr Fernsby the news as Mr Fernsby then decided to remove any threat from Mr Blakemore - permanently. Given the history of the co-conspirators, I suggest to you that the attempted murder of Mr Blakemore was also a joint decision.

In considering all the evidence that has been laid out before you, you cannot come to any other conclusion other than Ms Gilbert was unlawfully killed by Fernsby and Smythe and that they are both also guilty of the attempted murder of Mr Blakemore. In addition, there is sufficient evidence to convict Mr Smythe of the blackmail of Mr Blakemore."

The lawyer looked at the jury, looking from one face to another, and then sat down, satisfied that he had made his mark.

Fernsby's barrister then stood up and tried his best to discredit the lawyer's interpretation of the evidence given. He suggested that the enhanced audio evidence was deliberate misdirection and that there was no hard evidence that his client had put the poisonous mushrooms into a pie intended for Ms Gilbert. He steered clear of trying to rationalise Fernsby's involvement in sending Blakemore the poisonous muffins, just directing the jury to find his client innocent of murder.

Smythe's lawyer tried to blame everything on Fernsby and argued that his client should be acquitted of the charges of murder and attempted murder, but you could see from the jury's faces that they didn't believe him. He made no attempt to explain away Smythe's blackmail of Blakemore, just concluded on Smythe's former good character and his service to his local community as a councillor and mayor.

The prosecution lawyer was then given the opportunity to respond to the defence before the jury were sent to consider their verdict.

"Ms Gilbert was not a good person," he said. "She was a sex worker hiding behind a supposedly legitimate business, using banned drugs to lower the inhibitions of her clients so that she could video them and use those recordings to blackmail them. She committed crimes that deserved punishment, but she didn't deserve to die a horrible and lonely death. She had all her life in front of her, but that life was cut short by a callous and cowardly crime.

Mr Blakemore was perhaps weak and foolish, but when he realised that he found the moral strength to walk away: crimes had been committed against him, yet he ended up fighting for his life. He has a wife who has forgiven his lapse, a son that adores him and he has everything to live for, but he so nearly didn't get that second chance to be a good husband and father.

Ladies and gentlemen; I leave it in your hands to ensure that justice is done for these victims."

There was a short silence as the solicitor let his words sink in and then he thanked the judge and sat down. He felt he had done everything he could to ensure Ms Gilbert got a fair trial: it was up to the jury now.

The judge instructed the jury that they must reach a unanimous decision on each of the counts of murder, attempted murder and blackmail for each of the men on trial, and failing that, a majority decision on each count. They were then sent to the Jury Room to consider their verdict. An hour passed and they had not returned, so, being late in the afternoon, the judge instructed the court to resume the following day.

Chapter Sixty

The next morning Josie and Hugo, Kara and Jack, Ben and Zoe all came to the Crown Court to hear the verdict but found that the resumption of the trial was delayed. They waited outside with the press and other interested parties for over an hour, drinking takeaway coffee and discussing the case, before eventually being let in. They soon realised what the delay had been: Fernsby stood alone in the dock - Smythe had absconded.

The Judge explained that there was a warrant out for Smythe's arrest, but as the foreman of the jury had just informed the court that they had reached their verdicts, their decision would be heard, and if necessary Smythe would be sentenced in his absence. The jury filed back in and the foreman, a youngish man who had the serious demeanour of a much older person, stood up, the paper in his hands shaking a little.

"Foreman of the jury, have you reached decisions on all charges in front of you?" the judge asked.

"Yes m'lord, we have," the foreman replied.

"Have you reached a unanimous decision on the charge against Mr Julian Fernsby for the murder of Ms Pauline Gilbert?"

"Yes m'lord. We find Mr Fernsby guilty of the murder of Ms Pauline Gilbert," said the foreman in a loud clear voice.

There was a gasp from the courtroom, but Fernsby stood impassive.

"Have you reached a unanimous decision on the charge against Mr Julian Fernsby for the attempted murder of Mr Nigel Blakemore?" asked the judge.

"Yes m'lord. We find Mr Fernsby guilty of the attempted murder of Mr Nigel Blakemore," replied the foreman.

A flicker passed across Fernsby's face, but he otherwise looked unmoved.

"Thank you, Mr Foreman. I turn now to the charges against Mr Eustace Smythe. Have you reached a unanimous decision on the charge against Mr Smythe for the murder of Ms Pauline Gilbert?" asked the judge.

"No m'lord, we were unable to reach a unanimous decision," replied the foreman.

"Where you able to reach a majority decision on the charge against Mr Smythe for the murder of Ms Pauline Gilbert?" asked the judge.

"Yes m'lord. By a majority of eight to two we find Mr Smythe guilty of the murder of Ms Pauline Gilbert" replied the foreman.

Fernsby smirked at the news, not bothering to hide his delight that Smythe had also been found guilty.

"Have you reached a unanimous decision on the charge against Mr Eustace Smythe for the attempted murder of Mr Nigel Blakemore?" asked the judge.

"No m'lord, we were unable to reach a unanimous decision," replied the foreman.

"Where you able to reach a majority decision on the charge against Mr Smythe for the attempted murder of Mr Nigel Blakemore?" asked the judge.

"Yes m'lord. By a majority of six to four we find Mr Smythe not guilty of the attempted murder of Mr Nigel Blakemore."

A ripple of surprise ran round the courtroom. Jack saw the surprise and annoyance on Fernsby's face and realised that he knew far more about Smythe's involvement than had come out in court.

"Did you reach a unanimous decision on the charge against Mr Smythe for the blackmail of Nigel Blakemore?" asked the judge.

"Yes m'lord, we find Mr Smythe guilty of the blackmail of Nigel Blakemore.

"Thank you, Mr Foreman, and thank you ladies and gentlemen of the jury," said the judge. "We will now proceed to sentencing. In relation to Mr Fernsby, does he have any previous convictions?"

"Yes m'lord," replied the prosecution lawyer. "Mr Fernsby was fined for attempting to bribe a council official to secure a land deal."

"Does that case have any bearing on the case in hand?" asked the Judge.

"Not directly, m'lord. But it may be of interest that the person he was trying to bribe was Mr Smythe."

The Judge nodded and turned to Fernsby's barrister.

"Are there any mitigating factors in relation to your client?" he asked.

"Yes m'lord," replied the barrister. "Five years ago, Mr Fernsby suffered a substantial financial loss due to the actions of Mr Smythe and Ms Gilbert and was also fined heavily, as mentioned by my learned colleague. His business has not recovered from these losses and Ms Gilbert blackmailing him for a substantial amount would have been the final straw. I am not condoning his actions, but in sentencing please consider the provocation my client was under."

"Thank you. I will now proceed directly to sentencing," responded the judge before turning to face Fernsby.

"The mandatory sentence for murder is life imprisonment. In setting the minimum term, I have considered that there was a significant degree of planning or premeditation in committing this crime which I do not believe any provocation off-sets. The appropriate sentence for the murder of Ms Pauline Gilbert is life imprisonment with a minimum term of thirty years. For the attempted murder for Mr Nigel Blakemore the appropriate minimum term is twenty-five years. However, I am setting an *in cumulo* minimum term for both offences taken together of forty years."

The Judge paused and looked Julian Fernsby straight in the eyes.

"That means you cannot be considered for parole until after you have served a full forty years. Take him down, officer."

Julian Fernsby stood frozen in the dock. His expression of careful arrogance slipped and was replaced with a look of pure horror. He looked beseechingly at his barrister who simply shrugged and then turned away as Fernsby was forcibly removed from the dock and taken, struggling, to the cells.

Smythe's previous prison sentence for attempted fraud involving Fernsby and Gilbert was outlined by the prosecution lawyer. Smythe's lawyer appeared to have given up and just shook his head when asked if there were any mitigating factors. The Judge sentenced Smythe in his absence to a minimum term of twenty years for murder and six years for blackmail, to run consecutively. Once he was arrested, the length of sentence would be extended by at least another year for failing to surrender to bail.

The judge thanked the jurors again and dismissed them, the court stood, the judge left, and reporters rushed out to file copy. As the courtroom emptied, the six friends sat down again and just looked at each other.

"Well, I think justice has been done," said Josie at last.

"I feel almost sorry for Fernsby," said Kara. "Smythe and Poppy lured him into all this and now he's going to be locked up probably for the rest of his life."

"I don't. He got what he deserved," said Ben.

"I'll feel a lot better once Smythe is inside as well," said Zoe.

"He couldn't have gone far as he doesn't have his passport," said Hugo. "He's an old man, unlikely to be sleeping rough, so once they've checked relatives, friends, hotels, B and B's, etcetera, they'll find him."

"I hope so. He's a vindictive bugger and I don't like to think of him being out there," said Zoe with a shudder.

"I'll protect you, darling," said Ben, pulling her close.

"Hah! You'd be hiding under the duvet if you heard a noise in the night!" replied Zoe.

"Too true," said Ben with a grin.

Seeing the court ushers coming their way, the friends left the courtroom, glad it was all over. Nigel and his wife were waiting outside and shook all their hands warmly.

"I want to thank you all for bringing Fernsby and Smythe to justice. Your persistence has freed me from a nightmare," said Nigel.

"And I wanted to thank you again for saving my husband's life," said Mrs Blakemore, hugging Jack.

Chapter Sixty-One

The search for Smythe continued for many weeks, his picture was on Facebook, shop windows and even on the main TV news. Ports and airports were on alert for him, but as he didn't have his passport, it was thought unlikely that he would try to skip the country, so more focus was put on local trains, buses and taxi firms, hotels and bed and breakfast establishments.

There had been very little money in his bank account, but a few days later his ex-wife was outraged to find that all the money had been withdrawn from what had previously been their joint savings account. This account had been awarded to Mrs Smythe as part of the divorce settlement, but she'd never thought to remove Mr Smythe's name from the account.

After a few months, the local search was called off, and as posters peeled off windows and new sensational news stories filled the media, the search for Smythe faded from importance. An appeal on Crimewatch a few months later reignited some interest and brought a smattering of 'sightings', as far away as Spain and as close as Kirkby, but police follow-ups never uncovered anything new.

Josie found it difficult to stop wondering where Smythe was, glancing at the face of every man she passed in the street just in case. Sitting outside her hut on the allotments in the spring sunshine, cradling a mug of tea, Josie racked her brains as to where he could have gone. Fernsby was in prison paying for his crime and it seemed so unfair that Smythe had got away unpunished. Josie didn't know why it bothered her so much, but she knew it would always remain a niggle in the back of her brain.

Josie sipped her tea and made a deliberate attempt to forget the wretched man. She turned her face towards the sun and closed her eyes, letting the song of a nearby blackbird flood her brain instead. She could smell the freshly turned soil, feel a gentle breeze on her face and hear the happy voices of children who were with Jack planting seedlings on the children's allotment.

Smythe had always thought he was so important, but the truth was that he was an insignificant man of no consequence. He had none of the things that were really important in her life: a loving partner, dear friends, the joy of watching seeds grow into wholesome food, helping others thrive and a place within the community of Kirkby. She was content, and for once, she would let a mystery go unsolved.

Epilogue

It was almost a year since the first residents had moved into the square and Josie and Kara had been asked to help them plan a surprise party as a thank you to Jack. They were delighted to do so, and met with Bert, Nadia, Elsie and Joy one afternoon to plan the event. After a bit of a discussion, they agreed it was best to keep it simple as Jack would be embarrassed with anything fancier. Bert suggested that they plant a rose bush to mark the anniversary, and they agreed that apart from that they would just share a relaxed meal in the garden, which everyone would contribute to.

"Could we plant a rose called 'At Peace' and say a few words for Poppy Gilbert," asked Nadia suddenly, much to everyone's surprise.

"What on earth for!" exclaimed Bert. "That woman made everyone's life a misery."

"My mother feels her restless spirit in the apartment," said Nadia, a bit embarrassed to mention it. "She's not complaining," Nadia was quick to add, seeing Kara's concerned face "but forgiveness is a key Islamic teaching and mum thinks we all need to forgive Poppy, so she can rest."

"I think your mother's right," said Josie. "It's been worrying me that her ashes remain in a box at the funeral directors. It doesn't excuse her behaviour, but she had a terrible start in life and a terrible end to her life and no one mourns her. I agree with Nadia's mum that we need to forgive her to free her and ourselves from the evil that happened here."

The others stared at Josie and Nadia for a moment, but then slowly nodded in agreement, feeling a little guilty that in the back of their minds they thought that Poppy had got what she deserved, but recognised now that no one deserved to be murdered.

A week later, Nadia and Bert selected a sunny corner of the flower garden for the rose and Bert dug compost into the soil and dug a deep hole ready for the ashes and the tree. The day before they had visited a specialist rose grower in Pickering together and had chosen a perfect specimen of the rose 'At Peace', a lovely pale cream tea rose with petals that swirled in the centre, emerald-green foliage and a delicate perfume.

On the morning of the anniversary Josie visited the funeral directors and collected Poppy's ashes. It felt very strange having the box on the passenger seat next to her, but Josie had an overwhelming feeling that they were doing the right thing. Jack had been told they were burying the ashes and planting a tree for Poppy, but nothing else about the event. He had suggested that the vicar was asked to say a few words, and Josie readily agreed as she'd been struggling to know what exactly to say.

The vicar was already there chatting to Jack when Josie arrived, and the residents of the square soon started to gather around. Josie handed the vicar the box of ashes and then moved to stand next to Hugo who put his arm around her. Bert stood ready nearby with the rose tree and his spade and, following a glare from Elsie who was sitting on Dorothy's bench, he removed his flat cap and stood almost to attention. Jack and Kara stood hand in hand, as did Ben and Zoe whilst Will and Joy had their arms around each other. Nadia and Amir, each holding a sleeping twin, sat next to Nadia's parents on Hope's bench.

"The Lord said 'Bear with each other and forgive one another if any of you has a grievance against someone. Forgive as the Lord forgave you'," said the vicar. "It's easy to forgive friends small annoyances like forgetting your birthday, but it's difficult to forgive someone who delighted in making trouble for others. The bigger the sin, the more difficult the act of forgiveness is, and the more important that it is done, otherwise the hurt continues to fester and will remain as a stain on this lovely community. Forgiveness is letting go, and I want you all to let go of all the hurt and hatred and say in your hearts and minds 'I forgive you, Poppy.'

The vicar paused a moment before making the sign of the cross over the box of ashes.

"I forgive you Poppy," she said. As she carefully poured the ashes into the prepared hole, she heard others echo the same words.

"Almighty God, as you once called our sister Pauline Gilbert into this life, so now you have called her into life everlasting. We therefore commit her body to the ground, earth to earth, ashes to ashes, dust to dust. In the hope of resurrection unto eternal life, through the promise of Our Lord Jesus Christ, we give her over to your blessed care. Amen," intoned the vicar.

"Amen," the group replied.

Bert carefully placed the tree into the hole and filled in the earth around it, patting it down well, and then stood, holding his cap in his hands, his head bowed as if saying a prayer. Nadia handed the baby she was holding to her father and then, taking her mother's hand, came forward and together they said a prayer for forgiveness and peace in Arabic.

A gentle breeze suddenly moved through the garden, bringing everyone the scent of roses and a feeling of lightness. Josie wiped her eyes and Hugo hugged her, Kara squeezed Jack's hand, Joy kissed Will's cheek, Ben pulled Zoe close, and Dottie and Mia let go of their parent's hands and ran off to play.

Jack sat next to Elsie, forbidden to move whilst everyone helped to set up tables and pile them high with the food that they had each bought or baked. He ran his hand over the smooth wood of his great-grandmother's bench and thought that she would have approved of what they had just done. Bert appeared and handed them both a glass of wine and then helped Elsie to her feet: holding onto the arm of her dear friend, Elsie turned to face Jack.

"Jack, on behalf of all the residents of the square, I want to thank you for what you have done for us, for building this beautiful place and giving us all the chance to start again, the chance of happiness and the chance to be part of a community that cares about each other," she said. "Your great-grandmother would have been so proud of you, and we are all proud to call you our friend. Ladies and gentlemen, a toast to Jack, Lord Kirkby."

"Lord Kirkby," they all echoed, raising their glasses.

Jack looked at each of the faces he had got to know over the last year and thought of their stories; the abused wife, the lonely old lady, the ostracised young couple, the bereaved old man, the young man leaving home, the parents supporting their daughter - a mishmash of ages and ethnicity, but one community.

"Thank you," he said, raising his glass to them all, and then taking a minute to think about what he wanted to say.

"Five years ago, I was homeless and lost, and the people of Kirkby welcomed me into their community. The friendship and love given to me by Josie and Hugo, Ben and Zoe, my beautiful wife, Kara, and my amazing great-grandmother, Lady Dorothy Kirkby, was the inspiration for the square - to pass on that kindness.

We only have one life: we can choose to live it as Poppy did, selfishly, hurting others as she'd been hurt, or we can choose to forgive, to let go of past pain, to live kindly, to find joy in the everyday.

A toast, please, to helping others along the way - to paying kindness forward."

The friends, old and new, looked at each other, some wiping away a tear, and then raised their glasses and made the toast.

"To paying kindness forward."

THE END

Jean Illingworth

ABOUT THE AUTHOR

Jean Illingworth lives in North Yorkshire with her husband, DJ, and son, Jamie. She has written several books for children and young adults, most of them illustrated by Jamie: this is her second book for adults.

When not writing, Jean enjoys photographing the stunning Yorkshire coast and countryside, is a passionate gardener, and enjoys live music and socialising with family and friends.

OTHER BOOKS BY JEAN ILLINGWORTH

Short stories for young children

(Colour illustrations by Jamie Illingworth)

Danny's Bonfire Night

Danny's Christmas

Dragontide

Danny's Easter

Danny's Summer Holiday

Novels for mid-grade readers

(Illustrations by Jamie Illingworth)

Beach Beings

Beach Beings – Distant Shores

For Young Adults

Two Degrees

For Adults

The Allotments

ACKNOWLEDGEMENTS

This book would not have been written if my dear friend, beautiful Susan Cawthorne, hadn't insisted that I'd been too kind to Poppy in The Allotments. Thank-you Susan for, once again, pushing me to write a follow-up (as she did with my children's book 'Beach Beings'), for being the very first person to read it, and for all the positive feedback and support you continue to give me.

Thank you too to all my other beta readers, especially my darling husband, DJ, whose liberal use of a red pen has saved you, dear reader, from my many errors.

A big thank you to all my friends and neighbours in Kirkbymoorside for their support, for taking The Allotments to their hearts, and for asking 'when's the next one coming out?' Well, here you are – I do hope you like it!

If you have comments about the book, please get in touch via my website: *www.jeanillingworthauthor.com* or Instagram *www.instagram.com/theallotmentsauthor*

Jean Illingworth

DISCLAIMER

The fictional town of Kirkby is based upon the friendly North Yorkshire town of Kirkbymoorside, which does have allotments on the hill above the town, but Kirkby Manor does not exist and there is not a square of houses as described in the book.

All people and events in this book are fictitious: any similarity to events or to people alive or dead are purely coincidental

The Square

Printed in Great Britain
by Amazon

84244210R00169